THE GREAT WALL

Also available from Titan Books

The Great Wall: The Art of the Film

THE OFFICIAL MOVIE NOVELIZATION

THE GREAT WALL

Novelization by MARK MORRIS

Directed by ZHANG YIMOU

Story by MAX BROOKS and EDWARD ZWICK

& MARSHALL HERSKOVITZ

Screenplay by CARLO BERNARD & DOUG MIRO and TONY GILROY

LEGENDARY
TITAN BOOKS

The Great Wall: The Official Movie Novelization
Print edition ISBN: 9781785652981
E-book edition ISBN: 9781785652998

Published by Titan Books
A division of Titan Publishing Group Ltd
144 Southwark Street, London SE1 0UP

First edition: February 2017
1 3 5 7 9 10 8 6 4 2

A CIP catalogue record for this title is available from the British Library.

Printed and bound in the United States.

THE GREAT WALL

The mountains looked like something from a dream. The many layers of sandstone and multi-colored minerals had been compressed together over millions of years, creating rock formations both bizarrely garish and breathtaking in their beauty. Beneath the desert sun they glowed in vivid stripes of red and yellow, green and blue. It was an artist's palette of color, a phantasmagoric feast for the eyes.

Despite its beauty, though, this was a harsh landscape. People died here every day. The unprepared and the foolhardy expired from hunger and thirst; others fell prey to wild animals or brigands. Vultures wheeled in the sky, knowing that carrion was never far from their hooked beaks. The desert dust beneath the sparse clumps of greenery was rich with the powdered bones of the dead.

For now the air was still, the desert undisturbed. A lizard basked motionless in the heat of the slowly setting sun. Then, sensing vibrations beneath its feet, it darted for cover. Next moment a blot of darkness appeared on the horizon, wreathed in a churning cloud of dust.

Anyone standing where the lizard had been would have heard, faint at first, wild cries and approaching hoof beats. They would have seen the blot of darkness emerge from the heat haze and resolve itself into a tightly packed group of eight horses, five of which had men mounted on their backs. The men were hunched over, urging their chargers on. They were heading for the range of Painted Mountains, hoping that, under cover of the coming night, they would find safety in its deep ravines and steep valleys.

One of the men, William Garin, narrowed his eyes against the stinging onslaught of desert dust. He was lean, scarred and sinewed, his beard and hair wild and matted like those of the rest of his companions, his clothes a filthy patchwork of well-worn leather, threadbare animal hide and light armour. Born in England thirty-seven years earlier, he was currently a long way from home. But then William was a nomad; he regarded the entire world as his home. In the last three decades he had fought his way across continents. His past was steeped in the blood of countless battles. His vast experience of warfare had not only hardened his resolve, but had sharpened his senses and turned him into a master tactician. Glancing at his companions, he realized he was going to have to call on every one of his countless skills to get them out of their current predicament.

Of the twenty-strong party that had embarked on this possibly foolhardy quest, only five were left. The rest had been cut down by the thirty or so brigands who were now on their tail. Out in front was Najid, the Saracen mercenary, his dust-smeared robes flying behind him. If it came down to a case of every man for himself, then Najid was the one most likely to escape the flailing blades of their pursuers. He was a master horseman, and when in the saddle he and his steed seemed like one creature, a perfect fusion of man and beast.

Least likely to escape was Rizzetti, or possibly Bouchard the Frank. Rizzetti, the Italian, was an adept soldier, and fearless in battle, but he was badly wounded. He had taken an arrow through the leg, and was now pale and sweating, hunched grimly over his horse, his teeth clenched against the pain. William glanced at the untended wound, and saw that blood was still pouring down the Italian's boot and leaving a trail on the sand behind him.

At least, though, Rizzetti had the grim, determined mind-set of a soldier. Bouchard, on the other hand, the master of their ragtag crew and the only non-soldier left alive, was nothing but a soft-bellied blusterer, a smooth-talking entrepreneur, who had enticed them here with wild tales of a magical black powder that would bring them fame and untold riches. Confident, even arrogant, when spouting his empty promises, Bouchard was now terrified and much reduced. No longer a leader, but a gibbering wreck, he couldn't prevent himself from glancing continually behind him.

William caught the eye of Pero Tovar, the fifth member of their group, and the only one among them he would tentatively call a friend. Pero was a fiery Spaniard, a beast in many ways. Yet although he could be wild and unrestrained in temperament, and brutally efficient in battle, he nevertheless possessed a resilience, an intelligence and a humor that appealed to William— and indeed, that led him, if not to fully trust the man, then at least to know he could rely on him when they were faced with a common enemy.

Pero's expression right now was easy to read, not least because William himself was thinking exactly the same thing. Bouchard was a liability. He was slowing them all down with his persistent backward glances. Twitching the reins of his horse, William brought his steed flank to steaming flank with Bouchard's own.

"Stop looking back!" he yelled at the Frank. "If you can see them, we're dead men!"

Bouchard's only response was a flicker of his wide, panicked eyes.

Leaning over in the saddle, William whipped

Bouchard's horse, urging it to go faster.

"Ride!" he yelled at the Frank. "Ride or die!"

As Bouchard's horse, stung into action, eased ahead of him, William broke his own rule by glancing quickly back. He couldn't see the brigands behind them. Yet. Which meant there was still a chance of escape.

"Najid!" he bellowed into the dust.

Ahead of him, the Turk looked back.

William pointed at the ridge of multi-colored mountains ahead, which were looming ever closer, and then at the three riderless horses that were pounding along beside them, full saddlebags jouncing.

"Cut loose the horses on my signal!"

His words penetrated Bouchard's brain-freezing barrier of mortal terror, and now the Frank looked panicked for a different reason.

"The bags?" he gulped. "Non! Pas les sacs!"

But William didn't give a shit about the Frenchman's precious bags, not when their lives were at stake.

"Now!" he yelled.

Bouchard let loose a high-pitched wail of denial and distress, but Najid didn't hesitate for a moment. Drawing his scimitar, he sliced through the lead tethering the three unmanned horses to the rest of the group, and then whipped the animals to encourage them to run faster.

"Yahhh! Yahh!" he shouted almost gleefully. "Run for your lives, ladies!"

The three untethered horses pulled ahead, making for the nearest ridge. Bouchard's eyes bugged with distress and rage as he watched them go.

As they dipped towards the valley Najid twitched his reins and led his party in the opposite direction to the three untethered horses. With luck, by the time the brigands crested the hill, the five survivors would be out of sight among the jagged peaks, and their pursuers would follow the distant trail of decoy dust kicked up by the trio of unmanned and still blindly fleeing horses.

• • •

The fire flickered feebly in the darkness. Advertising their presence was a risk, but a calculated one. Out here, in this dazzling but inhospitable landscape, the temperature dropped like a stone at night. If they were going to survive they needed at least a little heat to prevent themselves freezing to death.

Although all of them were shattered, and their horses all but hobbled after the headlong chase through the desert, Rizzetti was the member of their party who was most at risk. He was now stretched out beside the fire, bundled with coarse blankets to keep him warm. William, Pero and Najid had extracted the arrow from his leg, and cleaned and bound his wound as best they could, but the Italian's grizzled, bearded face was now slick with sweat, his body shuddering with fever.

William knew he couldn't ride in his present state—but nor could the rest of them afford to linger here beyond the break of dawn. So either Rizzetti's fever had to break overnight, enabling him to recover quickly, or they would be forced to leave him behind to die.

It was a harsh choice, but it was reality. In reduced circumstances, survival was all. There was no time for mercy, for hesitation, or for sentimentality. They all knew it—even Rizzetti himself.

With Rizzetti stretched out between them, slipping between consciousness and unconsciousness, the other four survivors huddled around the fire. They were too tired to speak, and they were hungry and thirsty too. When the brigands had attacked they had escaped from the caravan with little more than a few skins of water between them and a pouch of dried goat's meat. That meat was now gone, as were the two small lizards they had managed to capture and share between them.

William looked up as something gave a harsh, cawing cry out in the desert—a nocturnal bird or some as-yet-unseen predator? He had encountered many strange beasts on his travels, and hopefully, if he survived this night and the following days, would encounter many more. He stared into the darkness beyond the fire, but could see nothing. It was as if the world had been swallowed in a black void.

Suddenly, perhaps stirred into wakefulness by the

night cry of the unknown animal, Rizzetti opened his eyes. His dry lips parted.

"Tell the story," he croaked, looking at Bouchard.

Bouchard stared back at him silently. Since escaping the brigands he had kept himself to himself—sitting alone, not helping them hunt, find wood or tend to Rizzetti. William wasn't sure whether the Frank's mood was caused by the trauma of the brigands' attack or whether he was simply sulking over the loss of his precious saddlebags. Perhaps it was a little of both.

"Tell me," Rizzetti said, his voice desperate—as though Bouchard's story was the only thing that could provide him with the impetus he needed to recover.

Bouchard sighed, then caught Pero's eye, who nodded at him fiercely.

His voice flat and weary, Bouchard began. "North of the Silk Road... past Xian... north northeast... three hundred leagues north, there is a mountain of jade. Pure jade. And a... a fortress..."

His voice tailed off. He stared into the fire. He picked up a handful of sand and let it trickle through his fingers.

"The powder," Rizzetti said. "Tell us about the powder." When Bouchard didn't respond, his voice became harsh with anger, the warrior in him breaking momentarily through the fever that was weakening his body. "Tell us!"

Bouchard looked around the fire, registered the flinty gazes of the other men staring at him. Clearing his throat, he said, "The black powder is stronger than arrows. Stronger than siege walls. It is a weapon so powerful it can destroy a dozen men at once…"

As he began to speak, William saw a change come over Bouchard; saw that the Frank's own words were galvanizing him. He listened to Bouchard's heavily accented voice slowly growing stronger, powered by his own enthusiasm. An enthusiasm born of greed.

"It is an alchemist's potion that transforms air into fire. A fire that reaches out so quickly that it blinds all in its path. A fire so loud that it makes men deaf."

His eyes were shining now, his excitement growing.

"Two dozen men are all I need. Hard, blooded men to make a journey in this life of shit that is finally worth the gamble. Together we will find the fortress and the powder and make the world our own!"

He leaned over the fire, eyes aflame and teeth gleaming as he smiled his wide smile.

"Why risk your life for princes or priests who care not whether you live or die? Why wager your souls for gods you don't believe in, in wars that prove nothing but making other men rich? Let us take hold of our own destinies, *mes amis*! Let us journey together to the hidden fortress of black powder and the fortune th—"

It was here that his spiel came to an end. Without warning, Najid's arm swept forward and across, the blade of his scimitar flashing in the firelight.

The movement was so swift, so precise, that for a split-second William wondered whether he had imagined it. Bouchard was still kneeling on the other side of the fire, staring at them. Now, though, his eyes were bulging and his mouth wide open in shock.

Then a black line appeared across his throat. A black line that immediately began gushing dark fluid. The fluid spattered into the fire, making it sizzle and spark. The Frank's hands fluttered towards his opened throat as he began to gurgle.

With shocking suddenness the life fled from his eyes and he keeled over, his body thudding heavily to the ground. His right foot twitched for a moment, and then became still.

William and Pero looked at Najid, who was staring sourly at Bouchard's body. The Turk calmly wiped the blood from his scimitar and re-sheathed the weapon. Then he looked at his companions and shrugged.

"I've grown sick of his story. He has been telling it for six months now, and still we are no closer to finding this precious powder."

Pero and William looked at one another, as if uncertain how to respond.

Then Pero said, "I want his boots."

"I want his saddle," croaked Rizzetti from his recumbent position beside the fire.

William saw Najid's face harden, saw his hand

straying once more to the hilt of his scimitar. Quickly he rose to his knees, hands upraised in a calming gesture.

"Fair plunder," he said quickly. "Choose and challenge."

There was a moment of tense silence, all eyes on him. Then Pero and Najid both nodded abruptly, and Rizzetti murmured his weary assent.

• • •

Bouchard's possessions—those, at any rate, that he hadn't lost in the raid or when the horses had been cut free— were strewn across the ground close to the fire. After much negotiation the choice items (the silver talents, gold coins and precious stones; the weapons and bags of seeds; the drawings of the Holy Land and the diagrams of medieval machinery) had been divvied up into four equal piles. Now all that was left were the personal items, a random collection of wax seals and copper eating utensils, a sewing kit, an ivory comb, a pewter flask.

Pero was perched on a rock close to the fire, one of Bouchard's trading bags between his feet. Reaching in he said, "And now we come to the final item." His hand emerged, clutching a lump of dense black rock. "The magnet. Who wants it?"

"Not me," Najid said. "Too heavy."

"Rizzetti?"

Weakly the Italian shook his head.

"I'll have it," William said, and grinned at Pero. "Unless you want to fight me for it?"

Pero pursed his lips a moment, then tossed the rock in William's direction. Instead of opening a hand to catch it, William simply raised his iron-gauntleted arm. The rock flew towards him, and—*clank!*—stuck hard to the metal. The magnetic attraction was so strong that William had to grit his teeth and pull hard, the muscles bulging in his arm, before he was able to pry it loose and tuck it beneath the folds of his tattered and grimy chainmail Hauberk.

"I'll take the map as well," he said.

Pero narrowed his eyes.

"Come on, Pero," William said good-humoredly. "You know you can't read. It's wasted on you. Hand it over."

Pero let out a ragged sigh, and then grudgingly reached into his new left boot—one of the ones he had pulled from the feet of Bouchard's corpse—and extracted the map he'd secreted there. With the resignation of a man who knew he'd been out-maneuvered, he handed it to William, who slipped that too into his Hauberk.

"It's a strong moon tonight," William said, looking up at the fat white disc in the sky. "When the horses are fresh, we move."

"To where?" Najid asked.

"North. If they keep after us we'll kill them in the mountains."

Pero glanced at Rizzetti, who appeared to be dozing again, and sidled closer to William. In a low voice he said, "Rizzetti won't have recovered by morning. Force him to move and we'll find ourselves dragging a corpse."

William's face was grim. "Well, that's up to him, isn't it?"

Pero frowned, which prompted William to add, "He's earned the right to die where he wants."

When Pero still looked unconvinced, William sighed and said, "Look, I've been left to die twice. It was bad luck."

"For who?" Pero muttered.

"For the people who left me."

William smiled, inviting his friend to join in, but Pero merely turned away and spat on the ground. "*Bien*," he said, his voice flat. "It is your call."

Before William could respond, a sudden, ear-splitting scream tore through the darkness. It was a hideous sound, like nothing he had ever heard before. Despite his experience of war, despite having witnessed the awful depths of man's inhumanity to his fellow man, the sound chilled him to the core. He spun towards the blackness beyond the flickering firelight.

"What—"

And then all hell broke loose.

Something came at them out of the darkness. Something huge and savage, but that moved so fast it was little more than a blur. In less than the time it took to blink, William was aware of both Rizzetti and Najid being plucked from their positions beside the fire and disappearing into the blackness. Najid's brief scream was one of agony and mortal terror; Rizzetti made no sound at all. As if in sympathy, the horses began to scream too. There was a brief, confused thrash of panic as they tore themselves free of their restraints, and then William was half-aware of the sound of pounding hooves receding into the distance as they bolted.

A flash of green, and then Pero, who had leaped to his feet and instinctively run into the darkness in pursuit of whatever had taken their companions, was flying through the air. He landed in the fire, scattering logs and extinguishing flame, plunging the camp into near-impenetrable darkness.

William spun instinctively, sword in hand, as their attacker turned its attention to him. He sensed it rather than saw it—a vast, thunderous presence bearing down upon him. Then it seemed to stop—and that was worse. Now he had no idea where it was. Moving forward, he swung his sword desperately, and felt it connect with something; felt it judder in his hands as the blade slashed through bone and tissue.

The animal—the thing—remained oddly silent. Pressing home his advantage, William swung again and again, slashing and thrusting and hacking, his reflexes lightning fast. As his sword blade flashed with reflected moonlight from above he saw vivid green splashes in the darkness. The beast stumbled, and William swung his sword towards the sound, and again felt it cut through tough living tissue.

And then the thing, whatever it was, was falling back. William got the impression, as it thudded away from him, that it was vast and meaty and weighty. At least as big as an elephant that had reared up on its hind legs, if not bigger.

Could this be what it was? A rogue elephant? A rogue elephant that moved like lightning and bled green blood? Tingling with terror and the exhilaration of battle, William stepped forward, still thrusting and slashing with his sword.

There was a tumble of rocks, and then suddenly, as the creature moved back from him, an awful, otherworldly scream.

But the scream was fading, receding, as if the thing was falling back into the hell from which it had come. All at once William realized what must have happened, and he came to a halt, his heart thudding madly. Sure enough, limned by moonlight, he saw the edge of a chasm a few feet in front of him. And peering hard he glimpsed—*thought* he glimpsed—the silhouette of something huge and monstrous falling down and down.

Stepping back he heard a crash of rocks, followed by a distant splash. And then…

Silence.

Still gripping his sword, William sank to his knees. Although he was a veteran of a thousand battles, he had never faced an enemy of such speed and ferocity. He began to shake with reaction.

Then a voice came from the darkness behind him. It was Pero's voice, though William had never heard it sound so lost, so plaintive. It called his name, once and then again.

William roused himself. He clambered shakily to his feet.

"Aye," he called, turning.

Pero emerged from the darkness, blood trickling from a wound on his forehead, his dark eyes wide. Standing beside William, peering into the blackness of the chasm, he muttered in Spanish, "What fresh hell is this?"

William didn't answer. He couldn't. Still gripping his sword in both hands, his breaths came hard and fast.

The two men stood shoulder to shoulder in the black night, listening to the eerie wailing of the wind in the canyon.

2

When the sun rose over the Painted Mountains, the two men were able to clearly see what their attacker had fallen into—and what they themselves had narrowly missed in the darkness. Less than a hundred steps from their camp was a narrow but horribly deep crevasse, the inner walls jagged with rocks, a stream or river just visible as a dark thread far below.

Their attacker, whatever it had been, was gone, its body presumably swept away in the turbulent waters. In its wake, though, it had left devastation—the hideously mutilated bodies of three horses that had been unable to break free of their restraints, and all that remained of Najid and Rizzetti.

The two men had been torn apart, their guts and limbs strewn across the dusty ground. At first light

William and Pero had performed the grim task of tramping through the blood and gore to collect up the pieces and lay them out in a manner more befitting a pair of fallen warriors.

It was a token gesture only. William and Pero had no intention of burying their companions. The task would be too arduous and time-consuming. If they had any chance of surviving this ordeal, they had to conserve their energy and move on quickly. The remains of the three men would become a feast for the vultures, insects and wild animals. Their bones would bleach in the sun and eventually crumble into the sand of the desert.

Such is the fate of us all, William thought, staring down dispassionately at Najid and Rizzetti's mutilated bodies. He thought of the time and care they had taken to bathe and dress Rizzetti's leg wound yesterday. Pointless. Utterly pointless.

The news wasn't all bad, though. At some time in the night the two horses that had bolted during the attack had returned. Rising from a fitful and exhausted sleep, William had spotted them grazing on the meager scrubland nearby. Though skittish, the horses had been unharmed, and by working together and speaking gently to the animals, William and Pero had eventually been able to coax them back to camp. Now the horses were waiting, their saddlebags stuffed with the most valuable and useful items that the two men had selected from the packs of their dead companions.

Before they could leave, however, there was still one task left to perform. It was a task William had been putting off since waking that morning. Cleaning the thick green fluid from the blade of his sword had been bad enough. The fluid had been as thick as blood— thicker perhaps—and it had a foul stench, worse even than the high stink of rot that William was used to from the many battlefields he had fought on over the years. A thick trail of the green fluid, copious spatters of it, led from the area where William had clashed with the creature to the edge of the crevasse it had fallen into. But right on the edge of the chasm was something even more alarming than a pool of green fluid. There was a piece of their attacker. A trophy. Something that William must have severed in the darkness with a slash of his sword.

He had seen it that morning, but hadn't wanted to touch it. Now, taking a deep breath, he once again followed the trail of stinking green ooze to the edge of the chasm. He came to a halt and stared down at the huge taloned claw, twice as big as his own hand, which sat in the middle of a pool of drying gore beneath the desert sun.

The claw was green and scaly, almost armour-plated, and the hooked talons on the ends of its stubby appendages (fingers?) were as black as the magnet that William carried in his tunic. It was a fearsome thing.

Savage and somehow evil. Though inert, it seemed to give off an aura of hostility and potential violence, as if, like a desert scorpion, it might suddenly rise up on its talons and scuttle forward to attack.

William looked down at the claw for a long, long moment. Behind him he heard the horses snort and stamp, eager to be off. He had been through so much peril in his life that at times he had felt almost armour-plated himself; had considered himself no longer capable of fear. But this thing frightened him. It was unknown and unknowable. He wouldn't let it defeat him, though. He wouldn't let *anything* defeat him.

Clenching his teeth, eyes narrowing, he bent down and picked up the claw.

It was heavier than he had expected. It had a dull, meaty weight. Green goo drooled from its severed end and spattered on the dusty ground, splashing his boots.

He turned with it to see Pero staring at him. His friend looked momentarily troubled, then nodded at the claw with disdain.

"I'm not eating that. We have plenty of horsemeat to keep us going."

Ordinarily William would have smiled, but right now he wasn't in the mood. Still gingerly holding the claw, he walked past Pero and approached the horses.

"What are you doing?" Pero asked.

William's horse shied and whinnied, its eyes wide

with fear, as he carefully worked the huge taloned claw into his saddle bag.

Pero rolled his eyes, but said nothing. With the claw out of sight, William wiped his hand on his trousers, then glanced across at the bodies of their fallen comrades.

"You want to say something for the dead?" he asked.

Pero muttered in Spanish, "Better them than me."

William nodded, then squinted up at the cloudless sky. Vultures wheeled overhead.

"Let's saddle up and move on."

• • •

The men were exhausted.

The horses were exhausted.

But still they rode on.

The camp was five hours behind them. Five hours in which they had seen nothing but sand and rock and sky. Five hours in which the only other life had been the vultures wheeling constantly overhead and the occasional darting movement of a nearby lizard.

They were hungry and thirsty, their clothes reeking and stained, their skin and hair ingrained with sweat and sand and dust. They were currently straining up a steep slope, their horses sweating and panting beneath them. If they didn't find water soon, William knew their steeds would simply collapse beneath them—and then where would they be? They'd be stranded in the Painted

Mountains. Caught in a breathtakingly beautiful, multi-colored death trap.

Maybe there'll be something over the next rise, he thought. An oasis. A village.

He glanced back over his shoulder to see how far they'd come—and his heart sank.

Down below them on the trail, perhaps a mile back, was a cloud of dust. And within the dust…

"Pero," he said.

Pero pulled up and turned to William. His bearded face was drawn, his dark eyes hooded with fatigue. William nodded down at the trail behind them. Pero twisted on his horse to follow his friend's gaze. His expression didn't change, but he spat on the ground.

A group of riders, packed in a tight bunch, were urging their horses along the trail in pursuit of the two men. They were desert tribesmen, and they looked like black beetles against the vividly striped mountains, their dark robes flying behind them.

William turned his attention away from their pursuers and scanned the route ahead in search of some tactical advantage. A place that was easily defendable. Even some loose rocks that they could set rolling down the mountainside.

But there was nothing. Nothing but the steep, even slope stretching before them.

Looking back at the riders, squinting to make them

out more clearly, he said, "Looks like five to me."

Pero patted the neck of his panting steed. Its skin was foamy with sweat. "The horses are shot. We can't outrun them."

"Then we'll have to kill them," William said.

He reached behind him and started to unstrap his longbow from its sheath, which was attached to the back of his saddle. Although he was an excellent swordsman, the bow was his real weapon of choice, the one with which he was most adept.

"William," Pero warned.

William looked up to see that their problem had doubled. From a different crevice in the canyon below, another five-strong group of black-clad riders had appeared and were now thundering up the slope towards them.

"How many arrows do you have left?" Pero asked calmly.

William glanced again at the ten riders pursuing them. "Nine."

Pero sighed. "You think these are the bastards from before?"

"Does it matter?"

Pero shrugged.

William tightened the reins in his hand, readying himself and his horse for one last effort. "We'll take the rise," he said. "Make a stand there."

Pero looked at the slope stretching ahead of them.

Who knew whether the ridge they could see outlined against the sky was the crest of the mountain, or whether there would be still further to go once they reached it?

"What a long stinking way to go to die," he said wearily.

Then he and William looked at each other and simultaneously dug their spurs hard into their horses' flanks.

"Away!" William yelled.

"Yah!" shouted Pero.

Their horses shot forward.

The race was on!

Dust and stone chips flew as William and Pero urged their steeds on to one last desperate effort. From the way it shuddered and gasped, its eyes rolling in its sockets, William could tell that his horse was almost spent, that its legs could give way at any moment. He looked behind him and saw that the tribesmen were gaining, their strong and compact ponies flying up the steep slope like mountain goats. The desert people had wild, nomadic faces, eyes like black flints that were fixed on their prey. Opening their mouths, they let loose a series of crazed, ululating war cries. In their hands they carried mallets and spears, which they waved above their heads.

William faced front again, urging his horse ever onward. They were a hundred yards from the summit now...

Seventy-five...

Fifty…

But the tribesmen were gaining. With each exhausted, lunging step that his horse took, William could hear the thundering hoof beats of their pursuers getting closer and closer.

Twenty yards… and suddenly William's horse stumbled. He felt himself sliding forward, had to dig his heels and knees into his mount's hot flesh to prevent himself flying over its head and on to the rocky slope. He hauled on the reins, and through sheer force of will, encouraged his horse to regain its footing, to keep going.

But their pursuers were closer than ever. Their battle cries reverberated in his ears. William kept expecting a spear to thud into his back, a mallet to crash down on his skull.

Ten yards to the summit now… but it was hopeless. There was nowhere they could run to, nowhere to hide.

Eight yards… five…

Leaning low over his steed, William gritted his teeth and urged it to clamber up and over the top.

He had no idea what was awaiting him beyond the peak of the striped mountain. It could have been a further slope, or a plateau, or even a sheer drop to certain death.

What he and Pero *did* find, as their horses scrambled up and over the top of the ridge, was so unexpected, and so incredible, that they both came to a sudden and instinctive halt. For a split-second, hit by the majesty and the scale of the thing before them, they forgot their pursuers and simply gaped in awe and shock, their eyes widening in their filthy faces, their mouths dropping open.

Towering above them, so high they had to crane their necks right back to see the top, was a vast stone wall. And it was not *just* a wall, but a wall that went on and on, stretching out in both directions, undulating over mountains and valleys, for as far as the eye could see.

It was a wall, William thought, which might encompass the whole world. And beyond the wall was… what? A vast city? A mighty kingdom?

Certainly there was *something*. Squinting against the sky, the top of the wall almost lost in the heat haze from the sun way above, William saw what appeared to be the tip of a vast tower or fortress.

"Mother of God," Pero muttered in a hushed voice beside him.

William lowered his gaze, looked at his companion. He felt dizzy and disorientated, and not merely from thirst and exhaustion.

Then something caught his eye at the base of the wall, a flash of brilliant purple in his peripheral vision. He turned his head again, this time in the opposite direction.

And—wonder of wonders—he saw a group of at least thirty horsemen, sitting atop magnificent steeds and watching them silently, who had appeared seemingly from nowhere. The horsemen's gleaming purple armour was so beautiful, so immaculate, so intricately decorated, that William was quite prepared to believe they served whatever god ruled these provinces, and had been sent down from the heavens to offer divine justice. Each of the purple-clad horsemen wore a purple helmet from which antlers curled, and each was armed with an unusually long lance. William and Pero were so overawed that even when the soldiers, in one smooth motion, unsheathed their swords and raised their long lances, the two mercenaries simply stared, making no move to defend themselves.

Another flash of color, red this time, made William look up. And now he saw that above them, equally positioned along the top of the wall, a row of red-clad archers had appeared, their heads encased within crimson helmets. The archers were poised, their bows readied, countless gleaming, deadly arrow heads pointed in the direction of the two men.

Before William could speak, there was a *zing!* as dozens of strings were released in unison, and the next second arrows were flying at them like a swarm of deadly insects. He watched them arc across the clear blue sky, and then fall, speeding towards them.

William knew there was no point in retreating, no point in throwing himself from his horse and ducking for cover. The arrows were too fast and too plentiful.

Gripping the reins, he sat up straight in his saddle and waited calmly for death.

But death didn't come. Instead the arrows thudded into the dusty earth around them, enclosing them in a perfect circle, a fence of slim, scarlet-feathered arrow shafts.

"*Por dios…*" Pero murmured.

They don't intend to kill us, William thought, and his heart leaped. *Maybe there is hope, after all.*

Pero was clearly thinking the same thing. Now that the immediate danger was over, he was perusing the vast wall once again, his grimy, haggard face etched with awe.

"You are a well-travelled man, William…" he said quietly.

But William shook his head. "No. I've never seen anything like it."

Pero looked almost wistful now. On his scarred and brutal features the expression was an unusual one to see. "If only the Frenchman was here to see this."

William barked a laugh. "The lying bastard was right."

There was a rustling of hooves behind them. Pero glanced back to see that the pursuing tribesmen had stopped at the crest of the hill, and were now glancing uneasily up at the wall and the still-silent, purple-armored horsemen. But they were not retreating. They were waiting patiently, clearly believing that eventually the two mercenaries would have no choice but to turn back, into their clutches.

"I have no desire to go down fighting," Pero said. "Not today."

William too looked back at the tribesmen, then nodded. "Agreed. I say we take our chances with the gents in front of us."

"I haven't surrendered in a while," Pero said with the ghost of a smirk.

William grinned, his teeth white in his filthy face. "It'll come back to you."

He sheathed his bow, then dismounted from his horse and, still holding the reins, raised his hands. He led his horse out through the encircling fence of arrows and began walking slowly towards the soldiers. Pero followed suit, walking a few steps behind William, hands held high. From behind them came a cry of disgust, and William turned to see the tribesmen wheeling away, spurring their horses.

He looked at Pero and nodded. Pero nodded back.

The purple-clad horsemen remained motionless as the two men approached. William eyed their lances and swords uneasily.

Let's hope we've done the right thing, he thought.

3

"General Shao requests Commander Wu of the Tiger Corps! Commander Chen of the Eagle Corps!"

The runner, clutching a black signal flag, was small and wiry. Dressed in a simple uniform of shimmering black silk, he scurried through the complex, intertwining corridors of the massive fortress like a worker ant through the tunnels of a colossal nest.

"Commander Deng of Deer Corps!" he shouted, scampering along a corridor lined with Deer Corps soldiers in their resplendent purple armour, metal antlers curling from their elaborate, tight fitting helmets.

Down another corridor, then another. He knew this vast interior structure like the back of his hand. A wave of red-armored soldiers, their helmets resembling beaked eagles, parted like a crimson sea before him.

Another corridor, and here was a set of downward-leading stairs, which in turn led to a long, wide tunnel, where a line of soldiers at least three hundred strong, their armour yellow, their helmets molded into the shapes of glaring tigers' heads, were passing crates of arrows and bolts and other weaponry from hand to hand with tireless mechanical efficiency.

"General Shao summons Commander Lin of Crane Corps!" the runner shouted. "Immediate request for Commander Lin of Crane Corps! Commander Lin is needed at once!"

He sprinted around another corner. Ahead of him stretched another staircase, leading upwards this time. Seeing him, a dozen guards jumped to attention, pushing open a pair of burnished, exquisitely embossed metal doors as he flew up the stairs. The runner shot through the doors and along another corridor, lined with soldiers in gleaming blue armour.

At the end of this corridor was yet another set of double doors, even grander than the last. A blue-armored soldier opened this door for him, and he shot through into a huge, high-ceilinged room.

"Commander Lin of Crane Corps!" he shouted again. "Immediate request for Commander Lin of..."

He halted. On the far side of the room, at least two dozen officers and adjutants, who were huddled around an expansive desk, turned to regard him.

The wiry little runner, still clutching his flag, stared back at them impassively. Then he opened his mouth.

"General Shao requests Commander Lin! Immediately!"

A huge powerhouse of a man, well over six feet tall, stepped forward from the throng, his black armour topped with a helmet molded into the shape of a snarling bear's head. The man's shoulders were so broad that the armour seemed to fit him like a second skin. He took another clumping step towards the runner, the deep blue, highly polished floor seeming to vibrate as he did so. Then he moved to one side, gesturing with his hand.

"Here she is."

Commander Lin Mae, visible now through the gap that the Bear Corps officer had created by stepping aside, rose elegantly from her seated position behind the desk. Like the rest of the Crane Corps soldiers, she was a lithe and athletic young woman, her shimmering blue armour more lightweight than that of her male colleagues in order to better accommodate the seemingly gravity-defying aerial acrobatics that the Crane Corps were renowned for. Her features were delicate, bird-like, beautiful, her hair framing her face like shimmering blue-black raven wings. Her movements, as befitting her stature, were so economical they seemed barely to disturb the air. She gave the runner a single sharp nod.

"Tell General Shao that I am coming."

• • •

The Great Hall was a huge gathering space, simply but beautifully furnished in black, white and gold. The stone floor was dominated by a massive ceremonial table, which could have sat four dozen people with ease, its dark lacquered surface gleaming.

Lin Mae was the last of the Corps commanders to arrive. Commander Wu of the Tiger Corps, Commander Chen of the Eagle Corps and Commander Deng of the Deer Corps were clustered around General Shao in their lavishly vibrant armour and flowing capes, and looked up at her as she walked in. Lin Mae was flanked by her lieutenants Xiao Yu and Li Qing and a number of Crane Corps soldiers, whose job it was to pass on through the ranks any information or instructions conveyed here today. Arrayed behind the commanders were at least fifty other officers and attendants, all of whom were standing in respectful silence, deferring to the central figure of General Shao, the man who had called the impromptu conference.

Shao, Commander of the Bear Corps, and overall leader of the Nameless Order, was, appropriately, a bear of a man. Taller, broader and a couple of decades older than the other Corps Commanders, the bearded giant cut an impressive figure in his black armour. When Lin Mae entered the room, he was leaning forward over the ceremonial table, his gauntleted fists resting on its edge, staring broodingly down at an object that had been placed on its lacquered surface. Lin Mae barely had time to register that the object appeared to be a massive green claw equipped with curved black talons, when her attention was snagged by two figures sitting off to one side, who were so filthy and ragged that they provided a startling contrast to the immaculately attired gathering and the ancient majesty of their surroundings.

• • •

Sitting on the cold stone floor, back to back, William stared at the grim faces of the soldiers as they looked down on the green claw on the table in front of them.

Turning his head towards Pero, he muttered, "They know what it is."

He felt Pero's long, straggly hair move against his own as he nodded. "And they don't look happy to see it."

"All the more reason to get the hell out of here," said William. He nodded towards a side table against the far wall. "Our weapons are on that table."

Pero's voice was full of incredulity as he realized what his friend was proposing. "Are you out of your mind?"

Stubbornly William said, "I can take out the guards on the perimeter with my bow. You cut the legs out from under the officers."

Pero looked around the room, at the dozens of soldiers in their resplendent armour, at the guards manning the doors. "I must confess, this is not my favorite plan."

Both men fell silent as the female officer in the blue armour suddenly rounded the table and stalked towards them. Indicating the claw she barked, "Where was this found?"

William and Pero looked at her in astonishment, their eyes widening in realization that she must have understood every word they had said to one another.

"You speak English?" William exclaimed, trying to sound as if he was pleased.

Pero sighed and slumped back against his friend. "Fantastic," he muttered.

• • •

Lin Mae regarded the two men with distaste. Both had straggly beards and matted hair, and faces that were brown with dirt and dust. Even though she was a good ten or fifteen yards from them, she could smell the high, rank stench that came off them in waves.

Nevertheless when one of the men—the less brutal-looking one—grinned as he asked his question, she couldn't help but find it disarming. All the same, she would not get drawn into conversation, not here with General Shao and everyone else looking at her. Her voice hardened. "Where was this found? Where?"

The grin slipped from the man's face. He looked abashed. "It wasn't found. It was taken. This... thing killed two men and three horses before we took it down."

"Where?" Lin Mae asked again.

The man gestured vaguely. "North. The mountains."

Lin Mae looked at General Shao, who stared back at her impassively. In Mandarin she said, "He says north in the mountains. They claim to have killed it."

General Shao's eyes narrowed. "A scout? That's earlier than we expected." He looked to his right and raised his voice. "Strategist Wang?"

Lin Mae followed her leader's gaze. She hadn't even noticed that on the far side of the room, a short, round-faced man, dressed in simple, black scholarly robes and a black skullcap, was bent over a side table, carefully examining a disparate scattering of objects, which Lin Mae guessed were the men's possessions.

Without looking up, Wang said, "I'm listening, General."

• • •

Unbeknownst to everyone else in the room, a shadowy figure was watching proceedings from an upper walkway. With thin, almost ascetic European features, but dressed in an eclectic mix of Eastern and Western garb, the man was crouched behind a pillar, his eagle eyes darting here and there to take in every detail of the scene below, his sharp ears listening to every word.

He perused the two prisoners with interest, noting

that despite their ragged clothes and the layers of filth that coated their bodies, they possessed the brute poise of trained soldiers. The one who was doing all the talking seemed to be English like himself, whereas the other appeared to be… what? Spanish? Portuguese? He guessed the men were mercenaries—and good ones too. Neither was especially young, which meant they knew how to survive.

His eyes darted over the men's possessions, which Wang was currently examining at the side of the room. He saw weapons, of course—knives, swords, daggers, a longbow and nine arrows—and also wax, pitch, a mixture of strange coins and precious stones, flints and tinder…

There was nothing surprising here, nothing out of the ordinary… except for one item—well, two, if you counted the taloned claw on the ceremonial table. In the center of the side table, dominating it in many ways, was a peculiar black stone. As big as a man's clenched fist and glittering, as though studded with flecks of crystal.

• • •

On the floor below the interrogation was still going on. William wondered when and how it would end. He and Pero had not exactly been treated roughly, but neither had they been greeted with open arms. His attempt to establish a rapport with the beautiful woman in the blue armour, the one who spoke English, had not been entirely successful (much to Pero's amusement, no doubt), but the green claw had caused a great deal of excitement, which meant it might still provide the key to their continued survival, or even their eventual freedom. William was all too aware that he and Pero were currently standing on very uncertain ground. But at least, for the moment, they were still standing.

"What time of day?" the blue-armored woman asked him now.

"Night," said William. "Our camp was pitched next to a chasm—not that we knew it at the time. With a river below. It was the night before last."

He saw the woman hesitate, and then translate his words. He knew very little Chinese, though he had picked up a smattering of words on his travels. He heard her use the word "black". Black Chasm?

The big man in the bear armour scowled and barked something. Lin Mae turned back to William to translate her commander's words.

"There were just the two of you? You alone did this?"

Pero looked uncertain, as if he didn't know where this was going. William wondered whether the creature he had killed was sacred in some way, and whether whoever killed such a creature was destined to face a terrible punishment.

"Well… that's…" Pero was saying, but before he could wrongly incriminate himself, William jumped in.

"I killed it."

The blue-armored woman's eyes widened incredulously. "You alone?"

William felt all eyes on him. He didn't need the woman to tell him that the air was thick with hostility and suspicion. He nodded.

The blue-armored woman turned back to the black-armored commander and spoke in Mandarin, presumably telling him of William's claim to have killed the creature by himself.

Now the eyes that looked at him were full of incredulity, scorn. The little man in the black robes and hat on the far side of the room was gazing at William with an intensity that he found unsettling.

Pero leaned towards him. "What if that's the wrong answer?" he hissed.

The commander in the purple armour, metal antlers curling from his helmet, asked what was clearly a question, his manner full of astonishment. The red-armored commander responded with equal disbelief. It was clear that they were questioning William's claim to have killed the creature single-handed.

Confirming his assumption, the blue-armored woman said, "Tell me how you did this."

William nodded at the other commanders, who clearly didn't believe a word of his story. "Is that what they were asking?"

"Yes. They want to know how you alone killed the creature."

William shrugged. "With a swing of the sword." He demonstrated as best he could. "Sweep, thrust and full carry-round. The piece on the table… the hand… it came away clean. The beast fell back into a chasm. It landed somewhere in the river below."

Now the blue-armored woman's eyes widened even more than they had previously. "It fell back?"

"Yes."

She shook her head fiercely. "They do not fall back."

William looked at her in frustration, and then at the others. Was she the only one who spoke English? The only one he could talk to?

Pero spoke up for the first time, addressing the blue-armored woman. "It had no choice but to fall back. William was attacking it. If it hadn't fallen he would have cut it apart."

The blue-armored woman was silent. Now she was regarding them both suspiciously.

Frustrated, William said, "Well, aren't you going to tell them? You're not telling them what we're saying."

"I think you lie," she said fiercely.

William rolled his eyes. "Are *you* in charge?"

Instead of answering his question, the blue-armored woman responded with a question of her own. "Why are you here?"

"We came to trade," William said quickly. "We were ambushed."

The blue-armored woman barked an order, and William and Pero were grabbed by the soldiers flanking them and hauled to their feet. The soldiers then wrenched aside their ragged outer robes, exposing the chainmail tunics beneath. Before either William or Pero could react, the female officer had drawn her sword in one slick motion and pressed the point into William's throat, forcing him to tilt his head back.

"You lie!" she hissed. "You are soldiers! Why are you here?"

The bearded, black-armored General lifted a hand and barked a command, and after a moment the woman reluctantly sheathed her sword and stood back.

Ruefully William rubbed his throat. "Seems to me he's the one in charge. Maybe you should tell *him* what I said."

The woman's eyes flashed dangerously. "Hold your tongue."

For a moment there was a stand-off between them, each staring into the other's eyes.

At last William said mildly, "I think your General is waiting."

The blue-armored woman's pale cheeks flushed. She took an aggressive step back towards him, fixing his gaze with her own. "And I think *you* lie." She gestured disdainfully at the green claw. "I think you found this in the mountains."

The black-armored General asked a brief question, his voice curious, concerned. One of the words he spoke was "Lin". Was that the woman's name?

The woman's eyes flickered, and then her expression became steely. She turned to the General, speaking in tight, clipped phrases. William supposed she was telling her superior, and the rest of the room, how he had disposed of the creature, exactly what had happened. He didn't for a moment believe she was repeating what he had said after that.

• • •

Lin Mae was angry at the stinking foreign soldier for making her feel flustered, but trying not to show it. Her voice business-like, she said, "They claim to be traders who were ambushed. He says he killed the creature with a sword and it fell into the Black Canyon at the mountain pass."

Commander Chen of the Eagle Corps was scornful. "He expects us to believe that? These barbarians are liars!"

Across the room Strategist Wang had been examining the glittering black rock. Now he placed it carefully back on the table and looked up.

"I believe him."

His voice rang across the room. Everyone looked at him in surprise.

Indicating the green claw with an economical twitch of his hand, Wang said, "They brought the claw here. The wound is fresh. He has green blood on his sword and clothes. These details verify his story."

Now attention swung back to the two men, who looked uncomfortable and concerned beneath the steady gaze of at least fifty blank-faced soldiers.

"They travelled thousands of miles and encountered Tao Tei as soon as they entered China," Wang continued. "Does that sound likely to you?"

Still brimming with anger, Lin Mae barked, "Does it matter?" She looked at William. "I say we kill them now to preserve our secret and escape the trouble they will bring."

Commander Wu's snarling yellow tiger helmet flashed as he nodded. "I agree. Let's get rid of them and get back to work."

Commander Chen too added his support to the views of his colleagues. With a dismissive glance at the two filthy men, he said, "General, we have no time for this nonsense."

General Shao, though, was not so impetuous as his younger, hotheaded subordinates. He looked silently to Wang for his input. The wily strategist, his age closer to the General's own, said quietly, "I advise we keep them alive for a few more days… at least until we all arrive at the same truth."

General Shao gave an abrupt nod. "Agreed."

Lin Mae scowled. She glared at the two men, who clearly had no idea what was happening. That, at least, gave her a little satisfaction. Unless the General gave her a direct order to inform the foreigners of his decision, she would leave them stewing in their own uncertainty as to whether they were to be executed immediately or allowed to live a little longer.

All at once, from outside the doors to the Great Hall, but approaching rapidly, came the steady pounding of a drum. The discipline of all those in the room dissolved for a moment, and they began to chatter among themselves. Then General Shao held up a hand and they were silent once more. But Lin Mae could not blame them for their momentary loss of control. The drum meant only one thing. It was a warning of dire peril.

As the pounding came closer, General Shao ordered, "Open the doors."

A couple of soldiers hurried to do his bidding. Next moment a runner rushed down the corridor that led to the Great Hall, and dropped to his knees before the General's feet.

"General Shao," he gasped, clearly trying to retain his composure. "Signals from the smoke towers. We are under attack!"

Though the news was not entirely unexpected, Lin Mae sensed a collective intake of breath among those present, a suggestion of increased tension, of hushed anxiety. The only person who did not seem to be affected was General Shao himself. Calmly he said, "Take the prisoners to the North Tower stockade. Get them under lock and key. We have no time for this now."

Lin Mae nodded, whereupon the General turned and bellowed, "All stations on full alert!"

As the runner raced out, continually repeating the General's order at the top of his voice, the room suddenly burst into swift and efficient motion, everybody rushing to their posts. Although those currently manning the Wall had never faced a real attack, they had planned and trained for this moment for many years, and now that the reality was upon them, Lin Mae had no doubt that the operation would be carried out with the utmost precision and efficiency.

First, though, she had to ensure that the prisoners were put under lock and key, as the General had ordered.

"You two!" she barked. "Come with me!"

The more talkative of the two men, the insolent one, was watching the flurry of activity around him with bemusement. "What's going on?"

"Never mind! With me! *Now!*" she yelled.

• • •

In the shadows of the walkway above, the man who had been avidly watching proceedings in the Great Hall glanced up fretfully, his blade-thin nose twitching, like an animal sensing danger on the air. Then, muttering darkly to himself, he slunk away, silent as a ghost.

4

The pounding of drums echoed through the vast interior complex of the Great Wall. Smoke rose in precisely controlled signals from engraved copper vats on every turret, conveying messages far and wide. The corridors rang with shouted orders, and troops rushed in all directions, heading for their stations. In the midst of this manic but rigorously rehearsed pandemonium, William and Pero, hands bound behind their backs, were being hustled towards an unknown fate.

In front of them the blue-armored woman—Lin?—was leading the way, flanked by her two captains, or lieutenants, or whatever they were. Behind them, just in front of William and Pero, was the small, neat figure of the scholarly man who had been examining their possessions, moving with such economical steps that he seemed almost to be gliding along. Behind William and Pero, at the back of the group, cutting off all hope of escape, were eight huge, heavily armed soldiers in black bear armour, their faces set like stone.

A little breathlessly, Pero called out, "Are you about to kill us, sister?" His voice was all innocence. "Two lost travellers?"

The blue-armored woman didn't reply, didn't even glance back at them.

Turning to William, Pero said in Spanish, "What are we doing here, my friend? Is this cold bitch walking us to the gallows?"

"I think she'd like to," William replied, eyeing her sweep of raven-black hair, the way she moved, nimble and quick as a bird, despite her armour.

Raising his voice, Pero said sweetly, this time speaking in English, "If it's death we're heading for, my dear, then I need time to pray. I'm a very religious man."

But still his words met with no response.

They turned to their left, passed through a wooden gate, and began to climb a set of steep stone steps. The steps were divided into groups of twelve, at the top of each of which was a stone landing. Gaps to their left offered them brief glimpses of different levels of the Wall, and of soldiers preparing weapons and taking up positions, readying themselves for battle.

"I know this, sister," Pero said. "I know siege

preparations when I see them. Who comes at you so hard that you need a wall like this?"

The blue-armored woman continued to lead them resolutely upward, acting as if Pero hadn't spoken.

The ominous pounding of the drums went on and on. William was starting to lose patience with the woman's silence. Angrily he said, "If we're to die, what's the harm in telling us why?" When she *still* failed to respond, he bellowed, "What the hell did we kill out there?"

The scholarly man turned to regard him. He had the air of a man of science examining a new and interesting species of insect. "Tao Tei," he said. "You killed a Tao Tei scout."

William and Pero both gaped. Until this moment they had had no idea that the man could speak English. William opened his mouth to respond, but before he could, the man spoke again. Raising his eyebrows a notch—his only concession to incredulity—he said, "*You* killed it. You killed it alone."

William and Pero looked at one another. What William had done was obviously significant. But when it came down to it, the beast, though big and fearsome and full of green blood, had been nothing but a wild animal. And he had been armed. So why all the fuss?

"What is a... Tao Tei?" Pero asked.

Up ahead the blue-armored woman finally responded—but only to bark an order at the scholar in Mandarin. The little man looked affronted, and responded coldly. William didn't need a translator to tell him that the woman had told the man not to speak to the prisoners, whereas he had clearly said something to the effect that she wasn't *his* boss, and that he would do as he saw fit.

Sure enough the little man turned back to them and said, "You are correct. We are under siege. But we did not expect the attack for another nine days. Many things about your story have importance." He puffed out his chest a little, and as though the choice was his, declared importantly, "You are not to die today!"

If he expected gratitude, he was to be disappointed. William, for one, didn't like his use of the word "today". If he and Pero *were* to be killed, he'd rather get it done quickly than live under the shadow of death for however long it might be until he was no longer considered useful.

"That's great," Pero said with more than a hint of sarcasm, "but can we go back to the Tao Tei? Or did I miss something?" He enunciated his words carefully. "What *is* a Tao Tei?"

Before the little man could respond, the blue-armored woman raised an arm and barked an order. Immediately the soldiers both at the front and back of the group came to a halt, forcing William and Pero to do the same. William looked up to see they had arrived at a large solid-looking door with a circular handle below an oversized keyhole.

"Must be the stockade," he murmured to Pero.

From behind them, one of the Bear warriors detached himself from their eight-strong escort and marched forward, carrying a huge dusty ring of keys. William glanced at him as he strode past, and was surprised to see that beneath the fearsome black helmet molded to resemble a snarling bear's head was the face of a young and nervous boy. In fact, now that he looked more closely, it was clear that the boy's armour, which was snug on his muscle-bound comrades, was a little too large for him. Despite the circumstances, William almost smiled.

The young bear warrior reached the blue-armored woman and nervously pushed a key into the lock. He tried to turn it, but it didn't turn. As he withdrew the key and began to search for the right one with trembling hands, William saw his eyes widen in panic, saw sweat begin to trickle down his face. The blue-armored woman stood motionless, glaring at him. With the din of battle preparations audible from the nearby Wall, it was clear she was eager to get this job done and enter the fray. The young bear warrior muttered what could only have been an apology, and the woman released a gasp of exasperation. She said something to her two lieutenants, and they hurried away—clearly she had been giving them leave to join the oncoming battle.

Pero looked at William, amusement dancing in his eyes, and mouthed: *Wrong keys*.

William grinned back at him, but there was a part of him that couldn't help feeling sorry for the boy.

• • •

General Shao stood on top of his command tower, his black cape with its bear emblem snapping in the desert breeze. Flanking him on both sides were several of his commanders, resplendent in their brightly colored armour. Though the group stood in solemn silence, staring out at the desert beyond the Wall, the air seemed to vibrate with tension and fear, but also with excitement. They all knew that what they were about to face was savage and terrible—but it was a moment they had all anticipated for as long as they had lived. A moment they had trained for, ceaselessly and tirelessly, since they had been children. A moment they had been *born* for.

In the distance, across the valley, a thread of river glistened under the sun. Beyond the river was the jade green Gouwu Mountain. At first glance the scene seemed a picture of beauty and tranquility. But beneath the whisper of the breeze was another sound, almost indiscernible at first, but quite definitely *there*. It was a sort of churning. Or rumbling.

Like distant thunder.

As the rumbling grew louder, it was accompanied by

yet another sound, carried forth on the wind. This new sound was shriller and far more disturbing. It almost sounded like… babies.

Thousands of babies.

Wailing in terrible distress.

. . .

The group in front of the stockade door suddenly tensed and raised their heads, each of them half-turning in the direction of the outer wall. From beyond it, faintly, they could hear a terrible sound, a hideous screeching wail, as if thousands of children were being tortured.

Lin Mae was the first to recover. Turning to Wang she said urgently, "Strategist, the Crane Corps needs me. I must go. Please forgive me."

Without waiting for a response, she hurried after her lieutenants, Xiao Yu and Li Qing.

Wang sighed, and then turned his mounting ire on the young Bear warrior, whose name was Peng Yong. "Hurry!" he snapped.

But his irritation did not encourage the boy. In fact, it had the opposite effect. Peng Yong jumped, and dropped the ring of keys, which hit the floor with a tinkling clatter. Sweating heavily, Peng Yong patted his own body, as if the missing key could somehow have magically worked its way beneath his armour without his knowledge.

"Sir, I…" Suddenly he blurted it out. "I cannot find the key!"

Wang sighed again, heavily, then spun to indicate the two prisoners. "Forget it! Bring them to the Wall and have the Bear Corps watch them!"

He stomped away. Still sweating, Peng Yong turned to the two prisoners and the group of impassive Bear Corps soldiers behind them. He gave a jerky nod, and saw the two men's eyes widen in alarm as gauntleted hands clamped down on their shoulders.

• • •

Moving nimbly and almost silently for a man of his age, Strategist Wang sprinted up the steps of the command tower. He emerged into daylight to find General Shao standing there alone, staring broodingly at what looked like a dust storm, bowling towards them from the far-distant jade mountain.

Shao turned and nodded a greeting. Wang moved forward to stand beside him, his head barely coming up to the clawed bear paw epaulette on the General's right shoulder.

"So General," he said, "it's finally happening."

Shao nodded again. "Sixty years," he said. "Sixty years spent in preparation for this one moment."

• • •

Lin Mae hurried up the steps of the Crane Corps command tower, followed by several blue-armored warriors. At the top a nervous but clearly relieved Xiao Yu moved forward to greet her.

"Commander Lin," she said, "the sky rigs are ready to deploy."

• • •

William whistled in admiration as, escorted by the bear warriors, he and Pero passed through a pair of huge wooden doors and onto the wooden platform of a vast space just behind the outer surface of the Wall itself. The area—it couldn't really be called a 'room'—was deep and high, and stretched as far as the eye could see in both directions. William couldn't help but feel he was standing within the workings of some colossal timepiece, albeit one that was infinitely more intricate and complex than anything he had seen before. Wherever he looked, his eyes were dazzled by numerous, vast mechanical components working in perfect harmony. There were enormous wooden and iron bearings, a cornucopia of wheels, winches, gears and levers, some propelled by gushing spumes of water. And among all of this, like busy but autonomous cogs in the machine, were dozens, perhaps even hundreds, of yellow-clad tiger warriors, each of whom were working furiously, operating an array of cranks and pulleys and rotating wooden handles.

He and Pero were ushered to the edge of the platform, and just for a moment William wondered whether they were about to be pushed into the maelstrom of grinding cogs and cables he could see below—blood sacrifices to the great devouring Wall. To his right he saw weird contraptions, five of them, slowly rising from hollows within the depths of the machinery. They were long and thin, and made him think of part of a ship's rigging, its sails and spars tucked in tightly for now, though ready to expand, to unfurl, when given space to do so.

The five contraptions were being hauled upwards by chanting, sweating soldiers, but before they could reach the level on which William and Pero were standing, an iron cage slid down from above on pulleys and opened directly in front of them. The young soldier who had dropped the keys, as if anxious to make up for his earlier mishap, barked at them and shoved them forward. He and another bear warrior followed them into the cage, the young soldier closing the door behind them. Then several soldiers on the platform began to turn a winch, and the cage rose smoothly into the air.

William might have been alarmed if there hadn't been so much to distract his attention. Through the bars of the cage he watched the narrow contraptions, which were now beside them and still rising rapidly—more rapidly than they were, in fact. Pero's astonishment matched his own as the huge, folded bundles of sails and spars slid past their cage, ascending to the high ceiling. Just as it seemed the five contraptions would either have to come to a halt or collide with the ceiling, five separate sections of the ceiling opened with a cracking sound, and the contraptions rose majestically up through the holes, beyond which they could see daylight.

William and Pero looked at each other, blinking in awe. They had seen many wondrous sights on their travels, but never had they seen anything so advanced as this, and on such a vast scale. William couldn't help but feel he and his companion were primitive and uneducated cave dwellers in comparison to their hosts. Whoever the enemy of these Wall warriors might be, they would surely have no chance of victory against such an incredible display of ingenuity and organization.

The cage reached its apex and clanked to a halt. The big bear warrior opened the door and the younger bear warrior, overly aggressive now, shoved William and Pero forward. They stumbled a little, squinting in the sudden bright sunlight that shone down on top of the Wall. To their right the battlements, which faced the desert, were a hive of activity as troops made their final preparations for war. William veered in that direction, hoping to catch a glimpse of whoever was foolhardy enough to attack the Wall and its many and varied defenses. He had taken no more than a couple of steps, however, when sunlight flashed on steel, and a moment later the tip of a sharp lance was pressed against his neck.

The young bear soldier's face was apoplectic with rage. His show of aggression and hostility wasn't quite convincing, though. Beneath the boy's bluster William sensed fear and uncertainty. If they hadn't been surrounded by myriad armored soldiers, he would have found it a simple task, even in his exhausted state, to have snatched the lance, flipped it round and rammed it through the young warrior's guts. He decided, though, that in this instance it was better to comply than to retaliate and end up dead. And so, curling his lips in a disarming grin, he raised his hands in surrender.

Clearly buoyed by his mastery over the foreign prisoner, the young soldier yelled an order at them. Although they didn't understand his words, the fact that he jabbed them with the end of his long lance made it clear that he wanted them to sit against the wall. William and Pero did so, their backs pressed up against the rear parapet. They watched the proceedings around them with a mixture of professional curiosity, apprehension and utter astonishment.

What astonished them the most was the fact that the Wall, incredible structure though it was, was not simply a barrier against attack, but a brilliantly conceived war machine. Peering over the parapet behind them, they saw that attached to the Wall below was a seemingly endless row of huge trebuchets, like gigantic, jointed arms that were even now slowly straightening, that stretched as far as the eye could see in both directions.

They both jumped as the surface of the Wall at the bottom of each of the trebuchets suddenly began to crack open. William's first thought was that the Wall was somehow breaking up, that the enemy, whoever they were, had launched a stealth attack, which was now undermining the structure. But then he realized that, like the ceiling through which the sail-decked contraptions had risen, the Wall was *supposed* to break open. He watched, amazed, as from the channels that had been created rose a series of vast iron chutes.

This, though, was perhaps only the least of the wonders they were destined to witness over the next few minutes. No sooner had the chutes appeared than, with a further series of cracks, the stone floor in front of them opened in multiple places once again, and what appeared to be numerous nests or platforms rose up from below. As soon as they were in position, rows of red-armored eagle snipers lined up and began to climb onto the platforms. Each of them was holding a weapon William had never seen before. It was similar to his own bow, but shorter, stubbier, and held horizontally rather than vertically. Odd though the weapons were, he and Pero had seen for themselves how accurate they could be. Again William wondered how an attacking force could hope to win against such firepower.

With the archers in position on their raised platforms, the floor cracked open yet again—in different sections this time—and the contraptions that William and Pero had seen earlier rose up through the gaps. There were not just five of them this time, but dozens—hundreds perhaps. They rose up into the air like giant spikes, and then, when they were in position, a flood of female crane warriors, fluid and nimble as dancers in their vibrant blue armour, flooded forward to tug on ropes and pulleys dangling from the undersides of the contraptions.

As they did so the contraptions opened up, like vast elegant birds spreading their wings. Immediately crane warriors began to step up onto the bird-like rigs, to buckle and strap themselves into harnesses that were attached to the structure, to become a part of it. As soon as they were in position, yellow-clad tiger warriors came forward to toss the crane warriors long lances, which they caught nimbly, before taking up their positions on massive winches to which the bird-like rigs were attached. The tiger warriors began to haul on levers and ropes, hauling the rigs higher, causing the great wing-like sails to spread wider, to fill with air. Now the crane warriors looked ready to launch themselves from the battlements, to fly and swoop through the air like gigantic birds.

William glanced at Pero, and saw that his dark eyes were as big as saucers.

Just as amazed himself, he muttered, "This is…"

"Unbelievable," Pero supplied.

William spotted one of the crane leader's captains or lieutenants clambering atop one of the rigs and strapping herself in, but he couldn't see the crane leader—Lin?—herself.

And then he *did* see her, further along the Wall, barking orders, organizing her troops. She was perched on one of the rigs, which was being hauled into position by tiger soldiers. As the wings of the rig spread she stood proudly, stretching her body out as though eager to launch herself into battle, a long lance in each hand, as if she was prepared to fight twice as hard as everyone else.

She looked magnificent, dazzling, beautiful. Her black hair flowed in the wind. William couldn't take his eyes off her.

And then, from behind a shadowy buttress in the Wall close to them, half-concealed by one of the trebuchets, a head suddenly appeared, snagging his attention.

The head was followed by the upper part of a lean, almost scrawny body. William blinked in surprise as the newcomer turned to regard him. What surprised him the most was not that the man had appeared, but that he was a Westerner, like himself! Who was he? Where had he come from? He didn't seem to be a prisoner here. The man was cadaverous, with sharp, almost fox-like features. He clenched his teeth in a grin and nodded. Then, as quickly as he had appeared, he was gone again.

William turned to Pero, feeling slightly dazed. "Did you see that?"

Pero nodded. "I did."

Beyond the din of preparations—the clank and creak and scrape of machinery, the pounding of drums, the bellowing of orders—the sound that had pulled them all up short in front of the stockade door, the screeching and wailing, as of a thousand tormented children, had been growing steadily louder. Now it was loud enough to start drilling into their heads, to send shudders of primal fear through their bodies.

"Who the hell are they fighting?" William asked, raising his voice above the ululation.

Pero shook his head. "No idea. But they look nervous."

William surveyed the well-drilled activity still taking place in front of them. Admiringly he said, "They know how to follow orders."

What Pero had said, though, was true. The soldiers *did* look nervous. And as the ceaseless wailing grew louder and closer and more ear piercing, they looked more nervous still, their eyes flickering with fear, sweat running down their faces.

"It's a big wall to be so nervous," Pero said.

Their bear guards had now turned their attention from their two prisoners and, like everyone else, were focused on the oncoming threat beyond the Wall. William nudged Pero and indicated the buttress to their right, from behind which the scrawny Westerner had appeared.

"Let's get a closer look," he said.

The two men sidled across to the buttress and, awkwardly because of their bound hands, scrambled up on to it as best they could to get a better vantage point. As soon as they were high enough, they peered over the heads of the hundreds of waiting troops at the desert beyond.

What they could see made them gasp. The river in the distance, which seemed to mark a border between the Wall and the jade mountain, was seething and churning, as if the water had turned boiling hot. Foam and spray were rising in the air, sparkling in the sun. But there was something *in* the spray, something dark that seemed to move with a kind of frantic purpose. Was it a single entity or…

"Dios mio…" Pero muttered.

William gaped, but couldn't speak. He literally couldn't believe what he was seeing. The creatures now bursting from the smothering cloud of spray, revealed for the first time beneath the unforgiving desert sun, were not animals but *monsters*. They barreled en masse towards the Wall, hundreds of them, *thousands* of them. And as they came they screamed their terrible, wailing war cry; a sound of rage and hunger and misery. It was as if they had burst from the very depths of Hell, bringing the screams of the tormented with them.

The closer they came to the Wall, the more William

and Pero could make them out. Each one of the beasts was the length of a grizzly bear, or a great ape, with a solid, muscular body that was nevertheless lithe enough to propel them across the desert sand at an incredible speed. Their skin, plated like armour, was green and crocodile-tough, with a ruff of hyena-like fur on their backs, and although it was hard to tell at a distance, each plate seemed to be marked or inscribed with a translucent pattern of swirls. Their heads were massive and shark-like, dominated by huge, blood red mouths filled with countless rows of sharp, jagged teeth. Their eyes, by contrast, were small and deep-set, and were positioned not on their heads but on either side of their wide, barrel-like chests. Although the creature William had fought and killed the previous night had reared up on two legs to attack him, these monsters were racing across the desert on all fours, impeded not in the slightest by the fact that their claws were huge, club-like, and inset with curved, black, razor-sharp talons.

A shudder of primal terror ran through William's body, yet mixed in with that was a scintilla of admiration, even awe. In all his travels he had never seen a creature so well equipped to fight and kill. He only hoped the Wall would stand firm against what was destined to be a devastating attack, and that the many and ingenious weapons of their captors would be enough to repel the invaders.

5

Up on her sky rig, Lin Mae gripped her two long lances tightly and tried to stay calm. The wind, which she could feel blowing through her hair, brought the awful screeches of the Tao Tei, which alone would have turned an ordinary man or woman's guts to water. But she had trained for this. She had been born for it. She took long, deep breaths and tried to find the point of stillness in the center of her body. When it came to the battle she would draw her strength and her focus from that stillness. Whatever happened today, she would not be found wanting.

• • •

Still standing on top of his command tower, Wang beside him, General Shao silently observed the oncoming horde. He was anxious, though not for himself. He feared for the city of Bianliang, which the Wall had been designed to protect, and for the one million people who lived there. If the Tao Tei breached the Wall... If they reached the city...

He quashed the thought.

The Tao Tei *would not* breach the Wall.

He and his troops *would not* fail.

He would not allow it.

He watched the Tao Tei approach. He stood silently, waiting for them to get a little closer... a little closer...

Wang looked at him anxiously, but still Shao waited.

Come on, he thought, *come on...*

And then suddenly he sprang into motion, startling Wang.

Wheeling first left, and then right, he bellowed the order:

"Long distance weapon!"

• • •

As the war drums quickened, and General Shao's order was relayed quickly along the Wall in both directions, the Tiger Corps warriors, responsible for engineering and artillery, leaped to the fore. Within the machine-like workings of the inner Wall, huge cannon balls were winched carefully from cauldrons of boiling oil and placed on iron chutes. Beside the chutes waited more

Tiger Corps soldiers with burning brands, who set the cannon balls aflame and then launched them, trailing flames and heat, down the metal slopes of the chutes towards their destination. The chutes passed through channels in the Wall, allowing the flaming cannon balls to roll into the iron holders of the dozens of trebuchets ranged along the battlements. As soon as the cannon balls were in place, a trigger was activated and the trebuchets fired. Once their cargos had been released the trebuchets were primed again and the action repeated.

• • •

Perched precariously on the buttress, their hands still tied behind their backs, William and Pero watched as the sky became filled with massive iron fireballs. The noise as the trebuchets, one after another, launched burning metal death towards the advancing horde of green monsters was tremendous, almost but not quite loud enough to drown out the ceaseless screeching of the creatures themselves. And the effect of the fireballs was devastating. They rained down on the horde, smashing many of the creatures into instant extinction, and creating a barrier of rising flame between the Wall and the incoming tide of attackers.

Yet unbelievably the creatures kept coming. Many dozens of them, undeterred by the rain of missiles, burst through the flames leaping up around them, as if unaffected by the blistering heat. From his perch William could see that the creatures' advance guard had suffered serious casualties. Yet he could also see that the creatures were *so* numerous that in the long run the death toll they had suffered from the fireballs alone would be so small as to be virtually negligible.

Another cry went up from the black-armored General on the command tower, his stentorian voice cutting through even the screeching of the creatures and the din of battle. William glanced up and across at the General, a distant figure whose black armour glinted in the sunlight, and wondered what he had said.

Whatever it was, he hoped it would prove effective against the enemy.

• • •

The drums changed tempo in line with the General's new order, which in turn was relayed swiftly along the length of the Wall in both directions: "Raise the mirrors! Raise the mirrors!"

Perched on the battlements at the very front of the Wall, effectively standing on the edge of a precipice and peering down at the desert far, far below, Commander Chen of the Eagle Corps gripped his crossbow and waited grimly to be called into action. If all went to plan it would not be long now. The order to raise the mirrors had been given, and already, leaning forward, he could see bricks in the Wall flipping over rapidly, to reveal that on their backs were smooth reflective surfaces that caught the sunlight and deflected it in a shimmering wave of golden light over the advancing hordes of the Tao Tei. Within moments every single brick in the Wall had flipped around, to create a smooth mirrored surface that stretched the length of the Wall. It undulated and meandered through the Painted Mountains, absorbing the blinding sunlight and casting it back as a white glare.

He braced himself on his perch as the first of the Tao Tei approached the Wall at lightning speed and then hurled itself forward. It tried to scramble up the mirrored surface, digging in its talons, but the mirrors proved every bit as effective as it had been hoped. Unable to get any traction on the smooth surface, the Tao Tei sank back to the ground, its claws making a hideous screeching sound as they slid over the glass. Immediately more of the Tao Tei hurled themselves at the Wall, but they too fell back. Soon hundreds of the creatures were packed against the base of the Wall, writhing and squirming over one another in their desperation to rend and tear and devour. Chen smiled grimly. The Tao Tei were now exactly where the Corps wanted them to be. He raised his head, looking to his left and right, and gave the order.

"Fire! Aim for the eyes!"

Immediately a lethal rain of bolts poured down on the

mass of Tao Tei below. Those creatures that were struck in the eyes died instantly, their life force extinguished in a split second. However those that were struck in other parts of the body only became more enraged, tearing and biting at the bolts, ripping them from their plated bodies and casting them away, as if they were nothing more troublesome than thorns or the stings of insects.

Still firing arrows, his hands moving so quickly they were almost a blur, Chen heard Commander Shao, up on his command tower, issue another bellowed order: "Crane Corps attack! Now!"

Watching another of his bolts strike home, he felt like a small but vital component of a great war machine.

Soon, he thought with grim satisfaction. *Soon we shall have victory.*

• • •

Lin Mae conveyed the General's orders, and watched with pride as the red-armored Eagle Corps drew back, allowing the sky rigs of the Crane Corps to be wheeled forward. The mechanisms and controls of the rigs themselves would be manipulated by the Tiger Corps, each of the different disciplines among the warriors of the Nameless Order working together like harmonious parts of a single entity.

As she was moved into position she looked right and left, and saw that the first wave of her Crane Corps soldiers were as poised and ready as she was. Each of them was standing upright on their rigs, proud and fearless, lances in their hands ready to strike at the enemy. Lin Mae knew how eager each of them would be to do their duty, the exultation they would feel as they launched themselves from the battlements. As a Crane Corps soldier, to fly was everything. To soar was the closest one could get not only to freedom, but to divinity. Facing front, she gripped her lances and took a long deep breath, searching again for that point of stillness in the center of her body.

• • •

As the blue-armored woman on her flying rig was wheeled forward to take her place at the forefront of the battle, William felt his stomach clench. They hadn't exactly become friends in the short time they had spent together—in fact, he was sure she would see him executed without a qualm—but he nevertheless couldn't help feeling there was a connection between them, and not simply because she spoke his language. The thought of someone so beautiful, so graceful, going head to head with the slavering, voracious beasts below seemed wholly wrong to him, obscene even. How could her elegance and purity survive in the face of such insatiable savagery? War was a filthy, bestial pursuit, best carried out by filthy, bestial creatures like himself and Pero.

As she braced herself to leap into the unknown his heart began to beat as fast as the pounding war drums, and he opened his mouth, as if to cry out.

But before he could say anything, the moment was gone. She yelled out an order, and then without hesitation dived from the battlements, lances extended.

William watched with horror as she plummeted towards the ravening horde below.

• • •

Launching herself from the top of the Wall, Lin Mae knew that her life was in the hands of the Tiger Corps warriors operating her sky rig. If they made the slightest mistake she would die, but she had the utmost faith that that wouldn't happen. As she soared into the air, she knew they would be operating the winches to slacken the ropes of the rig, allowing her to plunge towards the sea of green flesh and ravening jaws below. Holding on to the point of stillness within herself she readied her lances and focused on making her contribution count.

At the apex of her dive she felt herself tipping, falling, the desert wind battering her body and the sails of the sky rig with increasing force as she hurtled towards the ground. It was easy to panic here, to lose control, to spin and twist in mid-air. But she maintained her shape and concentrated on picking out her twin targets and sticking to them.

There! The eyes of the creature rearing up towards her, like a dog leaping to snaffle a scrap of tossed meat, were small and black, but as she plunged towards it, they seemed to grow larger, to fill her world. She adjusted the position of her lances slightly, and then, just at the right moment, thrust them downwards! The creature shuddered and died as the lances embedded deep in its eyes bent in two perfect arcs, slowing her fall. As her downward momentum was arrested, Lin Mae calmly and expertly flipped her body round in mid-air, from a diving position into a sitting position, at the same time bending her knees and drawing them into her body, tightening herself into a ball. She knew that up above the Tiger Corps soldiers would be frantically turning the winches in the opposite direction, pulling the ropes of the sky rig taut, so that she could spring back up into the air, out of danger.

For a couple of seconds, though, she was vulnerable. And sure enough, as she let go of her lances and watched the dead, impaled Tao Tei sink back into the morass of wriggling green flesh below, another of the creatures surged up from the throng, using the bodies of its comrades to propel itself towards her.

Lin Mae watched its widening maw grow larger beneath her feet, knowing there was nothing she could do. She saw rows of jagged teeth, a long red throat, smelled the thing's breath come boiling up towards her, hot and rancid.

Just as the creature's wide-open jaws began to close, the ropes of the sky rig reached their maximum tautness, and a split-second later she was shooting up into the air like an arrow fired from a crossbow. The Tao Tei's jaws snapped shut so close to the bottom of her feet that she felt the upward push of air created by it rippling through her lower body.

Nevertheless she composed herself as she hurtled upwards, stretching out her body, enjoying the sensation of the wind parting around her as she cut through it. As she neared the top of the Wall, she tilted her body, shifting her weight on to her right side so that the sky rig swung round with her in a graceful half-circle. She held out her hands and one of the Tiger Corps soldiers expertly tossed across two more lances. Lin Mae caught them, and without even catching her breath, flipped and dived again. Around her she was aware of other Crane warriors rising or plunging as they performed similar maneuvers.

Suddenly she heard a scream from below. Looking to her left she saw one of her warriors plummeting towards the open jaws of a rising Tao Tei. The girl was trying to twist in mid-air, to aim her lance towards one of the creature's eyes, but it was clear that this creature had not been her intended target, had instead risen unexpectedly from the mass and caught her on her blind side. Lin Mae looked on in horror as the girl frantically kicked her legs in an attempt to arrest or alter her course. But it was no use. The ropes of her sky rig were too slack.

Next moment the Tao Tei had her. The girl disappeared into its maw, still clutching her lance, and the Tao Tei's jaws snapped shut. With a couple of sickening crunches it devoured both the Crane Corps warrior, her lance and half of her sky rig, leaving the remainder of the rig dangling in mid-air, blood-stained and mangled.

Awful though the sight was, Lin Mae knew she couldn't let it affect her. They had all of them been resigned to dying a heroic death. They had known it was inevitable that once battle became joined with the enemy there would be casualties. As she plunged once again towards the seething green sea below, she tried to focus, to rediscover the point of stillness at her center.

But as she tried to home in on her new target, she realized that something was happening beneath her.

More than that, she realized that something was *wrong*.

• • •

High up in his command tower, General Shao had been watching the battle with a great deal of satisfaction. Their tactics had been working well. They had thinned out the advance guard of the Tao Tei with their fireballs, many of which were still burning; they had used their mirrors to prevent the Tao Tei from scaling the Wall, thus causing the creatures to mill about mindlessly at its foot; and now his Eagle Corps, Tiger Corps and Crane

Corps warriors were working together with devastating effect to pick off the rest of the creatures at will.

It was almost *too* easy. Like spearing fish in a barrel.

But then perhaps they deserved an easy victory. They had been working tirelessly for many years to produce the most effective weapons and the most highly trained fighting force imaginable. And the Tao Tei, formidable though they were, were really nothing but mindless beasts. Perhaps they had finally met their match. Perhaps this victory would mark an end to…

Then Wang, standing beside him, drew his breath in sharply, and everything changed.

Shao looked at Wang. But Wang's eyes were fixed on the battlefield below, where the Crane Corps were still diving and swooping. Wang, though, was not looking at their own troops. Instead he was observing the Tao Tei with narrowed eyes. General Shao followed his gaze— and then he too gasped in astonishment.

Something was happening among the Tao Tei. The mindless beasts that had been packed so tightly at the base of the Wall it was almost as if they'd been *offering* themselves up for slaughter, were now thinning out, pulling back—and not haphazardly but uniformly, like soldiers following orders. Indeed, General Shao saw an increasing number of the creatures lifting their massive heads and extending their surprisingly long necks, as if receiving some form of signal. The Crane Corps were still diving, but now there were fewer and fewer of the creatures left for them to kill. Almost meekly, considering how voracious, how utterly savage they were, the majority of Tao Tei were not only retreating but moving into formation, lining up in ranks.

• • •

William and Pero too were watching the Tao Tei with astonishment.

"Jesus," William murmured. "They're forming up."

With nothing left to kill, the Crane Corps soldiers were leaping back up onto the battlements, detaching themselves from their sky rigs. William was relieved to see that the Crane Corps commander, whose name might or might not be Lin, was one of them. Not all the Crane Corps soldiers had made it. William had seen several flying rigs hauled back up over the battlements shattered, bloodstained and empty.

Pero was peering beyond the ranks of Tao Tei, squinting into the sun. Now he nodded to indicate the distant desert.

"Look there," he said. "Further back."

William looked where he was indicating, wishing he could raise his hand to shield his eyes. Some way back beyond the furthermost ranks of the Tao Tei another group of creatures had emerged from the cloud of mist that now all but shrouded the boiling river. There were around a dozen of them, similar to the Tao Tei but taller and more powerful looking. Impressive and terrifying though these new creatures were, it wasn't they that drew the eye, however. Like a ring of bodyguards, the larger creatures were surrounding a being that was truly monstrous. Its body was massive, with dark, translucent skin and a huge, distended belly. Its eyes were a vivid green, flashing in the sun, and even though he was some distance away William sensed that a fierce, unknowable intelligence burned behind them.

As he watched, the creature raised its head and opened its vast mouth, as though chewing the air. William saw endless rows of curved, glinting, razor-sharp teeth, each of which looked as long as his forearm. Indeed, the maw itself, opened to its full capacity, looked capable of swallowing half a dozen men with a single gulp. He looked on with awe and revulsion as horn-like appendages on the creature's head, linked by a web-like film of connective tissue, suddenly began to vibrant, and to produce a hideous, high-pitched ululating sound, which caused many of the soldiers in front of him to cover their ears with their hands. As the sound drilled into his head and seemed to set his skull vibrating, William wished he could do the same.

• • •

Watching from her perch atop the battlements, Lin Mae saw that the awful, elongated screech of sound issued by the vast creature in the distance was having a marked effect on the now eerily ordered ranks of the Tao Tei. Straightening up, row after row of them, like soldiers going into battle, they each raised their heads and let out an answering wail of their own. Then, in perfect unison, the first row charged headlong at the Wall and crashed into it with all their might.

Lin Mae tensed as she felt the stone battlement tremble beneath her feet. She knew, though, that no matter how hard they tried the Tao Tei would never smash their way through the Wall using sheer brute force. Did they honestly think they could?

Nevertheless they kept at it. After the first row had moved out of the way, seemingly none the worse for wear, the second row charged. Then the third row. The fourth. The fifth. Despite being bombarded by fireballs from the trebuchets and hails of arrows fired down from the top of the Wall by the Eagle Corps, the barrage went on and on.

It was only when the sixth or seventh wave of Tao Tei had smashed into the Wall that Lin Mae suddenly realized with horror what they were doing. They weren't trying to smash their way through the Wall at all. They were trying to smash the mirrored surface, which had prevented them from climbing it!

And they were having a great deal of success too. Peering down between two Eagle Corps archers, who were perched on their "nests," firing arrow after arrow into the Tao Tei ranks, she saw that the mirrored surface was already cracking, splintering, falling away. And with each successive wave of Tao Tei pounding their considerable combined weight against the Wall, she saw more and more of the smooth mirrored surface disintegrating, revealing the bare—and climbable—stone beneath.

• • •

Wang was a man who usually kept his emotions on a tight rein, but at this moment his face was etched with anxiety. Shielding his eyes with one hand, he pointed at the vast creature in the distance with the other.

"That must be their Queen. She commands them."

General Shao diverted his gaze, peering in the direction of the Strategist's pointing finger.

"Attack the Queen!" he bellowed. "Attack the Queen!"

• • •

Tiger Corps soldiers buzzed around the trebuchets like wasps around a nest, making alterations. Meanwhile, within the vast machine-like workings of the inner Wall, ammunition was being made ready. This time the oil-coated cannon balls were linked together and embedded with dozens of razor-sharp blades. They were lit and then propelled, burning, along the iron chutes, towards the waiting scoops of the trebuchets.

• • •

General Shao watched as the trebuchets were loaded, one by one, with their deadly cargo.

"Fire!" he yelled, and the counterweights of dozens of trebuchets were released almost in unison, the great firing arms flipping up and over. His eyes narrowed in grim satisfaction as razored fireballs flew through the air towards the distant Queen. Surely nothing could survive such a deadly barrage. Within moments the Queen would be cut to flaming ribbons and the Tao Tei would become mindless beasts once more. Then it would simply be a matter of employing their superior firepower to dispatch the creatures until there was not a single one of them left.

The razored fireballs flew up and over the main mass of Tao Tei who were still hurling themselves in ordered ranks at the mirrored surface of the Wall. Some of the fireballs, Shao saw, would fall short, whereas others would overshoot their target. More than enough, however, would reach their intended destination. He clenched his fists, knowing it would only be a matter of seconds. Already the first of the razored fireballs was beginning its downward arc.

But then Wang gasped beside him. One of the larger beasts surrounding the Queen had risen to its full height and unfurled what appeared to be great fan-like shields on either side of its head. Shao had no idea what the shields were composed of, but they must have been tougher than steel, because as the first fireball reached the Queen and her cortege of Paladins, Shao saw it hit the shield in a shower of sparks and bounce harmlessly away.

Within seconds the rest of the Paladins had risen to their full height and extended their own fan-like shields. Shao saw fireball after fireball hit the shields and deflect away, leaving barely a mark. Enclosed within the protective barrier, the Queen remained entirely unharmed. Directly below, meanwhile, the Tao Tei continued to follow her bellowed instructions, hurling themselves relentlessly against the mirrored surface of the Wall.

Then they stopped. And for a moment an eerie silence fell. Wang and General Shao looked at one another. Down below them, on the Wall, the thousands of Corps soldiers seemed to pause too, as though readying themselves for the next stage of the battle.

The mirrored defenses had fallen. Now they were just so much glittering shrapnel at the base of the Wall. The stone surface had once again been exposed, leaving the Wall vulnerable to renewed attack.

The Queen used the vibrating web between her horns to issue another order, and all at once the Tao Tei surged forward en masse and hurled themselves at the Wall once again. But this time they dug their taloned claws into the crevices between the stones and began to haul themselves upward. Some fell back, but many didn't. The Tao Tei were climbing the Wall!

Trying to hide his anxiety, to appear calm and authoritative, General Shao stepped forward. "Close combat!" he shouted.

Immediately his order was conveyed up and down the length of the Wall. "Close combat! Close combat!"

Although General Shao had hoped it would never come to pass, this was another eventuality for which the soldiers of the Nameless Order had prepared themselves. Over and over again they had practiced their strategy for what would happen if the Tao Tei ever managed to breach the Wall. They had practiced it until every single man and woman could have performed their designated tasks in their sleep. And now the day had finally come when they were being forced to put that strategy into operation.

Within the inner Wall the Tiger Corps were busily pulling levers and adjusting mechanisms. As a result of their endeavors, the raised "nests" on which the Eagle Corps warriors perched with their crossbows suddenly cracked open, releasing great coils of barbed wire netting. As this was happening, the Crane Corps soldiers, now uncoupled from their sky rigs, moved back to form themselves into a defensive barrier, the rigs themselves, no longer needed for the time being, folding up and descending through trapdoors in the floor that had opened to receive them. The forward positions vacated by the Crane Corps were now taken up by the purple-armored Deer Corps, who advanced to a point directly behind the raised nests of the Eagle Corps archers. At an order from Commander Deng, which was relayed along the length of the Wall, the Deer Corps warriors raised their turtle-shell-like shields in unison, creating a formidable barrier between themselves and the enemy.

Despite the anxiety he was feeling, General Shao watched the preparations with pride. His soldiers had trained well, and now, with conflict against a terrifying enemy looming, they were acquitting themselves admirably. Whether they would win the upcoming battle was an impossible question to answer, but he was sure of one thing: whatever happened today, the men and women under his command would fight with courage and conviction, and would not give up until the very last one of them was dead.

6

William and Pero had a grandstand view of the action as battle was joined. Despite the best efforts of the red-armored archers, the first wave of screeching, green-skinned Tao Tei suddenly appeared at the top of the Wall, scrambling and clawing their way over the battlements. There was no reticence about them, no hesitation. They were insatiable creatures, who wanted only to tear and kill and devour. They had no notion of fear or pain or death. Each and every one of them was purely and simply a compact, ferociously equipped war machine.

William had been in enough battles to know how chaotic, how disorientating they could be. He knew that to survive you needed to keep a clear head, to keep your eyes and ears open, to react quickly and efficiently. As the first wave of Tao Tei swarmed up and over the battlements he took in all that he could, his mind simultaneously assessing his and Pero's chances of survival. He knew that to have any hope of living through the next few hours, if not minutes, they needed to have their hands in front of them rather than bound behind their backs.

As had been the case for some time, the young black-armored soldier and his silent companion were now more concerned with what was happening in front of them, rather than with what their two prisoners might be doing behind their backs. Acting quickly, William jumped down from the buttress and pushed his shoulders back, stretching his arms as far as they could go. Gritting his teeth against the pain in his bound wrists, he forced his hands down his back, at the same time bending forward until he had managed to get his tethered hands over and beneath his backside. Crouching low, and eventually dropping to his knees, he then contorted his body still further until he had managed to push both his feet through the loop of his conjoined arms. By the time he struggled back to his feet his hands were in front of him. Although they were still tied together, and his wrists were slippery with blood as a result of his efforts, at least he could now use them to defend himself if needs be.

When he saw what William was doing, Pero followed

suit. It took both men around thirty seconds to perform their contortions, by which time the Tao Tei were cutting a swathe through the front line of red-armored archers. Some of the archers' arrows had pierced the creatures' eyes and killed them, but it hadn't taken long before the ascending Tao Tei were overwhelming the archers through sheer weight of numbers. The first thing William saw when he straightened up was one of the archers being swept from his perch by the massive taloned claw of a Tao Tei. The archer flew through the air, flailing and screaming, then sailed clean over the Wall and disappeared from sight, plummeting to his certain death far below.

Having broken through the line of archers, the Tao Tei leaped towards the barrier of shields held in place by the purple-armored soldiers. As though unaware of the danger in front of them, though, many of the creatures were instantly caught in the coiled barbed wire nets that had unfurled from the archers' nests. Although the coiled and razored nets didn't shred their flesh, as they would have done to any normal adversary, they did hamper their progress enough for the purple soldiers to use their long lances to impale many of the creatures through the eyes. Within minutes many of the Tao Tei lay dead, tangled in the nets, but that still didn't deter those that were following on behind from surging forward.

And eventually, again through sheer weight of

numbers, the Tao Tei began to gain the upper hand. From his vantage point, William saw that the creatures were beginning to bypass the barbed wire nets by trampling over their dead fellows, who had effectively done the job of flattening the nets for them. He winced as one Tao Tei opened a massive mouth and bit not only a purple soldier's shield in half, but also the man who was standing behind it. Another Tao Tei further along the Wall clambered up on to the dead body of one of its fellow creatures and used it as a springboard, leaping straight into a line of shields and scattering them and the soldiers behind them like skittles.

Soon many breaches were opening in the line of shields, despite the purple soldiers' best efforts to maintain its integrity. When the Tao Tei did break through, the purple soldiers, aided by the black-armored bear soldiers and the blue-clad female crane troops, fought fiercely, the deer and crane soldiers with their swords, lances and shields, the bear soldiers—who, despite being huge, muscle-bound men, appeared puny in comparison to the Tao Tei—bludgeoning the enemy with mallets and axes.

Within minutes the impeccable organization of the multi-colored army had crumbled, and the battle had become as William and Pero had always known battles to be: a desperate, bloody, brutal skirmish for both victory and survival. Screams of rage and pain combined with the clash of weapons filled the air; the flat, wide battleground on top of the Wall became choked with mangled bodies, and awash with blood.

Weaponless and with his hands still bound together, William pressed himself back against the parapet beside the buttress, feeling vulnerable. For the time being the soldiers in front of them were fighting a fierce rearguard action, holding the Tao Tei at bay, but it would surely only be a matter of time before the creatures broke through the ranks and came for them.

"We need to get these off!" William yelled to Pero above the din of battle, and turned to the stone parapet behind him. In some desperation he stretched his hands, pulling the bound rope taut, and began to rub it up and down against the sharp edge of the parapet.

Pero was looking frantically around. Suddenly his eyes widened. He lurched across to William and nudged him.

"There!"

William turned and looked. On the ground not far away, evidently dropped in the heat of battle, was a small curved hand blade. It looked like one of the knives that the blue-armored crane warriors carried in their waistbands. William would have scurried across to get it if it hadn't been for the fact that several of the bear soldiers, including the young one who had dropped the keys, were between him and the weapon. They were paying him no attention now, but if he shoved his way past them, especially if it was to arm himself, they would almost certainly do so. He spun towards Pero, frustrated. What could they do? With every second that passed the soldiers in front of them were being pushed further and further back, the Tao Tei surging forward.

Suddenly, from a dark, narrow opening in the Wall, the Westerner they had seen earlier appeared again. He was like some nocturnal animal, emerging from its burrow to sniff the air for signs of danger before darting back underground. On this occasion he had clearly poked his head out to see how the battle was progressing, and from the expression on his narrow, wrinkled face it was evident he didn't like what he was seeing. His lips puckered and his eyebrows came together in a scowl, deepening the wrinkles on his forehead.

"Hey!" William shouted to attract his attention, though not loud enough to make the bear soldiers turn round. The lean Westerner, who was only a few feet from the blade, flashed a glance in William and Pero's direction. As soon as he did, both men indicated the knife with urgent rolls of their eyes and exaggerated nods of their heads. Pero held up his bound hands and grimaced, then mimed as best he could his wish that the man should grab the knife and toss it towards them. The man hesitated a moment, then he scuttled forward and gave the blade a kick, sending it sliding in their direction. As he retreated back into the dark slit from whence he had come, William revised his opinion of the man. He wasn't like a nocturnal animal at all. He was like a cockroach.

The man, whoever he was, had done them a favor, though, for which he was grateful. Sliding across the stony ground, the knife came to rest against the toe of Pero's boot. Quickly he dipped to pick it up—but as he did so, the melee of struggling, battling soldiers in front of them suddenly seemed to burst apart, bodies flying everywhere. One of them stumbled against Pero, who fell forward, his foot inadvertently knocking against the knife and sending it skittering away. As Pero scrambled after it on his elbows and knees, there came a shattering, high-pitched screech of rage, and a Tao Tei leaped into the space occupied by the scattered soldiers. It homed in on William, who backed away, his hands still bound and weaponless. With another triumphant screech, the Tao Tei lunged for him.

The black-armored bear soldiers, who had had their backs to William and Pero, now turned. The young one, seeing the Tao Tei at such close quarters, instantly froze, but his bigger, silent companion and two other black-armored men rushed forward. The two newcomers swung the mallets and axes they held in their hands, while the other—William and Pero's erstwhile guard—snatched up a discarded lance and thrust it at the advancing creature. The lance pierced the creature's shoulder, causing it to bellow with rage and swing away from William and towards its three attackers. The men bravely waded in to the fray, but they were no match for the massive Tao Tei.

Moving like lightning, the Tao Tei swept out a massive claw and instantly shredded two of the men. Its black hooked talons ripped through their armour as though it was paper, and through their bodies beneath as though they were nothing at all. The men's faces instantly went slack with horror and agony, and blood and innards began to gush from the rents in their midriffs. Both fell forward simultaneously, their armored bodies falling on to slippery piles of their own unraveling intestines. The third man hesitated, horrified at the ease and abruptness with which his companions had died. It was a fatal hesitation. The Tao Tei lunged like a shark and grabbed the man in its mouth, rearing up and shaking him as a dog might shake a rabbit.

The man screamed, his upper body inside the Tao Tei's mouth, his legs kicking in desperation. Then his screams were abruptly cut off as the Tao Tei bit him in half. The man's legs, still twitching, dropped to the ground with a clanking thump.

Pero had taken advantage of the distraction to grab the knife, which he was now holding awkwardly, the blade turned inward as he attempted to saw at his own bonds. It was a difficult process as his hands were both slippery and sticky with the blood oozing from his chafed wrists. He winced as the blade slipped again, nicking his skin and opening a fresh wound.

Then William yelled, "Pero!" and he looked up, to find the Tao Tei, its open maw blood-stained and dripping, bearing down on him.

Pero quickly turned the blade round, holding it out before him, already knowing how pathetically inadequate it would be against such a creature. Even so, he was a fighter and he would go down facing his enemy. He braced himself as the Tao Tei barreled towards him, thinking that this, at least, would be a far better way to go than dying ignominiously on the end of a rope.

Before the Tao Tei could reach him, however, help appeared from an unexpected source. The young bear warrior, who had frozen in terror as his comrades were torn apart in front of him, suddenly found the courage to lunge at the creature from the side, his long lance held out before him. With a shrill shriek, as though channeling all his terror and rage into one decisive action, he plunged the lance deep into the creature's back.

The Tao Tei howled, swinging round so violently that the lance was not only torn from the young warrior's hands, but actually became dislodged from the creature's back and flew through the air. Although the lance-wound was nothing more than a scratch as far as the Tao Tei was concerned, it was still enough of an irritant for it to turn its attentions from Pero to the young bear warrior. Watching the creature veer towards him the boy's eyes went wide with terror, and he desperately grabbed a discarded, bloodstained shield from the ground. As the Tao Tei attacked, its jagged-toothed maw opening wide, the bear warrior thrust the shield forward, and more by luck than judgment managed to jam it between the creature's massive jaws.

The Tao Tei roared in frustration and bit down, the thick metal shield already bending and twisting in its powerful jaws. The momentary delay, though, helped save the young warrior's life. Behind him William had leaped, and though his hands were still bound in front of him, managed to catch the bear warrior's jettisoned lance as it flew through the air. As he came down from his leap, William spun in an almost balletic parabola, a maneuver that ended with him standing side by side with the young bear warrior, facing the looming Tao Tei. Even as the shield, under enormous pressure from the creature's massive jaws, began to splinter, William rammed the lance forward directly into the center of the monster's exposed throat. As the Tao Tei gurgled and staggered back, Pero, who had finally succeeded in freeing his hands, jumped forward with a round, sharp-edged shield, and using it like a massive blade, slammed it with force against the side of the creature's neck.

The result was spectacular. The creature's massive

head flew from its shoulders, spun into the air and landed with a thud at Pero's feet. Acting instinctively, Pero leaped back, putting himself out of range of the still chomping teeth, then smashed the head with the heavy shield, as though crushing an oversized bug. The skull cracked and the head caved in, green blood gushing from its mouth as its grinding maw finally became still.

As Pero stepped forward to cut William's bonds, William glanced at the young bear warrior, who was gaping in shock at the spectacle before him. He could tell instantly, from the boy's thousand-yard stare, that this was his first experience of battle, and that it had traumatized him.

But there was no time for sentiment or reassurance. All around them the battle was still raging. Looking around for weapons, William spotted a fallen archer, his eyes open in death, his red armour stained redder with blood. Close to his outstretched hand was his crossbow. William scrambled across to it and snatched it up. He examined the weapon for a moment with expert eyes, then smashed the crossbow against the stone ground, knocking its trigger and stock free. When he was done he was holding a weapon he felt far more comfortable with—a conventional bow. As he helped himself to the dead archer's supply of arrows, Pero rushed up to him, having grabbed a pair of lances.

"Not a time to be choosy, William," he yelled above

the din of battle, his white teeth showing through his beard in a grin of adrenaline-fuelled exhilaration.

"No, just quick," William said.

As if to prove his point, several Tao Tei suddenly broke through the massed defenses of the warriors in front of them, and charged at the two men.

With weapons in their now unbound hands, William and Pero switched to full fighting mode. Using his experience, skill and versatility, Pero darted and spun, thrusting forward with his lances, aiming for the creatures' exposed and vulnerable parts—their throats, their eyes. William, meanwhile, showed his prodigious skill with the bow, grabbing a handful of arrows from the dead archer's purloined quiver and holding them between the fingers of his pull hand, before loading and firing with such dazzling speed and accuracy that his movements were almost a blur.

Between them the men dispatched half a dozen Tao Tei in less than a minute, the creatures' dead bodies, their eyes reduced to leaking jelly, tumbling so heavily to the ground that the impact seemed to shake the foundations of the Wall itself.

In a momentary lull Pero pointed to his left. William looked, just as a weird, high-pitched scream reached his ears, to see the skinny, cadaverous Westerner scuttling towards them, having apparently been wheedled from his hiding place like a rat from its hole. He had a Tao

Tei on his tail, and was running in an odd, panicked zigzag fashion in an obvious attempt to shake his pursuer. Spotting William, who was drawing his bow, he scrambled towards him, but in the act of looking up fell headlong, his skinny arms shooting out. The Tao Tei roared in triumph and sprang towards its helpless prey— just as William let loose one arrow, then another, each of which found their mark, puncturing the creature's eyes and killing it stone dead.

The Westerner scuttled forward as the Tao Tei fell, barely avoiding being crushed by the creature's body. He ducked behind the two men and cowered there as they continued the battle, Tao Tei bearing down on them from all angles.

Pero, as skillful and adaptable as he was strong and ferocious, was grabbing anything he could use from the ground, converting whatever he touched into a lethal weapon. He slashed and pummeled and thrust and stabbed, until his body was liberally doused in the stinking green blood of his enemies.

William, meanwhile, continued to grab arrows from the quiver that he had slung over his shoulder, to load and fire them with almost supernatural speed and accuracy into the advancing creatures' eyes.

But the Tao Tei kept coming. It was an endless tide of jagged teeth, hooked black talons and green, plated flesh. Grabbing another handful of arrows, William heard them clattering about loosely in the quiver behind him, and realized he was running out. And the advancing horde of Tao Tei, now trampling over the heaped bodies of Wall warriors and their fellow creatures alike, were still coming too fast for him to try to retrieve some of the arrows he had already fired.

If we don't retreat, he thought, *we're finished.* But retreat where? They were hemmed in. They had nowhere to go.

He was just wondering whether it was worth leaping for one of the trebuchets, scrambling up it to get a more elevated vantage point, when, without warning, a black-armored warrior in front of him was smashed aside and a massive open mouth came out of nowhere, the multiple rows of jagged teeth stained with human blood.

William raised his bow in a flash, though even as he was doing it he knew he was going to be too late. His vision was full of nothing but teeth when a lance shot past his head from behind, so fast and close that it ruffled his hair and grazed his ear, and plunged unerringly into the creature's eye.

As the creature shuddered and dropped to the ground directly in front of him, William half-turned. A blue cape swept past his eyes, then settled in rippling folds, revealing its owner, who appeared to have dropped from nowhere. It was the commander of the blue-armored crane warriors who had interrogated him, and who he had last seen standing on top of the battlements just before the Tao Tei had swept up and over it. William barely had time to acknowledge her, however, before another Tao Tei broke through the ranks of soldiers and hurtled towards them.

The crane commander turned, but now she was unarmed, the lance she'd been holding still jutting from the writhing Tao Tei's eye. Ducking around her, William raised his bow again and fired two arrows in quick succession—one into the advancing creature's left eye, one into its right. As the Tao Tei dropped like a stone, the crane commander flashed William a look of gratitude. Momentarily he lowered his bow, acknowledging the look with a nod.

• • •

Splashed liberally in green blood, General Shao had descended from his command tower, leaving Wang up there alone, and was now standing shoulder to shoulder with the men and women under his orders, embroiled in the heat of battle. Fending off attacking Tao Tei with a lance and shield that were both coated in green blood, he instinctively glanced up as another high, ululating sound rent the air. It was so loud and piercing that it cut through the clashing din of battle as easily as a sword slashing through soft flesh. For a moment everything seemed to stop, Tao Tei and Wall warriors alike temporarily frozen into immobility. Then, without warning, the Tao Tei began to retreat, dragging their dead with them. Before the astonished eyes of General Shao and his fellow warriors, the Tao Tei drained from the battlefield in a green wave, swinging themselves ape-like over the battlements, before descending the Wall and flowing back towards their waiting Queen and the jade mountain beyond.

• • •

William and Pero watched, stunned, as the Tao Tei retreated en masse. All around them, Wall warriors in black, red, yellow, purple and blue armour were standing around open-mouthed, barely able to believe that the battle was over and that they had survived. The upper surface of the Great Wall was strewn with mangled bodies and awash with blood, both red *and* green. It was a typical battlefield in the aftermath of a savage conflict— except for one thing. There was not a single enemy body, or even a single body part, left behind. As the Tao Tei had retreated they had gathered up every single one of their fallen comrades and taken them with them.

Ever the soldier, and all too accustomed to premature victories, William wandered around, grabbing stray arrows from the ground as he kept a watchful eye on the retreating enemy. When he had picked up as many arrows as he could find, he rejoined Pero, who was still clutching a sword as he stared at the river in the distance, its water churning and boiling again as the Tao Tei army crossed it.

"What God made those things?" William muttered.

Pero waited until the last of the Tao Tei were out of sight, then he dropped the sword he was holding and slumped into a squatting position. "None we know."

A mist was rising up from the river now, like it had before when the Tao Tei had crossed over. William couldn't help thinking of the mist as a veil between this world and the next, or perhaps more accurately as a gateway that led from and into Hell.

Pero spoke again. "Think they'll hang us now?"

"I could use the rest," William said, smiling wryly.

He glanced at his friend, but then realized that Pero was not looking at him, but at something behind him. William turned slowly to find that the blue-armored crane commander, the big, black-armored bear commander, the dapper little strategist and a huge group of bedraggled soldiers spattered in green blood were standing motionless, staring implacably at them.

Realizing he was still holding the bow, William dropped it to the ground and raised his hands.

Still nobody moved. William swept his gaze across the array of exhausted, staring faces, trying to find something—some spark of emotion, be it friendliness or animosity. Beside him, still squatting, Pero's heavy-lidded eyes were drooping and his body was swaying from side to side. Despite the potential predicament they were in, the Spaniard looked almost drunk with fatigue.

Feeling an urge to break the silence, William nodded towards the boiling river and the distant jade mountain. "Will they be coming back?"

His voice sounded eerily loud on the now-silent battlefield. It was the blue-armored crane commander who answered.

"Yes."

William fixed his gaze on her. "Soon?"

She nodded.

Pero roused himself from his semi-stupor, though his words were still a little slurred. "Tao Tei. What does it mean?"

This time it was the little strategist who answered. "The Beasts of Greed."

The big, bearded commander in the black bear armour muttered something to the crane commander, who nodded.

"General Shao says he believes you now, and that you fought well. You have earned his praise."

William acknowledged the General's compliment with a nod of thanks. "Your army fights hard as well," he said.

Eyeing the young black-armored bear warrior who had frozen in fear during the battle before recovering to save William's life, Pero muttered, "But I'm guessing they haven't had much practice."

"Once a lifetime," the little strategist said.

William looked at him questioningly.

"Some never have the chance to fight," the strategist elaborated. "The Tao Tei rise only once every sixty years."

William blinked in surprise, and was about to ask a question when the young black-armored warrior cried out and ran forward. William wondered what was happening, wondered if he was about to be attacked, but then he realized that Pero, squatting beside him, was toppling forward, sheer exhaustion finally having got the better of him. Before Pero could land face-first on the stone floor, the young soldier caught him and lowered him with surprising gentleness to the ground.

Pero was muttering in Spanish. "Que... estoy... bien... estoy..."

General Shao barked an order, then turned and marched away.

The crane commander regarded William with her dark eyes, her expression softer now. "The General has ordered me to take you to the barracks," she said. "To find you a chamber in which you and your friend can rest."

7

Strategist Wang hurried through the bustling interior corridors of the fortress behind the Great Wall, his mind whirring. He dodged and weaved between the bodies of the injured and the exhausted; between soldiers with dented armour and haunted expressions; between those who were sitting against the wall or groaning in agony or lying still and dead on stretchers, their terrible injuries concealed beneath thin white sheets.

The aftermath of the battle was terrible, and tending to the dead and wounded would be a gargantuan task. But callous though it sounded, those who were still able-bodied enough to fight would have to rally quickly. They would have to fall back on every ounce of their training and discipline to recover their senses, re-mobilize, and focus on the task in hand. The Tao Tei would attack again, and they would do so sooner rather than later; there was no question of that. The men and women who dwelt within the fortress and fought on the Wall *would* be permitted to mourn their fallen friends and comrades—but not until the Tao Tei threat had been repelled, if not extinguished, for another sixty years.

Leaving the post-battle chaos behind, Wang bustled now along quieter corridors—corridors *so* quiet, in fact, that the atmosphere here was akin to a monastery, or an institute of learning and contemplation. He was nearing the Hall of Knowledge when, from behind a pillar in the corridor ahead, stepped a young man in green robes, his sleek black hair pulled into a topknot, his long face wearing an expression that was somewhere between shy and sulky.

Although the young man tried to look nonchalant, even arrogant, it was clear to Wang that he had chosen to hide here during the battle, no doubt crouched and quivering like a craven mongrel. Wang chose to overlook the young man's cowardice, however. There was nothing to be gained in antagonizing the imperial liaison officer.

"Ah, Shen," he said, as if the man had appeared at his bidding, "I want you to do something for me. Nine centuries past—the Year of the Horse—I recall an account of an incident at the Southwest Tower on the third day of the siege. Could you find it for me?"

Shen looked at first as if he was about to refuse, and then jerkily he nodded.

"Thank you," Wang said. "Oh, and Shen?"

"Yes?"

Wang smiled magnanimously. "Calm yourself. All is well."

• • •

The room was spartan. It contained little more than a table and two straw mattresses with a lantern on the stone floor between them. Peng Yong and another soldier carried Pero over to one of the mattresses and carefully laid him down. Stepping back out into the corridor and pulling the door closed behind them, Peng Yong saw the man who called himself William standing in front of one of the many long mirrors that were propped against the corridor wall. These mirrors were replacements for those on the Wall, should they get damaged—which of course, today, all of them had.

Peng Yong looked at William curiously. The man was gazing at his reflection, open-mouthed, a stunned expression on his face. Suddenly he noticed Peng Yong and the other soldier watching him, and turned towards them in a daze.

He looked undone, almost embarrassed. When he spoke he did so in a quiet, faltering voice. Although Peng Yong didn't understand what he had said, he could guess. It was there in the man's expression, his body language, his tone of voice.

Clearly, coming from a primitive country, he had never seen himself before, had never seen what he looked like, and was ashamed of his appearance. Peng Yong was not surprised. Brave though the foreigner undoubtedly was, he looked like a beast. He was caked in blood and filth both new and old, his clothes were a patchwork of disgusting rags, and his hair and beard were matted and dirty. His face, raw from the heat and cold, was ingrained with dirt, his eyes were bloodshot and his lips were dry and chapped.

He smelled too. He smelled very, very bad—and not only because of the fresh Tao Tei blood that stained his skin and clothes.

Nevertheless Peng Yong, having witnessed the courage of this man and his companion on the battlefield, had developed a great respect for them.

Cupping his hands he said, "Thank you for saving my life."

The foreigner—William—looked at him for a moment. And then, as if he understood what Peng Yong had said, he smiled and nodded, his teeth very white in his filthy face.

• • •

Fires burned on the watchtowers all the way up and down the line of the Great Wall. Lin Mae, too restless to sleep, prowled the parapet, making a midnight inspection. The fires, evenly spaced, stretched out on either side of her as far as her eye could see. The furthermost ones were nothing more than sparks winking on the horizon, but she knew that there were more fires, unseen from here, that stretched further still, that many more thousands of soldiers were manning the Wall for miles in both directions, all of them knowing what had happened here today, and all of them ready and nervously waiting for a Tao Tei attack.

Right here, though, directly opposite the Gouwu Mountain, which glowed a sickly green in the darkness, was where it had always been thought the Tao Tei would make their first incursion—if not concentrate their entire offensive campaign—and so, up to now, it had proved. Several hundred soldiers of the Nameless Order had been maimed or killed in the battle today, but already reinforcements were being drafted in from other Corps regiments to fill the gaps.

Lin Mae had known many of the dead personally— had grown up with them, trained with them, eaten with them, laughed with them—but for now she was keeping her emotions in check. While the Tao Tei were a constant threat, she had no time to mourn. That would come later, when the war was over and the enemy had been vanquished.

That didn't mean she could sleep soundly, though. She had tried—her body felt exhausted enough—

but each time she had closed her eyes the memory of the battle had been there waiting for her, the clamor and horror of it seemingly magnified in the darkness, threatening to wriggle insidiously into her very core and devour her from the inside out.

And so finally, giving up on sleep, she had decided to walk the parapets, to occupy her mind with more than her own thoughts. The minute she had stepped out into the cool night air she had known she'd made the right decision. Because despite what had happened out here today, she felt instantly becalmed. She sought the still point at the center of her being, and was gratified to discover it remained intact.

For now, at least.

Already the evidence of that day's battle had been erased. The dead had been taken below to lie on cold stone slabs in special chambers that had been constructed underground. The blood had been sluiced away with gallons of water, which had then arced from drainage slits to spatter on the sand hundreds of feet below. Now, having been baked by the last of the day's sun, the stone ground under Lin Mae's feet was dry again, as was the desert sand at the base of the Wall.

As she walked she passed soldiers on guard, many dozens of them, their tense eyes fixed on the distant valley where the jade mountain glimmered like something diseased. The soldiers worked in groups of three, on rotational shifts, each one standing on guard for two hours, then resting for the next four until their turn came around again. Behind each soldier, with some of whom she exchanged brief nods, were therefore another pair of soldiers, stretched out on thin mats on the hard ground, sleeping beside their weapons. Some of them twitched in their sleep. One or two moaned, their faces creasing in horror or distress. Many, she knew, would be suffering nightmares tonight. Even though the Tao Tei had departed for now, the night was still full of teeth and claws.

Lin Mae rounded a bend in the Wall and halted at an unexpected sight. There, sitting cross-legged in the shadows, his back against a buttress, was the large, dark figure of a man, curls of steam shrouding his face. The steam was rising from a dainty china bowl that he held delicately in one huge, gnarled hand. Lin Mae moved closer and the man looked up. Despite the shadows and the steam, she could see that his bearded face looked drawn, haggard.

"General Shao," Lin Mae said gently. "You should be resting."

Shao took another sip of tea. "I've slept enough in my life." He turned his attention back to the Gouwu Mountain glowing poisonously in the distance. "Strategist Wang was right. He told us the Tao Tei would change. His warnings went unheeded."

Lin Mae sat beside him. She wondered about placing a hand on his arm, a touch of reassurance and support, but decided against it.

"We were ready," she insisted. "You prepared us well."

"We were prepared—we *are* prepared—for the enemy of sixty years ago. Pray that that's enough." His eyes flickered towards her again. After a moment he said, "You should know, Lin Mae, the Emperor's Council has done more than just doubt Strategist Wang. Forcing me to fight to keep him as my advisor… Sending Shen to spy on us…" His features hardened in distaste.

Lin Mae's face hardened too, in sympathy with her commander's. Decisively she said, "We will prevail as we have always done."

Shao smiled at her spirit. Then his expression grew somber again. "Keep the foreigners close. Make them comfortable. We will take what they can offer… but they must never leave here alive."

There was a beat of silence between them. Then Lin Mae cupped her hands in a sign of acceptance and obedience.

• • •

William flew awake, sensing danger. It was not something he had trained himself to do, but something that came instinctively to him after decades of sleeping among cutthroats, brigands and mercenaries.

And as always, his instincts were proved right. On the other side of the stone chamber, his gaunt features glowing a jaundiced yellow in the lamplight, was the wiry Westerner, perched on his haunches like a cat about to spring.

The Westerner did not flinch or jump back. Instead he regarded William coldly.

"You don't smell like heroes," he said.

His voice was a gravelly drawl, but it was enough to pluck the softly snoring Pero from sleep. He came awake as William had done—suddenly and violently. Jumping to his feet, he grabbed for the non-existent knife at his belt, calling out a challenge in Spanish.

William raised a hand. "*Calma*," he said.

The Westerner shuffled closer, reaching out a sinewy arm to prod at the equipment heaped on the table— their travel bags, their swords.

"They've given back your weapons. That's a most positive sign." He looked both impressed and mildly surprised. Then he fixed his darting, bird-like eyes on them and began to tell them his story as if they had asked him for it.

"I came with mercenaries. My caravan. Twenty-five years ago. I had four of them. Not a scrap of diplomacy between them. They didn't last very long. Doesn't play around here. They don't waste their resources."

He stared at them again. His stare was unnerving.

Then abruptly he rattled off a string of Chinese.

William and Pero stared back at him blankly. William shrugged.

The Westerner grunted, his expression not quite a sneer. "No, I thought not. I'm Ballard. I don't take you as learned men, so I don't expect you to instantly warm to the light of my reputation. But my name, although faded in memory, was known from Antioch to Cumbria." He looked at them with a hopeful, needy expression. "Ballard. You've not heard of me?"

William shook his head. "I'm afraid not."

Ballard was silent, though his lips hardened into a thin line. Once again he extended a long-fingered hand and began to poke idly through their belongings.

"The beasts…" Pero said.

Ballard glanced up. "What of them?"

"What are they?"

Ballard's lips peeled back in a skeletal grin. William watched him warily. The man looked amused, but also annoyed about something.

Suddenly he hissed at them, "You were supposed to be here six months ago! This was all supposed to be over by now."

William blinked in surprise. It was clear that Pero too had no idea what the man was talking about.

Then Ballard, scowling, said, "Where is Bouchard?"

Pero's mouth dropped open, which was how William

felt too. Recovering more quickly than his companion, William said, "He's dead."

"Drowned," added Pero before William could say anything more.

Ballard's eyes danced between them, his expression giving nothing away. Then, tightly, as though biting off the words and spitting them out, he said, "They think I'm squirrely. You understand? I play the fool. But I am not a fool."

William glanced at Pero, decided to take the gamble. "We came for black powder."

Again Ballard's thin lips curled into a ghastly, clench-toothed smile. "I bet you did. And Bouchard drowned, did he?" He regarded them thoughtfully, then abruptly changed the subject. "They'll draw a bath for you. You saved the west turret. That was extremely *diplomatic*."

William shook his head. "We weren't being diplomatic. We were trying to stay alive."

Ballard snorted. "You're very handy, but you smell like animals. Clean yourselves up and they'll feed you."

Picking up his lantern, he slipped out of the door like a shadow without another word.

When he had gone, Pero looked at William with eagerness in his eyes. "He knows where the black powder is."

"Then why is he still here?" William wondered.

"He needs help getting out?"

William pondered on this for a moment, and then nodded. "Right. We play our part, get the powder and go home."

Pero sighed. "I didn't sign up for this."

"Which part?"

"Any of it. But mainly the monsters."

William grunted and gave a wry smile. "There *are* a lot of them," he said.

8

After her talk with General Shao, Lin Mae had finally managed to catch a few hours sleep. Or to be more precise, it was sleep that had caught her. She had gone back to her quarters to mull over the General's words, but as soon as she had laid her head back on her thin mattress she had fallen into a place that was deep and black and without dreams.

Now she was in the Great Hall, eating breakfast with hundreds of other soldiers and officers. Not surprisingly the atmosphere was different this morning, oddly brittle. Some of those present were silent, staring into space, their faces still etched with the trauma of the previous day. Others seemed to be celebrating their survival with almost hysterical abandon, laughing and joking as if their lives depended on it. There was a sense of desperation about their glee, and Lin Mae felt her muscles tensing as their shrillness filled the room. Looking around she saw splints and bandages aplenty, faces marked with bruises and cuts. One of her own Crane Corps warriors had a dressing covering up one side of her face, where a Tao Tei talon had gouged a groove from her temple down to her upper lip. It was still uncertain whether the girl would regain the sight in her left eye. Even if she recovered fully she would be scarred for the rest of her life.

Finding a spare seat, Lin Mae began to work her way stolidly through her breakfast of sweet dumplings and rice porridge. She was not hungry, but she needed to fill her body with as much energy as possible—she might well be in need of it later. She had been eating for several minutes when she became aware that the chatter around her was beginning to dribble into silence. She looked up from her bowl to see that every head in the room was turning in the direction of the north-east entrance door. She looked in that direction too. Her eyes widened.

There were three figures standing by the door, having just entered the room. In the lead was Peng Yong, the young Bear Corps warrior who had mislaid the keys to the stockade before yesterday's battle—a misdemeanor for which he was still to be punished. Behind him were the two foreign prisoners who had been intended for the stockade, and whose imprisonment would surely have resulted in the fall of the west turret, not to mention a great deal more bloodshed and death, possibly even her own. But the astonished silence that had befallen the room was not due simply to the *arrival* of the prisoners, but to their appearance. Bathed and shaved, and wearing clothes that had been cleaned and repaired, they had been utterly transformed. Now they no longer looked like beasts, but men. More than that, they looked like soldiers.

The two foreigners stood and looked around the room, bemused and disconcerted by their reception. The silence stretched on for several more seconds—and then General Shao stood up from his seat and slowly began to applaud. Immediately Lin Mae jumped up too and followed the General's lead. Then Commanders Chen and Deng joined in, and soon chairs and benches were scraping back from long tables as every man and woman in the room stood and applauded the new arrivals.

The foreigners looked at first astonished, and then delighted. The bearded, darker-skinned man bowed while the other grinned, his eyes darting around the room.

Although her eyes were on the newcomers, Lin Mae suddenly felt different eyes on her and turned to see General Shao looking in her direction. His face was impassive, but his unblinking gaze spoke volumes: *Remember what I told you.* When he looked away she felt as though he'd left a sliver of ice behind, lodged in her heart. She tried not to let the discomfort it gave her show on her face as she continued to applaud.

• • •

William felt more relieved than anything when the applause eventually died down. Though Pero seemed to bask happily in the glory, William had never felt entirely comfortable being the center of attention.

Plus he was hungry. He wanted to eat. And the food arrayed along the long table on the far side of the room looked and smelled delicious.

But the formalities were not over yet. Once everyone had sat down, the blue-armored crane commander remained standing. When William looked across at her, she offered him a small (and, he thought, confidential) smile. Then she said, "General Shao welcomes you as honored guests of The Nameless Order and thanks you for your skill and courage."

Pero looked at William, who blushed and stammered, "We… er… we're honored to be honored."

As the crane commander translated his words for the benefit of the room, Pero leaned across to him and muttered under his breath, "That's the best you've got?"

Before William could reply, he saw that the young commander in the red armour, whose helmet was shaped like the head of an eagle, had risen from his seat and was now walking across the room towards him, holding out William's crossbow and arrows. Handing them to William, he turned and said something to the crane commander, who smirked.

"Commander Chen thinks your bow is not worthy of your skill."

"You mean he thinks it's an antique?"

Her amused silence was proof enough that William had got pretty close to the mark.

Although he dearly wanted to sit down, become anonymous and fill his belly, William's indignation got the better of him. "Tell him there's no better weapon in this building."

The crane commander conveyed his words, which generated a ripple of laughter. The bearded man in the black bear armour, General Shao, made what was clearly a good-humored comment and the woman nodded.

"General Shao says we have much to learn about foreign pride." She wafted a hand to encompass the room at large. "We would like to see you shoot."

William looked at her in surprise. "In here?"

The commander in the red eagle armour who the woman had called Chen said something and chuckled.

"What was that?" asked William.

This time she managed to keep a straight face. "He thinks you have fear. That you are afraid to look foolish in front of so many people."

That stung William's pride. His indignation rose another notch. Turning to Pero he pointed at one of the tables. "One of those cups."

Pero rolled his eyes. "Now?"

"Get one of those cups," William said, more insistently.

Pero sighed. "I want to eat."

But a look from William was enough to make him trudge across to the nearest table and pick up an empty copper cup.

William examined his bow, testing the tension in the string. "You remember how to do this?"

"I remember that last time didn't go so good," Pero muttered.

William selected his arrows. "We were drunk."

All eyes in the room were on the two men. Now that William had his bow back some of them looked wary.

"How high?" Pero asked.

William placed three arrows between his fingers. "Ten yards. And six hands to the right."

Pero hefted the cup in his hand, testing its weight. William turned to face the door he had entered by, his back to Pero and the rest of the room.

"Oh no," Pero said.

"I'm fine."

"Seriously, William. Do the easy one."

Obstinately William said, "On my count…"

Pero looked quickly around the room. Several hundred Chinese soldiers, their breakfast forgotten, looked back at him expectantly.

Lowering his voice, Pero made one last appeal. "Please, Amigo…"

"One…" William said firmly. "Two… Three… Pull!"

With a look of anguish on his face, Pero hurled the cup across the room. As he did so, William wheeled round, bow drawn. Spotting the cup, he waited for it to reach its apex and then let the first arrow fly. There was a clank as the arrow struck the cup in such a way that it sent it both spinning and flying backwards. In quick succession William released two more arrows, which zipped through the air, over the heads of the astonished spectators. With a pair of metallic *thwack* sounds the arrows hit the cup almost in unison, and next second the spectators were astonished to see that the cup was pinned top and bottom to one of the big oak pillars on the far side of the room, so neatly positioned that it was as if it had been carefully placed and nailed there.

There was a moment of silence, and then the applause was both spontaneous and deafening. Grinning again, William saw General Shao laughing and clapping his big, meaty hands. He looked across at Commander Chen, who smiled and bowed in deference. Then his gaze found the crane commander, who gave him a quick smile and a nod of respect. Feeling a hand clap down on his shoulder, William turned. Pero winked at him.

"Let's eat!" he said.

• • •

Ballard hovered on the periphery, taking everything in. As soon as he saw the bearded Spaniard break away from his friend and head for the food table, he sidled across.

By the time he reached the Spaniard's side the man's plate was piled high with dumplings, spicy noodles, rice and pork.

"Pace yourself," Ballard said. "The meals are plentiful and regular here."

The Spaniard helped himself to a generous portion of steamed vegetables. "I hope not to stay that long."

"I like your thinking," said Ballard, glancing around, "but I suggest you keep your plans private and your mouth under control. You're not the first westerners to come here looking for black powder. We'll discuss it tonight. Bring your partner."

• • •

After getting his food, William was beckoned across to the officers' table. With the crane commander, who told him her name was Lin Mae, acting as translator, he talked to General Shao and Commander Chen for a while, though was careful not to give too much away. Eventually Shao and Chen excused themselves and left the table to go about their duties, leaving William alone with Lin Mae.

"Who taught you English?" he asked her.

She nodded across the room. "Sir Ballard. English and Latin."

William wondered what good either would be way out here. "Why?"

"Duty to the Nameless Order demands a life of service," she said as though reciting a mantra. "We become ready in many ways. We have many foreign books. Many books on war."

"I heard Ballard has been here twenty-five years," William said. "You won't let him leave."

Lin Mae's face hardened. "He must stay here."

"What about us?" William asked, but Lin Mae stared back at him implacably. After a moment he tried a different tack. "How long have *you* been here?"

"Always. I was not five years old when I came here. I have no other family."

William nodded, feeling an affinity with her. "You came to fight?"

"To learn to fight." He smiled and she became indignant. "You think I lie?"

"Oh!" he said, surprised by her reaction. "No, not at all."

She frowned, confused. "You smile. You find me foolish?"

"No, no, nothing like that." He struggled to explain. "I smile because… I understand. Because we're the same. I was given to an army before I can remember. As a child."

"As a soldier?"

"Worse," he said. "A gleaner."

Again she looked confused. William's smile faded as he recalled those terrible times.

"Packs of children… we cleaned the battlefields. After. When the fighting was over."

She nodded. "I understand."

"I became a page, then a pikeman's boy. Then on and on until…" He raised a hand, indicating himself, a wry expression on his face.

"You fought for your country?" Lin Mae said.

"No, I fought for food. In my world you fight to eat. And if you live long enough, you fight for money."

Lin Mae's face hardened. "So all flags are the same for you?"

William smiled again, but this time the smile was an uncertain one. Had he offended her in some way? He realized that if he was going to maintain his standing here he was going to have to tread very carefully.

"How many flags do you fight for?" she persisted.

"Many," William said, but the answer clearly wasn't enough. She stared at him implacably, waiting for him to go on.

Unsure whether it would impress her or anger her, he said, "I fought for Harold against the Danes. I was captured and spared and sold to the Normans. I killed my first man in Scotland—*and* saved a Duke's life!—before I even had hair on my face. I fought for him until he died, and then I went to Europe as an archer. I fought for Spain against the Franks. I fought for the Franks against Boulogne. I fought for Pisa and Valencia and the Pope. I've fought from Swintetown to Antioch." He looked at her, but still her face was giving nothing away. Uncertain whether he was apologizing or boasting, he smiled thinly and said, "Many flags."

Lin Mae stared at him a moment longer, and then she stood up. "We are not the same," she said coldly.

William looked up at her, surprised. He wanted to reach out and grab her wrist, ask her what was wrong, how he could make amends. Before he could act on his thoughts, however, she said, "Meet me on the Wall later. I have something to show you."

Then she left without a backward glance, leaving William staring after her in bewilderment.

• • •

Across the room, Pero was eating like a man possessed, shoveling rice and meat and vegetables into his mouth with his fingers.

By contrast Ballard, sitting beside him, seemed to have no interest in the meager portion he had selected for himself. Instead his eyes were fixed on William and Lin Mae. At last he leaned into Pero, pressing his thin shoulder against the Spaniard's brawnier one. "He should be careful with her," he murmured. "She's very powerful here."

Pero glanced across at his friend and the Chinese woman. He grinned, showing Ballard a mouthful of mashed-up food. "Then it's a fair contest," he said in a muffled voice.

9

After breakfast William and Pero were summoned to the Hall of Knowledge, Ballard appearing at the door of their barracks to escort them. He led them through a complex maze of corridors that made William hope he would never have to negotiate the internal geography of the fortress on his own.

Eventually they arrived at a pair of ornate double doors that opened into a vast room filled with exotic and complicated devices. Ballard pointed out a few items as they stepped inside, but the words he used to describe them—"astroscope", "seismograph"—left the two men none the wiser.

As they entered the room, their footsteps echoing on the wooden floor, Strategist Wang hurried forward to meet them. Behind Wang, in the far left corner, another man sat behind a desk—a younger man in green robes, whose black hair was knotted tightly on top of his head, and whose long, sulky face was turned mistrustfully in their direction.

Wang, however, was uncharacteristically effusive. Greeting William and Pero warmly, he introduced the sulky-faced man as Shen, and told them he had requested their presence here this morning in order to relate to them the full story of the Tao Tei. As he beckoned them forward, Ballard peeled off, reminding William of a cat that had lost interest in its human companions. The scrawny man wandered among the instruments on their display tables, fingering and prodding them as if in search of something. Ignoring him, Wang led William and Pero across to an open area in the middle of the room where two young men in plain dark clothes stood in silent obedience, as if waiting for instructions.

"About twenty centuries ago," Wang began, "King Zhou forever stained the reputation of Imperial China. At the height of his corruption and depravity, a comet appeared, spreading its light across the night sky. At its center a single huge stone struck the earth."

Wang nodded at the two young men, who stepped forward in unison, each taking hold of a cord that hung from the ceiling. They tugged on their cords and a shimmering silk scroll unraveled from above. The scroll was about a yard wide and as long as the room was high. Images were painted on it in delicate Chinese ink, depicting the fallen comet from Wang's story.

"Its impact was heard for thousands of miles," Wang continued. "The great valley was created in its wake. The mountains where the comet came to rest began to glow green, releasing the Tao Tei. From that day on, with terrible regularity, the Tao Tei rise with the sixty year moon to scourge the North of China."

As he proceeded with his story, he nodded at intervals, whereupon his assistants released more silk scrolls from the ceiling. Soon there were a dozen or more, hanging down like tall thin trees in a translucent silk forest. Their appearance was impeccably timed, Wang strolling between the scrolls and referring to each one as he related his tale, the delicate images perfectly illustrating the narrative.

Moving between the hanging scrolls in Wang's wake, William's attention was snagged by a suggestion of dark movement in the gap between two of them. He glanced across to see that Ballard, who had doubtless heard this story before, was standing behind a large table which housed a model of the Great Wall and its internal workings. Like a child with a fascinating new toy, Ballard was pulling levers and turning dials, causing miniature flying rigs to open, the nests of the eagle archers to rise from the ground, the tiny trebuchets to fling their great arms forward, just as the real things had done when they had rained balls of fire down on the Tao Tei.

Ballard was grinning, clearly enjoying himself. William felt a thread of disquiet work its way inside him like a burrowing worm. He diverted his gaze from Ballard and back towards Wang and his story.

"The ancient Great Wall built by our ancestors has been reinforced," Wang was saying. "The Nameless Order guards this Wall year after year. It is the first—and last—defense for China.

"We are now in the Thirty First Cycle. What you see here in this room is but a fraction of the study we have made in secret for over eighteen hundred years. Throughout that time, to avoid creating panic among our people, we have kept the legend of the Tao Tei in the realms of folklore and rumor. Every sixty years, for eight terrible days, this Wall is the only barrier keeping China—and the world—safe."

His story was done. He looked at them, hands clasped together, as though inviting comment or questions.

Obliging him, William asked, "What do the Tao Tei want?"

Wang spread his hands. "Simply to feed. To grow."

"We've seen them eat," Pero said darkly.

"Yes," said Wang, "but there is a limit to the food north of the Wall. We know they scourge every scrap of meat through the Jade Valley. We believe the only reason they retire to their hive is because they have reached a balance between what they have taken and the damage we have rendered."

He gestured towards one of the scrolls, on which was depicted an image of a vast, bloated beast feeding, its massive mouth open and multiple tubes or cords extending into the open mouths of smaller Tao Tei who were presumably providing it with food from their own bellies.

Sure enough, Wang said, "The Tao Tei have their own Queen. Around her are the Paladins, the officers that protect her. The Tao Tei soldiers are her arms, legs and stomach. The Queen does not stalk her prey, but depends on the soldiers to continually feed her."

Wang turned from the scroll and looked from William to Pero, his face serious. "If the Tao Tei were to breach the Wall… Bianliang is only eight hundred li away. A city of two million people. The consequences should the Tao Tei find that much nourishment are too dark to consider. What would ever stop them? No corner of the world would be safe."

He beckoned with a finger and led them beyond the hanging scrolls, to a workbench close to Shen's desk. On the bench, surrounded by various measuring devices—calipers, weighing scales—and a scattering of sketches on rice paper, sat the severed Tao Tei claw. Even now, perched on its black, hooked talons it looked as though it might scuttle away at any moment. Perhaps Wang thought so too. Perhaps that was why it sat inside a heavy glass bell jar.

Gesturing at the claw, Wang said, "In thirty cycles, no man has ever taken a Tao Tei down alone. To be attacked at night, in the open…" He shook his head in wonder. "You are strong and skillful, and yet it is difficult to believe your story."

"I have no reason to lie to you," William said.

Wang produced something from within the simple black robe he was wearing and held it up. It was the magnet.

"Where was this?" he asked. "As you fought, where was this stone?"

William patted the left side of his tunic. "Tucked in my vest. Just here."

Wang looked thoughtful, then placed the magnet carefully down on the workbench and lifted his hand away. To Ballard's evident astonishment, the magnet shot across the wooden surface and with a loud clang stuck firmly to an iron rivet bolting the joints together. At his desk, Shen jumped like a startled rabbit.

Wang looked at them calmly. "The unseen force is powerful."

Ballard ghosted across to the magnet. He touched it, then gave it an experimental tug, but it was stuck fast. "Your point is what, Master?" he asked.

Wang shrugged. "Perhaps nothing." He indicated

Shen. "Master Shen has sent questions to the Emperor's Council. I seek the history of a strange battle nine hundred years ago on the southwest tower." All at once he looked weary. "We try everything we can."

"Where are the Tao Tei now?" William asked.

"They have gone back to the mountain, to regroup for the next attack," Wang said.

"Can't you hunt them?"

"Men have tried. They always disappear. We never find their bones."

Pero looked incredulous. "So sixty years you wait? *Sesenta años?* What are they doing all this time?"

"I think they change," said Wang. This was clearly a pet theory of his. "I think they sleep and slowly change. Many people disagree with me, but I have spent my life studying their history, and I believe they are not the same enemy our ancestors faced. How this can be I do not know, but…" He had wandered over to the magnet and was now trying to pry it loose from the iron bolt it had attached itself to. "…I will keep this stone close."

William didn't know if the Strategist was asking his permission, but he nodded all the same.

"Good luck," he said.

10

After the meeting with Wang, William and Pero were left to their own devices. Now that they were no longer prisoners, nor even confined to their quarters, William decided to look around before taking up Lin Mae's invitation to meet her on the Wall. After a few wrong turns, he eventually found his way to the vast gallery where he, Pero and their bear warrior escort had ascended in the cage to the top of the Wall. Here was housed the machinery that powered the Wall's defenses. In many ways, William thought, this was the beating heart of the Wall itself. He watched for a while as dozens of yellow-armored tiger warriors, overseen by Commander Wu, installed a succession of sharp, wide blades onto giant wooden blade carts. He thought about offering his services, but the men were so well drilled he decided he would probably only end up getting in the way.

After a while General Shao appeared, accompanied by a bevy of lieutenants, to inspect the work. The General nodded to William and William nodded back, but although the acknowledgement was a friendly one, it prompted William to move on. He was interested in the preparations for what would surely be further conflicts ahead, but he didn't want to outstay his welcome. As Shao and Commander Wu became embroiled in conversation, he decided to make a surreptitious exit.

He rode in the cage to the top of the Wall, emerging into strong sunlight. He raised his face to the sky and closed his eyes for a moment. After the comparative gloom of the fortress it was good to feel the warmth on his face, the slight breeze in his hair. Ahead of him, blue-armored crane warriors, Lin Mae among them, were training, the tall wooden cranes from which they launched their sky rigs spread out in a line along the battlements. He watched them, attached to a complex arrangement of hooks and ropes, swoop and dive and fly around the cranes, constantly adjusting ropes and hooks to give themselves more mobility. He watched them practicing with their long lances, spinning them, thrusting them into the bodies of imaginary enemies, pressing their flexible tips against hard surfaces to give themselves more impetus, more spring.

It was a dazzling sight, like watching a flock of

gleaming blue birds performing an air ballet. Eventually Lin Mae spotted him and beckoned him over. "Come."

He clambered up on to a sky rig, where Lin Mae was surrounded by a group of crane warriors, who regarded him curiously. Beside the pulley mechanism of the rig stood a pair of impassive bear warriors. Lin Mae had a harness in her hand, all hooks and ropes, which she held out to him.

"You want to try?"

One of the crane warriors muttered something, which made the others laugh.

"What did she say?" William asked.

Lin Mae was smiling. "She said men have so much to teach us."

The girls were still tittering, and flashing William mocking looks.

"I don't think that's what she said."

Lin Mae leaned in closer and stared into his eyes. "You know what I think?" she said softly. "I think you're afraid."

William smiled. Equally softly he replied, "You said that this morning. And yet here I am."

Lin Mae offered him the harness again. The hooks on it clanked together. "Yes. Here you are."

• • •

Ballard was playing the role of tour guide, showing Pero around. He was giving him a closer look at the inner

Wall workings, pointing out massive wheel gears, levers and pulleys, explaining what they were for, how they worked.

The area was quiet now after the earlier activity, the huge blade carts equipped and ready for action, standing in silent rows. Most of the Tiger Corps soldiers had departed. Those who had been left on guard nodded to Ballard as he passed them, evidently relaxed in his company.

"You'd have to run sixty miles west before you could consider yourself free," he said suddenly, as though continuing an earlier conversation. "That's how far they would chase you before they quit."

Pero looked at him in horror and slid a glance towards the nearest Tiger Corps guard, who was surely within earshot. Ballard laughed.

"Oh, don't worry about them. Not a single one of them speaks English." He looked around, grinned, raised his voice. "Not a wee wanking one of you, eh?"

A few of the soldiers smiled politely. They were clearly used to his eccentric foreign ways.

• • •

William looked down and immediately wished he hadn't. Perched on the end of one of the crane rig platforms jutting out over the battlements, with a warm breeze ruffling his hair, the ground seemed impossibly distant. His stomach flipped and his heart felt as if it was ballooning up into the back of his throat. He tried not to show his fear, but looking at Lin Mae's face, he realized he was fooling no one with his nonchalance. She knew perfectly well that he was nervous. She was even taking pleasure in it.

"Well?" she said, looking him in the eye as he stood there. "Will you jump or not?"

William glanced at the hulking bear soldiers who were standing beside the pulley mechanism, glowering at him. If he *did* jump his life would be in their hands.

"Those guys *do* know what they're doing?" he murmured.

She smiled a superior smile. "Wrong question."

She waited, looking at him, as if willing to give him another go. William, though, grimaced in apology.

She sighed. "Whether or not the cable is attached? That is the question."

"And the answer?" he asked.

"*Xin ren.* Say it."

Automatically he repeated what she had said, struggling with the pronunciation. "*Xin ren.*"

"It means to have trust," Lin Mae said, holding his gaze with hers. "To have faith." She gestured at the semi-circle of silent, watchful crane warriors standing behind them. "Here? This army? Our flag? We fight for more than food or money. We give our lives to something more. *Xin ren* is our flag. Trust in each other. In all ways. At all times."

She turned back to him. William stared into her eyes, held her gaze for a long moment. Then he looked once more at the ground far, far below.

Eventually, turning back to her, he said, "Well, that's all well and good. But I'm not jumping. I'm alive today because I trust no one."

Lin Mae regarded him with something like pity. "A man must learn to trust before he can be trusted," she said.

"Then you were right," replied William. "We're not the same."

11

Ballard's quarters reminded William of the cluttered, cave-like interior of a Turkish market stall. Lit by several lamps, it was crammed with books and trinkets; with maps, charts and wall hangings; with bits of machinery and strangely shaped stones; with bottles and jars and boxes containing who knew what variety of material?

Selecting a bottle of cloudy yellowish-brown liquid, Ballard poured three generous measures into a trio of copper cups, two of which he passed to each of his visitors. Pero sniffed dubiously at the liquid and exchanged glances with William. Grinning at their wariness, Ballard drank from his own cup. Pero watched for a moment before following suit, sipping the concoction tentatively at first, and then, raising his eyebrows, drinking more eagerly.

As William took a sip from his cup, tasting something potent and sweet that he guessed was made from stewed fruit, Ballard began to speak.

"You're stuck, gentlemen," he said. "I hope you realize that. You know their secrets. They'll never let you leave now."

He allowed his words to sink in, a smug smile on his face. Then he gestured at his quarters with a sweep of his hand. "Posit the future. See what becomes of even the best of us. Once renowned in the finest courts of Christendom, what am I now but a pampered drunk with a pen and a rice bowl? I make spirits for the elders, bore the young with Latin, and translate every piece of nonsense that comes down the Silk Road. I have spent half my life on this joy forsaken rock and yet I live only by the Oath of the Nameless Order." He intoned the words with solemn irony. "Discipline. Loyalty. Secrecy."

He raised his cup with a sneer. "I'm afraid, gentlemen, you have joined the choir. Your only hope is me."

As he gulped at the potent liquid in his cup, tilting his head back to savor every last drop, William looked at him. The light from the flickering candle Ballard held in his left hand turned his leering, skull-like face into a writhing yellow mask.

"The flavors of black powder are simple, gentlemen," he said. "Charcoal, sulphur and nitre. It is the recipe and profundity of their integration wherein the magic lies."

He lowered the candle towards a small pewter bowl perched on the end of a cluttered workbench. Without warning there was a flash of brilliant light that caused both William and Pero to cry out and leap back. For a few terrible moments William felt sure he'd gone blind—and then little by little the white disc at the center of his vision faded. Blurrily he saw a curl of pale grey smoke rising from the pewter bowl, and Ballard grinning wolfishly at the dramatic effect of his little demonstration.

"A taste. A glimpse," he hissed. "A few pilfered grains from Strategist Wang's hoard. He has mastered the transmutation of these elements. The tablets of his formulae I have seen with my own eyes in the gated heart of his Hall of Knowledge."

Pero was still watching the curl of now thinning smoke as if mesmerized.

"Bouchard spoke of a weapon," William said.

Ballard grew sly. "There are many weapons here."

"Why have we not seen them?"

"There are many things here you haven't seen. And many things you should pray will not be needed before this siege is over."

He fell silent as if inviting them to ask him to elaborate. But William refused to rise to his bait. The man reminded him simultaneously of a variety of repulsive creatures: rat, snake, spider, cockroach. In the end Ballard sighed.

Adopting the tone of a rather pompous teacher, he

said, "The Tao Tei siege has never lasted more than nine days, nor less than seven. The only certainty is this: they *will* return. And when the battle drums begin to sound, the guards of the various Corps—Tiger, Bear, Crane, Deer and Eagle—will leave their posts and take up their positions along the wall. That will be our moment."

He fixed his eyes on them like a mesmerist attempting to bend them to his will.

"We want to be riding away as the battle rages," he said.

"What about the armory doors?" William asked. "You have keys?"

Ballard rolled his eyes. "I have black powder. Enough for several doors."

"*He* brings us in," said Pero, his face flushed with alcohol. "*We* get us out."

"How?" asked William. "Do we have horses I don't know about?"

Pero nodded. "They have a stable here. A big one."

"And nowhere near enough guards," added Ballard.

William gave him an incredulous look. Was Ballard seriously proposing that they steal a couple of horses and fight their way out? With heavy irony he said, "That sounds like a busy morning."

Pero grinned a drunken grin. "Once we get that far, what else *is* there? Kill or be killed. Right, amigo?"

William said nothing. Pero leaned across, almost

toppling over, and punched his friend on the arm.

"To win the thing we came for? What would we not do, eh?" His eyes were shining, his voice exuberant, as if he hoped his enthusiasm would rub off on his friend.

But William simply looked at him, and then at Ballard.

And still he said nothing.

• • •

Escorted by a squad of Deer Corps soldiers on horseback, pine oil torches raised above their heads to cut through the darkness, General Shao and Lin Mae thundered along the length of the Wall. General Shao sat astride a huge, gleaming black steed, and Lin Mae rode beside him on a smaller but no less impressive animal that was as white as lotus blossom. The desert beyond the Wall was as black as pitch, the Gouwu Mountain glowing in the far distance with a bilious green light. Though there was not a single sigh of wind, the air rang with cries from the inspection towers that spanned the Wall at regular intervals, a message passed down the line: "Troops unaccounted for at the West Tower!"

Passing through the arch of the final tower before the one from which the guards on duty there had recently fallen ominously silent, General Shao reined in his horse and raised a gauntleted hand. As Lin Mae and the rest of the squad slowed, they saw a horrendous sight ahead of them. Scattered across an upward slope of the undulating Wall were at least a dozen bodies, and parts of bodies – all that had remained of the soldiers that had formed the night watch on the West Tower.

Lin Mae glanced at the General. His face was stern and watchful, his upper body stiff with tension.

"Something's wrong here," he said. "This is not a common attack. The Tao Tei never leave the bodies."

Lin Mae said nothing. For a few more seconds she and the General continued to scan the dimly lit section of the Wall ahead, alert for the slightest indication of movement.

Eventually General Shao hissed two words. "Dismount. Formation!"

Instantly, their reactions honed by years of training, the two dozen Deer Corps warriors slipped silently from their horses and flowed forward like a purple sea to stand in front of their commanding officers, their circular shields locking together to form an impenetrable barrier.

General Shao and Lin Mae crept forward to peer through a gap in the shields. With a single whispered command and a couple of economical gestures, the General ordered that all but two of the pine oil torches be extinguished.

That done, he whispered, "Forward."

In perfect synchronization the shield formation began to slowly advance, their breathing steady, the outer edges of their shields scraping gently together.

Bringing up the rear, General Shao and Lin Mae drew their swords. Ever cautious, General Shao held his up in front of him, using its polished blade as a mirror to check behind them. Sure enough, behind the tethered horses, he saw something dark and bulky at their backs, creeping towards them up the slope. Signaling Lin Mae with the slightest movement of his head, he angled the blade in her direction so that she too could see the impending threat.

Moving slowly, so as not to goad the enemy into action, the two of them reached down in unison, each drawing circular throwing blades, which were sheathed to the outsides of their boots. Despite their attempt to be surreptitious, the huge, dark shape at their backs suddenly began to accelerate towards them, causing the horses to whinny in panic. At the same time a massive black shadow rose above the apex of the slope ahead and began to rush, almost to *flow*, down the incline. The Deer Corps warriors, alert to the impending attack, advanced swiftly, shield formation unbroken, to engage the enemy.

Just as the shield formation neared the top of the slope, the Tao Tei, which had been moving with uncharacteristic stealth, let out a bellowing screech and leaped forward from the shadows, green skin vivid and the rows of jagged teeth in its gaping maw gleaming in the lamp light. As it pounced, the shield formation suddenly opened up from the center outwards, like a double door composed of overlapping panels, and eight long lances thrust out to skewer the beast in mid-air. Although the point of every lance hit home, piercing the creature's eyes and skin, and causing green blood to spurt from multiple wounds, the dying Tao Tei's momentum carried it forward, scattering soldiers as if they were toys. The creature's massive jaws snapped shut on the lance bearer directly in its path, ripping through his armour as if it were wet paper and grinding him into a mouthful of pulverized meat in an instant.

As the creature thudded to the ground and died, its last unfortunate meal still leaking from its mouth, the second Tao Tei at the rear of the group launched its attack. With a screeching cry that echoed its companion's, it lunged at Lin Mae and General Shao, who wheeled around, throwing their twin blades in unison. Two of the four blades struck home with unerring accuracy, burying themselves deep into the creature's tiny eyes on its massive chest. But as with the other Tao Tei, its unstoppable momentum continued to carry it forward, its jaws yawning wide to consume Lin Mae, who was standing directly in its path.

Although her reactions were second to none, she knew, even as she was drawing her sword, that the creature would be upon her before she had time to defend herself. As the Tao Tei's jaws gaped, she knew that what she was staring at was her own death hurtling towards her.

And then, without warning, something smashed into her from the side, sending her spinning out of the way. She fell, rolled and regained her feet in an instant—just in time to see her savior, General Shao, now standing in front of the creature. His sword was in his hand, and as the huge green mass of the monster bore down upon him, he thrust it forward, straight into the Tao Tei's mouth. It was dead before it reached him, but Lin Mae was still horrified to see it crash into his body with the weight and power of a dozen horses; to see him first go down and then disappear beneath its pulverizing bulk...

12

Removing a stone from the base of the wall behind his bed, Ballard reached into the hollow and withdrew a tightly rolled scroll of brown parchment. With long, deft fingers he untied the twine around it and carefully unrolled it. William caught enough of a glimpse of the scroll to realize it was a map, but before Ballard could explain exactly what *kind* it was, and why he was showing it to them, a simple, steady drum beat began to pulse through the maze of corridors within the fortress.

Like a rat sensing danger, Ballard froze and looked up.

"That's a tower call," he hissed. "A warning. Something's happened."

• • •

The top of the Wall was already thronged with soldiers who had answered the call. Yet still they flowed from every opening, illuminated by thousands of torches, which blazed in defiance of the night.

General Shao, lying on a stretcher, his black and now hideously crushed armour splashed with green Tao Tei blood, was being carried quickly but carefully through the milling crowd. Despite the chaos, soldiers moved back to make way for him, bowing reverently not only to their injured commander but also to Lin Mae, who was by his side.

The stretcher bearers were heading towards the opening in one of the towers, from where they would be able to descend to the fortress, when Shao weakly raised a hand.

"Far enough," he croaked.

Immediately the stretcher was lowered gently to the ground. Lin Mae and the other commanders knelt beside it, the rest of the soldiers in the crowd around them—including William, Pero and Ballard, who had rushed to the top of the Wall like everyone else—craning forward to see and hear what was happening.

Turning his head with obvious pain, General Shao swallowed and softly said, "Commander Lin."

Irritated by the buzz of alarmed and speculative conversation around them, Commander Chen turned and barked, "Quiet!"

Instantly the clamor ceased, to be replaced by a respectful silence.

Lin Mae leaned forward to hear the General's murmured words. "They led us into a trap. We underestimated their intelligence." His trembling hand reached beneath the collar of his armour and emerged holding a gold medallion attached to a length of silk thread. The rim of the medallion was studded with five precious stones, each a different color to denote the five Corps of the Nameless Order.

"Commander Lin," Shao said again, and although his voice was weak, such was the depth of the silence around him that it carried a good distance through the crowd in all directions.

Lin Mae leaned forward as General Shao, summoning the last of his failing strength, reached out towards her with both hands. His left hand found hers and cupped it so that her palm was facing upwards. With his right hand he pressed the medallion into her open palm, then closed her fingers tightly around it.

Raising his voice as much as he was able, he croaked, "The Nameless Order is yours to command. This is my final order." Turning to the rest of his commanders, he said, "From this day forward, Commander Lin will lead you."

Lin Mae looked alarmed. "General," she began, but he silenced her with the tiniest shake of his head.

"You are ready."

Through the tears, which first blurred her eyes and then began to run down her cheeks, Lin Mae saw blood on her beloved General's lips. She glanced around at the other commanders, and saw tears in their eyes too.

Moving forward, Commander Chen cupped his hands in a gesture of respect and obedience.

"It will be so, General," he said. "The soldiers of the Nameless Order will stand firm. The Wall must not fall. We will defeat the Tao Tei." His voice cracked, but with a gargantuan effort he held himself together. "Rest in peace, sir."

Kneeling beside the stretcher, he and the other commanders bowed their heads. All around them, the action spreading out like ripples from the center of a pond, every soldier present did the same. When the entire force was kneeling, an echoing rumble rolled through the crowd, gradually rising in volume and clarity.

"Rest in peace, General."

Lin Mae saw the General smile and close his eyes. His chest rose and fell one more time. Then his ravaged body relaxed as the life slipped away from him, and he was gone.

Wiping away her tears, swallowing her emotions, Lin Mae slowly rose to her feet and turned to address the silent, kneeling throng.

"There will be time for memories and offerings later.

Today we honor General Shao by letting our weapons do the talking." Her voice rose, ringing out in the night. "To your stations!"

Immediately the kneeling soldiers rose in unison and began to move in all directions, heading to their various posts. Within a minute or less the area around the General's stretcher was clear. One by one the commanders rose, turned to Lin Mae and solemnly made a gesture of fealty. After Lin Mae had bowed to each in turn and the commanders had silently filed away, she gestured to the stretcher bearers, a pair of Bear Corps warriors standing to attention nearby, and indicated that they once again pick up the General's stretcher and follow her into the fortress.

• • •

Observing proceedings from the rear of the now thinning crowd of soldiers, Pero turned to William.

"A woman?" he said scornfully.

But William said nothing. In truth he had been impressed, even overwhelmed, by the manner and consequences of the General's death. Never had he known such bravery as the General had shown in his last moments. Never had he experienced such a sense of community among warriors, or encountered such dignity in grief, such genuine compassion and love for a fallen leader. And as a soldier he had been overawed by the way every single member of the Nameless Order had accepted without question their dying leader's final wish, by their instant deference to their new commander Lin Mae, and by the discipline they had shown in instantly obeying her orders and returning to their duties.

He understood Pero's disbelief. A few days ago he would even have shared it. But now, having seen Lin Mae in action, and witnessed the level of respect she was shown by every other warrior on the Wall, he honestly couldn't imagine anyone *but* Lin Mae taking on the General's mantle. He watched her, spellbound, until she had disappeared from view—and it was only then that he realized Shen, the man he had previously seen behind his desk in the Hall of Knowledge, was standing at his shoulder.

Shen's voice was curt. He barked a string of syllables at them, only one of which William understood—the name Wang.

Before he could respond two hulking Bear Corps soldiers were lumbering forward, prodding both him and Pero in their backs, a silent but unmistakable command that they should follow Shen, who had already turned and was marching away. William flashed a look at Pero—*What the hell have we done now?* But Pero, scowling, looked just as mystified as he was.

As they were ushered through the now rapidly dispersing throng of soldiers, William caught a glimpse of Ballard, who had disconnected himself from their company (possibly when Shen appeared) and was now skulking in a shadowy alcove nearby. Ballard too looked disconcerted, and William knew instantly that the man was wondering whether their earlier conversation could somehow have been overheard, their escape plans discovered.

Then he was prodded once more in the back, hard enough to make him stumble, and biting back a rejoinder he focused on Shen, who was moving with a kind of fussy imperiousness towards the nearest tower opening. With their menacing escorts looming behind them, William and Pero followed their guide into the gloomy interior of the Wall.

• • •

Lin Mae, walking beside the General's stretcher through the labyrinthine corridors of the fortress, still protective of her leader even in death, looked up as Strategist Wang appeared around the corner ahead and hurried towards her. As Wang squeezed past the stretcher bearers in the narrow corridor, Lin Mae saw tears in his eyes, glistening with reflected lamp light. The expression on his face, though, was not one of grief, but of suppressed urgency, even excitement.

Reaching her, he bowed in fealty, and then to her surprise leaned forward to whisper something in her ear. She listened for a moment and then straightened up, the urgency on Wang's face now mirrored in her own delicate features. Knowing there would be runners nearby, ready and waiting to carry her orders far and wide, she shouted, "All Commanders and First Officers to the Great Hall! Immediately!"

13

The Great Hall at night was illuminated by hundreds of pine oil lanterns. The effect of the softly glowing light, reflected in the brightly colored armour of the assembled mass of officers, and of the wavering shadows that rose and fell on the walls like a soft grey tide, gave the vast room a tranquil, almost holy atmosphere. The fact that Shen was reading solemnly from a scroll of parchment spread out on the table, with Lin Mae and her staff silently surrounding him and listening intently to his every word, only added to that impression. Across the room, standing a little apart from everyone else, William and Pero were listening to Ballard's murmured translation of Shen's words.

Despite the brusque treatment they had received, the two men had quickly realized they were not in trouble.

Indeed, their presence in the Great Hall might even be construed as a courtesy, if not a privilege, extended to them by Lin Mae—though William suspected there was a more specific reason why they were here, one that had not yet been revealed to them.

In the meantime Ballard had revealed that Shen was reading from a nine-hundred-year-old battle report. In a low voice he was now translating the imperial liaison officer's words.

"…at the Hansha Gate, in the middle of a strong wave of Tao Tei, three beasts mounted the Wall. They killed many men as they came forward, threatening our flanks and raising panic…"

He listened a moment, head cocked to one side, and then he resumed.

"And then, by the Grace of the Ancient Gods, the beasts stopped and sat peacefully, never moving as we slaughtered them…"

Ballard fell silent a few moments after Shen. William looked up, to see that Wang, with Lin Mae and her commanders watching the strategist with interest, was walking determinedly towards them.

Still some twenty feet away he came to a halt and said, "I am the Tao Tei. The river is behind me." He gestured vaguely over his shoulder. "I will come towards you. I want to know the exact distance that was between you and the Tao Tei when you made your attack."

All at once William realized why their presence had been required here. This was an experiment. Strategist Wang was trying to recreate the moment when William had killed the first Tao Tei out at the camp in the desert, presumably in the hope of finding out exactly how and why he had managed it.

William nodded and stepped forward. Wang began to walk slowly towards him. When he had halved the distance between the two of them, William held up a hand, indicating that Wang was standing at roughly the right distance.

"And the beast stood its ground as I am?" Wang asked.

"A bit larger—but yes," said William.

Wang looked more than satisfied—in fact, he looked positively energized. Turning smartly he strode back to the table and picked up an ancient-looking book that was sitting there. As he began to speak to Lin Mae and the assembled officers, Ballard translated his words.

"He says the book is from the Library here. It's an equipment manifest from nine centuries ago."

Wang put the book down and turned again to the scroll, which was still spread out on the table, its corners weighed down with smooth, highly polished green stones. Once more Ballard translated for William and Pero as Wang began to read from it.

"At the Hansha Gate was an unusual winch, which

had been brought from Yunnan. A lodestone so powerful it was able to pull unbound iron up the rampart walls…"

Wang looked around, allowing his words to sink in. Then, with an understated but nevertheless orchestrated sense of drama, he picked up William's magnet and held it above his head.

As he began to speak, Ballard muttered, "He believes the magnet is the reason you were able to kill the Tao Tei in single combat. He thinks it has power over the Tao Tei." He listened to what else Wang was saying with a frown on his face, his lips moving slightly, as though silently rehearsing his translation before giving voice to it. When he next spoke, it was not to paraphrase Wang's words, but to offer a literal, though halting translation.

"I believe there is… hearing… sound beyond what we can sense… the ears of dogs and wolves… superior to man… the great birds… the owl… the bat… many sounds no man can hear… we know the Tao Tei… we see them listen to a voice we cannot understand…"

His frown deepened as Wang's words spilled out faster, his voice becoming more strident.

"I think the magnet makes them deaf. Without instructions from their Queen they fall still."

Instantly he had finished speaking, there rose a tumult of excited speculation. The black stone was passed from hand to hand, and although there was skepticism on some of the faces, there was a great deal of hope too.

Lin Mae listened to her commanders discussing the practicalities and implications for a few minutes, and then she raised a hand for silence. Looking at Wang, she said, "How can we be sure that you are right?"

Unsure whether he was breaking protocol, William stepped forward. "Why not try it?" he said.

Eyes turned towards him. Wang spoke a short sentence to the assembled throng, presumably translating his suggestion.

Lin Mae's question was a challenge. "How?"

"We capture a Tao Tei and see if it works."

She rolled her eyes dismissively. Wang translated his words and many of the officers snorted in derision; some laughed.

"What's the problem?" William asked. "Have you never captured one before?"

"No net is strong enough," said Wang.

"You don't need a net. You hunt him like a whale." He addressed Lin Mae. "You know what that is? It's a water beast. Many times the size of a Tao Tei." He demonstrated with his hands as he spoke. "I've seen it done in Spain. The hunters use a spear that grabs. It hooks the bone. Then they pull him up."

Now Lin Mae was listening intently, Wang behind her translating his words for the assembled officers. From their body language, facial expressions and tone of voice, William could tell that his suggestion was meeting with a variety of responses—from derision to excited interest, dismissal to contemplation.

There was only one response *he* was interested in, though. He focused his attention on Lin Mae, the new commander of the Nameless Order.

Her dark eyes stared back at him. She looked thoughtful.

• • •

In the corridor leading back to their barracks, the first moment they were alone, Pero grabbed William roughly by the shoulder and spun him around.

"What are you doing?" he hissed, his face furious. "Now you're *involved* with this? We need to be free when the attack comes! How many chances do you think we'll get?"

"I just—" William began, but Pero cut him off.

"No! Just nothing. We've already done enough. Get out of this. When the time comes, be injured. Be missing. Be a coward."

With an aggressive sweep of his arm, he turned and stormed off down the corridor, leaving William to stare after him.

• • •

The next morning William found himself up on the battlements, overseeing preparations for his plan to capture a Tao Tei. He had been summoned that morning and given the surprising news that Lin Mae was in favor of his suggestion, and that a strategy had already been discussed and agreed upon. When he emerged from the base of one of the towers, into early morning fog so thick that the world beyond the Wall was nothing but a densely swirling grey mass, it was to find that an assembly line had been set up and was already operating at maximum efficiency.

Shrouded by mist, which not only impaired vision but deadened sound into a suffocating silence, Strategist Wang was carefully pouring yellow powder from a gourd into a large bowl full of liquid. From the fact that he was wearing gloves, and that he turned his head away from the bowl every time he needed to inhale, it was evident that the concoction was pretty pungent stuff, if not downright toxic.

Indeed, William quickly noticed that everyone who came into contact with the stuff was handling it with extreme care. As Wang mixed the yellow powder into the liquid, various assistants, all similarly gloved, were scooping up smaller bowls of yellow paste and distributing them to a long line of Eagle Corps soldiers. The red-armored warriors, supervised by Commander Chen, were busy brushing the yellow paste onto the tips of newly forged metal harpoons, and then passing them on to Bear Corps soldiers, who were transporting them with utmost care to the Eagle nests along the Wall, where they were being loaded and chained to the winches.

It was clear to William, when he arrived, that the process had been going on all night. As he strolled along the Wall, nodding to Lin Mae and her officers, who were alternately monitoring the plan's progress and nervously peering out into the mist, he realized that the furthermost Eagle nests he came to had already been equipped with poisoned harpoon ballistas, and that all that was left to be supplied were the closest, most central nests.

Although everyone had been assigned a task to do, and was undertaking it with the usual industry and efficiency, the atmosphere on the top of the Wall was one of hushed anxiety—which was hardly surprising considering that the Nameless Order had no way of knowing when and how the next Tao Tei assault would come. After last night's stealth attack anything was possible. For all William and the rest of them knew, the Tao Tei, under cover of the fog, might even have been climbing the outside of the Wall that very moment. In anticipation of this, archers were positioned at regular intervals along the edges of the battlements, behind whom stood a long line of Deer Corps warriors, lances poised. With no specific job to do, William strolled up and down the length of the Wall, offering murmured words of encouragement and every now and again stopping to test the tension on chains and winches to which the harpoons had been attacked. He tried to appear calm, but under the surface he felt nervous, agitated. His encounter with Pero last night kept playing through his mind. What *was* he doing here? What *did* he hope to achieve? This wasn't his battle, and in a way Pero was right. Once the next big attack came, he needed to be out of there. He needed to be at his friend's side, helping him put their escape plan into action.

His reverie was interrupted by a sharp cry from over near the battlements. He looked that way, heart jumping, half-expecting to see a man missing from his post, perhaps plucked from his perch by some unseen horror below. But the archer who had cried out was still there, hand raised for silence, his head cocked towards the billowing wall of fog. Clearly he had heard something—but what? For several moments all activity ceased and the silence became so profound that not even a breath could be heard.

Then there came an almighty crash, which caused everyone to leap out of their skin and whirl round. The shamefaced culprit was the young Bear Corps warrior, Peng Yong, who, his hands perhaps shaking with nervousness, had dropped a china bowl containing yellow paste to the ground, where it had shattered into a thousand pieces, spattering the noxious concoction everywhere. Now he was blanching and trying to stammer out an apology as Commander Chen stalked towards him. Chen thrust his face into the young soldier's and hissed a string of furious words. Although William didn't understand what Chen was saying, the way Peng Yong lowered his eyes and nodded miserably suggested he had been dismissed. Sure enough the young soldier left his place in the line and began to trudge through a silent gauntlet of his fellow warriors, shoulders stooped and head down. When his walk of shame brought him parallel with William, William said, "Psst."

Peng Yong glanced up with an abject expression.

Winking, William whispered, "I used to throw up my supper before every battle. At least what you did isn't that bad."

It was clear that Peng Yong didn't understand him, but he recognized the note of sympathy in William's voice and gave a thin, grateful smile in response. Then he walked on by, lowering his head again as he passed through the door of the tower and out of sight.

• • •

In the corridor below, Pero heard someone coming. Grabbing Ballard's loose-fitting robe, he dragged him through an arched doorway, then into the black wedge of shadow against the inside wall.

They stood, motionless, hardly daring to breathe, Pero peering through the narrow crack between door and frame. He saw the young man who had mislaid the keys to the stockade a couple of days before trudging past, his oversized armour seemingly weighing heavily on his body.

The two of them waited until the Bear Corps warrior had rounded the corner at the end of the corridor, Ballard looking after him curiously. Then Ballard turned his attention to other matters. Waspishly he asked, "Where is William?"

"I don't know," said Pero, raising his hands placatingly. "But he'll be here."

Ballard looked at him sourly. "He'd better be."

• • •

William was watching Strategist Wang, who had stopped mixing the yellow paste and was now listening attentively. William listened too, and was able to discern a faint hiss coming from the fog.

What's that? he wanted to ask, but he didn't dare speak.

Many of the archers perched on the outer battlements now had listening devices pressed to their ears, which to William looked like long battle horns.

For several minutes there was almost complete silence, all eyes fixed on the men with the listening devices. One of them screwed up his face and leaned a little further out, as if trying to pin down an elusive sound…

Suddenly a shadow loomed from the mist beyond him, and an instant later he was snatched from his perch.

He screamed, and as he disappeared from view his listening device flew out of his hand and went spinning away through the murk. Next moment, like a massive shark breaking the surface of a grey sea, a huge red mouth appeared, snatched the listening device out of the air and swallowed it whole!

William had barely taken that in when a number of huge green claws tipped with black talons suddenly appeared over the top of the Wall, gripping on to the stone ledges like grappling hooks. Next moment several Tao Tei heaved themselves up out of the mist and over the Wall.

Instantly Eagle Corps archers began to fire at the Tao Tei, enveloping them in a blizzard of arrows. But although one of the creatures was knocked back immediately and sent tumbling over the battlements to plunge down through the fog to the earth below, the others were only marginally affected. Indeed, the arrows merely angered them rather than disabling them, and before the archers had time to reload the creatures were lashing out with their massive claws. They cut a swathe through the archers, ripping them apart, snatching and grinding them in their jaws.

As more Tao Tei appeared, the Deer Corps soldiers leaped to the fore, thrusting at the creatures with their long lances, aiming for the eyes. Simultaneously Bear Corps warriors ran forward with lines attached to their left wrists, the trailing ends of which they tied swiftly and expertly to hooks on the inner rim of the Wall. The tethered Bear warriors then climbed up on to and *over* the parapet, the lines enabling them to stand horizontally on the outside of the Wall. Armed with huge axes, they slashed and hacked furiously at the ascending Tao Tei, fighting with such frenzied and fearless purpose that it took William's breath away.

Despite their bravery, however, it was clear that the Nameless Order were fighting a losing battle. The enemy was simply too plentiful and too strong. Many Tao Tei fell, pierced by lances and arrows, or smashed into oblivion by axes. But for every one that died, another was immediately there to take its place.

The same could not be said of the Nameless Order. Their fighting force was impressive, but it was not infinite. And as the battle raged on, more and more Tao Tei began to break through, to cause devastation in the ranks.

William saw Bear Corps soldier after Bear Corps soldier, like a series of tempting worms for hungry fish, snatched from their moorings and devoured. He saw Eagle Corps and Deer Corps soldiers, their specialist weapons less effective in close combat, being trampled and ripped apart. He saw Lin Mae screaming orders, blue Crane Corps warriors darting about like dragon flies, stabbing and slashing at the enemy.

Every single one of them fought bravely. But it was not enough. It was never going to be enough. And although he was no coward, William thought of Pero and Ballard waiting for him below, of their plan to escape and take as much of the black powder as they could carry with them—and he decided it was time to go.

• • •

Pero was in the room he shared with William, grabbing his weapons and stuffing them into his belt, into his boots. Even here, this deep within the complex of corridors, tendrils of fog had infiltrated the interior of the Wall, and were curling and probing, hazing the air. As Pero armed himself he watched Ballard, who was prowling back and forth like a caged animal, his eyes blazing with rage. In the distance the war drums were pounding incessantly, a background beat to the sounds of battle: the clash of metal; the impact of flesh on flesh; screams both human and inhuman.

As an extra loud crash reverberated through the corridors—the unmistakable sound of shattered and tumbling masonry—Ballard whirled towards the doorway, as if half-expecting to see the green bulk of a Tao Tei standing there.

Spit flying from his mouth, veins standing out on his forehead, he snarled, "What curse have I provoked so deeply it plagues me thus?"

Calmly Pero said, "He'll be here."

Ballard rounded on him. "When? When it's over?"

Pero batted away his invective as if it were a troublesome fly. "We'll make a start. He'll find us."

"*Start?*" Ballard pivoted on his heels, eyes rising to the heavens as if he had never heard anything so idiotic. "As if what? As if we were descending a flight of stairs and might turn back if the fancy became us? *We're jumping from a cliff here!*" He waggled his head and began speaking in a simpering falsetto, mocking their earlier questions. "'Do I have keys?' 'Do I know the way?' I have *everything!* Keys! Powder! Tools! Maps! It's all hidden and arranged along the route! Once we *start* there's no turning back! *Understand?*"

• • •

Within the machine-like workings of the inner Wall, Tiger Corps soldiers were busily moving rows and rows of blade carts into position. As levers were pulled and slits opened in the Wall, so each cart was pushed forward until the sharp, broad blade mounted on the front slid neatly through the slit and into the open air on the outside of the Wall.

"Blades ready!" Commander Wu barked, his order being relayed up and down the line. "Left! Right!"

Like a highly trained rowing team, Tiger Corps soldiers began to work oar-like levers rapidly back and forth, causing the lethal blades to slash from side to side. Several ascending Tao Tei, caught between the huge blades, were instantly hacked to pieces, their dismembered parts, trailing green blood, spinning down through the fog to land with assorted thuds on the desert sand below. Those Tao Tei climbing the Wall that were still beneath the level of the blades were now unable to continue, their route blocked by the lethal, constantly moving barrier.

With the blade barrier erected and operational, more Tiger Corps soldiers now began to once again load the trebuchet chutes with spiked cannon balls dripping with boiling oil. As before, the balls were set alight just before being released. Within moments the trebuchets were launching fiery balls of death through the fog-shrouded air at the thousands of Tao Tei milling on the desert sand. Although the Tao Tei had drawn first blood in this particular battle, the Nameless Order were now fighting back.

• • •

William, poised on the stone exit ramp that led down to the nearest guard tower, was in an agony of indecision. Thick fog was swirling around him, hampering his vision, reducing the action on this part of the Wall into a kind of hazy chaos. Mingled with the ever-present pounding of drums were yells and screams as soldiers desperately fought those creatures that had managed to breach the parapet before the blade barrier had stymied their advance. But among the sounds of conflict William could also hear the rumbling of iron wheels and the clanking of heavy chains as the harpoon ballistas were wheeled into position. To attempt to capture a Tao Tei had been his idea, and there was a part of him that was desperately anxious to see it come to fruition.

On the other hand, this moment right now, while the Nameless Order were fully occupied with the Tao Tei attack, was the perfect opportunity to do what they had come to do—steal the black powder and make their escape.

What should he do? Stay or go?

As William hovered, unable to decide, he glimpsed a flash of blue armour through the fog to his right.

• • •

Lin Mae, in the thick of the action, her green-smeared sword clutched in her hand, ran forward to the edge of the parapet and peered over the Wall. She was satisfied to see that the blades had done their work, stemming the Tao Tei advance—for now at least.

As the huge harpoon ballistas were hauled into position, she turned and yelled, "Raise the harpoons! Prepare to fire!"

Her orders were relayed up and down the length of

the Wall, Commander Chen running the line to check that everything was in order. Eagle Corps soldiers were manning the huge crossbows, swinging them into position on their pivots. Behind them, Tiger Corps soldiers were loosening the winches with a jangle of heavy chains. As the harpoons, coated with yellow paste, were angled downwards into the fog, Strategist Wang, perched atop one of the command towers, shouted, "Make it count! Aim for the body!"

All they needed was one harpoon to find its target.

One captured Tao Tei on which to test their theories.

• • •

Pero strode towards the sounds of battle, Ballard at his heels, snapping like a vicious dog.

"Do you possess even a shadow notion of what it means to carry out an endeavor this challenging? What I've put into it? What I've endured? Or is that beyond your miniature, animal powers of conception?"

Pero swung round on him, hand moving instinctively to the sword at his belt. Ballard scuttled back, eyeing him with a mixture of outrage and wariness. For a moment Pero glared at the smaller man, whose eyes seemed to glint redly in the gloomy, fog-greyed corridor. Then he turned and strode on.

• • •

Lin Mae, still standing at the edge of the parapet, looked up and down the line as crossbow strings on the huge harpoon ballistas were pulled taut, creaking with tension. The metal harpoons, attached to chains, were arrowed down into the sea of fog.

"Fire at will!" she yelled.

The noise as multiple bolts trailing iron chains were released—*ZZZPPPTTTT!*—rang through her head and vibrated in her jaw, making her teeth tingle. Perched on what felt like the edge of the world, she watched as the harpoons looped out and down, bypassing the barrier of hacking blades, before disappearing into the fog. Some of the harpoons simply paid out the full length of their chains and then hung there, having encountered no resistance. Others thudded into what she could only assume was Tao Tei flesh, judging from the screeches of pain that rose up from the fog below.

As each harpoon came to a halt, whether because it had hit its mark or missed it, Tiger Corps soldiers immediately began to crank the winches, tightening the chains and hauling the harpoons back up.

"Put your backs into it!" Commander Chen shouted, though his order was unnecessary. Utterly devoted to the cause, the warriors manning the ballistas were working as hard as they could.

Suddenly Lin Mae jumped back with a cry as one of the taut chains snapped and flew back up and over the Wall at great speed, like a striking metal snake. The soldiers manning the ballista scattered as the chain lashed towards them. But Lin Mae had barely registered that when another chain snapped—and then another!

Moving back to the parapet, and leaning over to peer down through the fog, Lin Mae could see nothing at first. Then a section of fog thinned, broke apart, and blurrily, beyond the blade barrier, she saw a cluster of Tao Tei clinging to the Wall, their bodies punctured by harpoons. They were thrashing and writhing, trying to dislodge the metal bolts by tearing at their own flesh, causing the chains to whip wildly from side to side even as the men working the winches tried to pull them taut. Then she saw one of the Tao Tei, a harpoon sticking out of its belly, lean forward and bite the bolt in half, causing the chain to snap and whip upwards with lightning speed.

She ducked again—and then again as another chain snapped. Their plan was failing. The Tao Tei were chewing through the bolts before Wang's sedative, powerful though it was, could take effect.

A few ballistas away to her right, however, the chain was still taut, the soldiers there straining every sinew to winch it and its cargo in. Keeping her head low to avoid being decapitated by a flying chain, she ran across to help, arriving at the ballista at the same time as Commander Chen. Together the two of them helped haul on the winches, the clanking of the chain increasing as it rose a little faster. Then other soldiers were there—big, hefty Bear Corps warriors, who had abandoned their own failed ballistas—and Lin Mae moved aside, deferring to their greater physical strength. As the soldiers hauled the harpoon and its weighty cargo in, she rushed to the parapet and peered into the fog below. On the end of the chain, its abdomen impaled by a harpoon, was the vast green bulk of a Tao Tei, still struggling, but only weakly now as the sedative took effect.

Perhaps due to the fog, it hadn't been noticed by its fellow creatures, hadn't been torn or bitten free from the hooked barb in its flesh. She watched with trepidation as it rose higher with excruciating slowness, half-expecting at any moment for a gaping maw to rise up out of the fog and bite through the chain.

• • •

"Twenty-five years!" Ballard exclaimed. "Twenty-five years I've been braiding this together. Twenty-five years of smiling and scheming and burying my intentions in this forgotten graveyard."

Pero halted again. Took a deep breath. Although Ballard had backed away when he'd swung round on him earlier, it hadn't taken more than a few seconds before the skinny little man had been scurrying along behind him again, jabbering in his ear as if *he* was the one jeopardizing their plans.

If he didn't need Ballard's help…

If it wasn't for the black powder…

Pero was not a patient man, but he forced himself to stay calm. Though gritted teeth he said, "I've told you, I'll find him."

"And I've told you—forget him!" snapped Ballard. "Your friend would rather die trying to bed the new General than grab the key to every counting room and brothel in the world!" He darted around Pero to look briefly into his face, as if to check that he was listening. "Good God, man, the time is now!"

Pero's dark eyes flashed, holding Ballard's little ratty ones for a second. Obstinately he said, "We can't go without him."

Ballard's voice was suddenly sly, silky. "The more spoils for us should we live."

Then he quailed at the cold, murderous look that Pero gave him. "We need his bow."

Before Ballard could respond, a high, wailing screech came ricocheting down the corridor.

Pero started to run.

• • •

The wailing sound, eerie and high-pitched, almost child-like, had come from the harpooned Tao Tei. Still fighting the sedative, it was squirming on the end of the chain, making a last desperate bid to escape. Peering over the parapet, Lin Mae saw the blades protruding from this section of the Wall retract to allow her men to haul the creature up the last stretch of stone. She wondered whether the creature's wail was a cry of pain or anguish (she had thought the Tao Tei possessed no real emotions), but when she saw a swarm of green shapes rising swiftly up the outside of the Wall towards it, she suddenly realized what it really was—a distress signal.

Sure enough, instead of scaling the Wall towards their human enemies, the Tao Tei surrounded the impaled creature and tried to release it, their huge jaws biting at both the harpoon and the chain. Lin Mae turned and yelled at the winch bearers to hurry, knowing that within moments their potential catch would be lost.

But already the extra weight on the chain as several Tao Tei leaped and clung on to it was too much for the winch bearers to cope with. Try as they might to hold on, their contorted faces sweating and straining beneath their helmets, the chain which they had taken such pains to reel in slowly but surely began to unravel, sparks flying up as metal scraped squealingly over metal.

Suddenly she sensed someone beside her and turned to see the foreign soldier, William, his bow and a quiver of arrows over his shoulder. He glanced at Lin Mae and then peered over the parapet to see what was happening. To his right the chain was scraping and shrieking over the lip of the stone Wall as it continued to unravel.

As William moved across to the chain, Wang, still standing on top of the command tower, shouted, "What are you doing?"

William glanced up at him. "I'm going over. It's the only way."

He was aware of Lin Mae's eyes widening, of Commander Chen looking at him as if he was crazy. Then Chen turned to Lin Mae, as if silently asking her what the protocol was for this situation, whether the foreigner could do what he intended without her permission.

Lin Mae looked at William, and a moment passed between them—of respect, perhaps of understanding.

Then she gave the barest of nods, and the next moment William leaped up on to the edge of the parapet, wrapped his legs around the unraveling chain and plunged headfirst towards the ground.

14

Using his legs as a natural brake, he eased the tension
in them a little to allow his body to slither down
the chain even as the chain itself was plunging towards
the ground. As he descended through the mist, he
grabbed a handful of arrows, aimed his bow, and fired
off several quick shots.

His aim, as ever, was impeccable. Shot through both
eyes, the Tao Tei directly below him, that had been
attempting to gnaw through the chain, lost its grip and
fell away, tumbling into the murk below, dead before its
body had even reached the ground.

William fired two more arrows, and the Tao Tei that
had been trying to bite the harpoon from the impaled
creature's abdomen also fell away.

But now William was so low down the Wall—closer

to the ground than he was to the parapet—that the stonework around him was swarming with Tao Tei, some of which were still ascending and some of which were simply clinging there like giant green spiders, as if awaiting further orders from their Queen. Many of the creatures William dispatched before they even became aware of him, his body spinning and swaying on the descending chain as he fired off arrow after arrow with dazzling speed and skill.

By the time the now unconscious Tao Tei, its body still attached to the harpoon, reached the ground, William was no more than twenty feet above it. The Tao Tei's landing, slowed by those still working the winch at the top of the Wall, was a relatively gentle one. William slid down the last few feet of chain and swung round to land on his feet beside the Tao Tei's body.

He looked around him, but all he could see was thick white fog. Were the Tao Tei even aware that he was here? He looked up at the chain, which was swallowed by fog about thirty feet above him. Now that there was only the dead weight of the unconscious Tao Tei to contend with, would they have another go at winching it up? In fact, why weren't they doing it already? Because the winching mechanism was damaged? Because they were all exhausted from their earlier efforts and were pausing for breath before starting again?

Suddenly a Tao Tei loomed out of the fog, going down on all fours and springing at him like a dog. Reacting instinctively, William brought his bow round and fired two quick arrows, piercing its eyes and stopping it in its tracks.

But even as he jumped to the side to stop the creature's dead bulk from slithering into him and crushing him against the Wall, another Tao Tei lunged at him from his left hand side. He turned, trying to adjust his position and bring his bow up at the same time—and succeeded only in tripping over the outstretched claw of the creature he had just killed.

The Tao Tei bellowed in triumph, its jaws opening wide. William fell, his bow beneath him. He knew even as he twisted round to face his attacker that there was no way he'd be able to roll off the bow, grab it, load it and fire it in the couple of seconds it would take for the creature to crunch him in its jaws and devour him. There was barely even time to resign himself to his fate—which was probably a good thing.

Then there was a *thwack!* and the next instant the creature's severed head was flying through the air. Hot, stinking green blood from its stump of a neck splashed over his boots as it collapsed, shuddered for a moment and then became still.

Astounded, William looked up. Wreathed in fog, Pero looked like a wraith. He was scowling, an axe dripping green gore in his hand. As Pero hauled William to his feet he said, "I'm only saving you so I can kill you myself."

"How did you get here?" William asked.

Pero pointed at the chain ascending into the mist. "Same way you did." He looked quickly around to peer into the fog that surrounded him, and then back at William, anger and confusion on his face. "Have you lost your mind?"

"It's possible," said William, and then shouted a warning as a Tao Tei lunged out of the fog behind Pero. He spun, swinging his axe and smashing the creature to one side. Stepping smartly forward, William finished the beast off with two swift arrow shots to its eyes.

As the Tao Tei's body slumped into lifelessness, Pero asked caustically, "This is where you want to die?"

"Wherever we go, you always ask me that." William whirled and fired more arrows as another Tao Tei hurled itself out of the fog towards them.

Pero leaped forward to finish the Tao Tei off, then deflected the attack of another of the creatures, giving William time to fire another pair of arrows into its eyes.

"And *you* never answer!"

William grinned, exhilarated by the adrenaline pumping through his system, and in the lull between attacks rushed across to the unconscious Tao Tei. He examined the chain, which, though a little mangled by Tao Tei teeth, looked as though it would hold okay, and then the harpoon, the metal of which was splintered and frayed like old rope.

Quickly he looped the slack length of chain lying on the ground around one of the creature's stumpy, powerful legs and cinched it as tight as he could. He gave three hard yanks on the chain, hoping the winch bearers above would recognize it as a signal that they should reel the creature in. How he and Pero would get out of their current predicament he didn't know, but it was a question he'd asked himself a hundred times before. So far they had managed to get by on their wits, their skill and an awful lot of luck.

Another Tao Tei came out of the fog at them, and then, almost simultaneously, another. Perhaps they could smell his and Pero's blood and were starting to home in. Or maybe they were alarmed at the thought of one of their own kind in the hands of the enemy, and were swarming forward to prevent that happening.

It certainly seemed to William that those up above had received and understood his message. Slowly—*too* slowly—the chain was tightening and the Tao Tei's limp body was rising into the air. It hung upside down by one leg, its huge arms dangling either side of its head, black talons scraping the stonework of the Wall as it was hauled up, inch by painstaking inch.

William and Pero, meanwhile, were fighting a desperate rearguard action, spinning and jumping and firing and slashing, relying on their speed and their instincts to defend their valuable prize as the Tao Tei came at them from all sides. But whereas they were slowly but surely beginning to tire, the Tao Tei were not. And whereas William was running out of arrows, and didn't have time to retrieve any of the ones he had fired, the Tao Tei had teeth and claws to spare.

• • •

Although the winch bearers were working hard, and the chain was gradually being reeled in, Lin Mae knew it was taking far too long. She was also worried about William. If he wasn't dead already, he very soon would be.

"Prepare black powder weapons!" she yelled.

Chen, at the winch, looked up at her, shocked. "General?"

"Do it!"

• • •

The attacking Tao Tei were now little more than a blurred chaos of green flesh, black talons and teeth-lined maws rushing at them out of the fog. One of them bit down on Pero's axe blade as he swung it and jerked its head back, lifting him off his feet, and causing him to cry out as his shoulder was almost wrenched from its socket. William spun and let loose two arrows, piercing the creature's eyes. Pero fell back to earth as the creature collapsed. But before he had time to take evasive action, another Tao Tei came at William from the side, swinging a claw and knocking him over. He sprawled on the sand as the creature charged, its jaws yawning wide.

• • •

On the top of the Wall, Bear Corps warriors were carrying locked metal boxes from the towers. The instant the boxes were placed on the ground, they were unlocked and thrown open by Eagle, Deer and Tiger Corps warriors. The contents of the boxes—black powder arrows and lances—were rapidly lifted out and passed along the ranks.

"Light the fuses!" Lin Mae shouted.

• • •

Desperately William thrust his bow forward, jamming it between the creature's wide open jaws. It screeched and bit down, but although the bow bent it didn't break. Frustrated, the creature lashed out, its claw catching William on the shoulder as he tried to stand up and sending him spinning through the air again. He landed heavily, his fall partly broken by the dead body of another Tao Tei.

He had no idea where Pero was. The fog shrouded everything beyond a six feet radius. Suddenly there was a sizzling whoosh and a soft thud. William turned his head to see what looked like the shaft of an arrow sticking up out of the ground. Curiously the arrow was still sizzling and smoking.

Instinctively he turned away to shield his face, as with an enormous bang the arrow exploded in an eruption of crimson flame. William felt red hot sand pattering down on him, stinging the backs of his hands. When the sand stopped falling he swung back round, his ears ringing from the explosion. He saw a huge ball of fire rising and engulfing the creature that had attacked him, black grainy smoke mixing with the fog, reducing his vision still further. His body trembling, as though shock waves were still running through it, he struggled to his feet and began to stagger through the fog, calling Pero's name in a voice that felt thick and muffled in his ears.

As though from far, far away he heard Pero's answering cry. "William? Damn it, William!"

Standing among the burned remains of the creature whose mouth he had jammed with his bow—a blackened claw here, a lump of charred meat that might have been its head there—he swung this way and that, trying to locate the source of his friend's voice.

Then he saw movement in the gritty grey fog, something shambling slowly towards him. He tensed, but almost immediately realized the figure was too short and thin to be a Tao Tei.

But what was this? His friend or some kind of demon? The figure's skin was black, its clothes hanging in tattered rags.

"Pero?" William said uncertainly.

The figure slowly raised its head. But before it could answer, there was another enormous explosion from somewhere behind it, and propelled by a gout of fiery air it was thrown forward, smashing into William, the two of them landing in a choking sprawl of flailing limbs.

Coughing, his eyes gritty with smoke, William rolled on to his front, pushed himself up on his hands and knees. Beside him the ragged figure was lying on its back, its body racked by spluttering coughs. William wiped his eyes and looked at it more closely—and was delighted to discover that it *was* Pero.

He was about to say his friend's name when a shattering roar interrupted him. Turning to his right, he saw a Tao Tei charging towards them through the grimy air, head low and mouth wide open, as though to scoop them into its maw and swallow them whole. William grabbed at Pero's arm, trying to haul him up, but Pero was as limp as a corpse. He looked around for something he could use to defend himself with, but there was nothing except charred and burning meat. His bow had been lost when the creature had died in the explosion and Pero had stumbled into view with no weapon in his hand. Which meant that out here, in this environment, they were now as helpless as babies.

When the Tao Tei was no more than six feet away from them, another arrow sizzled down from the sky and lodged itself in the creature's mouth, burying itself deep within its rows of teeth. Perhaps in pain, perhaps by instinct, the creature clamped its jaw shut.

It was almost certainly this action that saved William and Pero's lives.

The arrow exploded inside the Tao Tei's mouth, blowing its head into a thousand pieces. Bombarded by a rain of flesh and green blood, William reeled and spun, his head ringing as if he'd been caught with a knock out punch. He tried to stay upright, but his vision was spinning and closing down, and he no longer had control over his limbs. The sky swooped away from him, but he didn't realize he'd fallen until he tasted sand in his mouth.

He only realized he'd been unconscious when his eyes snapped open. How long everything had gone black for, he had no idea. It could have been anywhere from two seconds to two hours. His guess, though, was that it was seconds, otherwise the Tao Tei would surely have eaten them for breakfast. Head still spinning, confused and disorientated, he struggled to his knees.

When he saw a flashing wall of yellow, like a piece of the sun fallen to earth, he thought at first he was hallucinating. Then his vision steadied, enabling him to focus, and he realized it wasn't sunshine he was seeing, but a contingent of Tiger Corps warriors in their yellow armour and flowing cloaks. Two of them were dragging a deliriously struggling and thrashing Pero towards a black doorway that had opened in the base of the Wall, while the others formed a protective guard, backing to the door with their long lances held out in front of them.

To his horror, William realized that they hadn't seen him, that his body had been hidden behind the slumped bulk of a Tao Tei. He staggered to his feet, his legs feeling as unsteady as splints, and raised a hand.

"Hey!"

His voice was a rusty croak. The Tiger Corps warriors, still backing towards the door, their faces set, gave no indication they had heard him.

Pero had, though—or at least, at that precise moment, he seemed to come temporarily to his senses and look up.

"William!" he yelled.

His cry alerted a pair of yellow-clad warriors, who glanced in his direction, their eyes narrowing against the smoky air. Summoning all his strength, William began to stumble across the sand towards them. The warriors, seeing him, beckoned him towards the open doorway, barking words at him in a language he didn't understand, but which he nevertheless knew was their way of urging him to go faster.

He broke into a shambling run just as a Tao Tei erupted from the grimy fog to his left. It would certainly have intercepted him before he reached the door if a pair of Tiger Corps warriors had not leaped forward and thrust their long lances into the advancing creature's eyes.

With a last burst of effort, William homed in on the black doorway and propelled himself towards it. He felt hands grabbing his arms, supporting him, hauling him forward.

Then the doorway swallowed him and he tumbled into the blackness beyond.

15

It was dusk. Lin Mae's first full day as General of the Nameless Order was almost over.

And what a day it had been. A day of blood and violence and fear.

But they had survived. Again. And with the foreigner's help they might even have achieved a significant victory.

Only time would tell.

Exhausted now, but trying not to show it, she followed a nurse into the huge infirmary, buried deep within the belly of the fortress. Most of the time, during the years when the Tao Tei slept, the infirmary was all but empty, the smattering of patients suffering from little more than fevers or training injuries. Now, though, it was a full and bustling place, the medical staff tending day and night to those wounded, some severely, in the recent battles. Nurses and doctors hurried here and there as Lin Mae followed 'her' nurse between the occupied beds, nodding and offering encouraging words as she went. Many of the men and women lying here had lost limbs or been so badly injured that they would never fight again. Some were *so* badly injured that they would not survive, and were merely being kept as comfortable as possible until the inevitable occurred.

The patient she had come to see, though, had suffered no more than cuts, bruises and concussion. His worst injury was a gash to his ribs, which a nurse was bandaging as she arrived.

Nevertheless, when she sat at the side of William's bed, Lin Mae was shocked to see the condition of his body. William, still groggy, was stripped to the waist, and she found it hard not to stare at the dozens of battle scars striping his torso. Together they seemed to make up a map of pain; they were testament to a life ruled by violence and conflict. Some of his more recent scars were still red and angry, whereas others were little more than tough old knots of white scar tissue. She exchanged a glance with the nurse tending him, who was also clearly shocked at the extent of his injuries. Finishing up, the nurse bowed and excused herself, as did the one who had brought her here.

"Tell them I won't be long," Lin Mae said as the nurse walked away. She bowed in obeisance.

William turned his head slowly on the pillow to look

at Lin Mae through heavy-lidded eyes. Drowsily he asked, "Did it work?"

"Yes," she said. "The beast was captured."

"And my friend?"

"He was unharmed."

He sighed in satisfaction and made an attempt to lever himself up on his elbows. His face, however, creased in pain, and Lin Mae moved forward to help. Eventually, grunting with the effort, he managed to raise himself into a sitting position. Once again Lin Mae's eyes strayed to the scars on his body. William noticed her looking, and became suddenly self-conscious, trying to tug his thin blanket up over his chest.

"I know. It…" He shook his head, embarrassed. "It looks worse than it is…"

Lin Mae lowered her eyes and offered a small smile of apology. When she next looked up, it was to find that *he* was staring fascinatedly at *her*.

To cover both their embarrassments she asked, "Why?"

"Why what?"

"Why did you go over the Wall? Why did you risk your life?"

He gave a crooked smile. "*Xin ren*. Did I say it right?"

She nodded. She looked stunned. She opened her mouth, then closed it again, as if uncertain what to say. Then she murmured simply, "Thank you."

He gave an awkward nod, as if the gratitude of others

was a new thing to him. Self-consciously he rubbed at a dark patch of soot, a powder burn, on his right forearm.

"Do you know what that is?" Lin Mae asked. Her voice grew heavy. "That black powder?"

William's eyes flickered. "I've never seen its like."

"It would be best if you had *never* seen it."

There was a deep sorrow in her voice, and perhaps also an implied threat. When William looked at her he saw how uncomfortable she seemed, how regretful. All at once he realized that she hadn't simply come here to thank him, or to see how he was. No, she had a different agenda. Something larger and more important.

A little hesitantly she said, "It is a terrible weapon. I know… very little of the outside world, but it seems to me that men are not so very different from the Tao Tei. Both are full of greed. Is that true?"

Despite her prowess as a warrior, the expression on her face was one of naivety and confusion.

"The strong take what they want," William admitted.

Tentatively she reached out. William didn't move as she trailed a finger gently down his cheek, then held the finger up in front of his face, showing him another smudge of black powder.

"Think of a world where that becomes this simple." She stared into his eyes, her face becoming serious. "Forget what you have seen."

Before William could answer, one of her lieutenants,

her blue armour flashing beneath the lamps, hurried through the crowded ward towards her.

The lieutenant said something, her tone urgent, and Lin Mae nodded.

As she stood up, William asked, "What is it?"

Lin Mae turned back to him. "The beast is waking."

• • •

Accompanied by Xiao Yu and Li Qing, Lin Mae strode into the fortress courtyard. It was a huge, torchlit square open to the skies, surrounded by high walls. It was currently packed with a full contingent of her commanders and hundreds of soldiers, all warily eyeing the massive iron cage in its center. Guarded by a quartet of soldiers, each of whom had their long lances aimed at the cage, it contained the captured Tao Tei.

As Xiao Yu had informed Lin Mae, the creature was indeed waking. It had been unconscious for many hours, but now it was groggily lifting its head, its nostrils opening and closing as it snorted the air. Lin Mae noticed that Shen, the imperial liaison officer who had been acting as Strategist Wang's assistant, was standing further forward than most, his eyes glittering with fascination as he watched the Tao Tei revive. As she came abreast of Shen, the creature made an attempt to climb to its feet, but skidded and fell, its legs not yet able to support it. Undeterred it tried again, and then again, its body seeming to shake itself further free of the sedative with each fresh attempt.

All at once, with a bellowing screech, it jumped up and threw itself at the bars. Every single soldier gathered in the courtyard flinched, many reaching for their weapons, but the iron bars were thicker than a man's arm, and although the cage rattled they held firm.

To the left of the cage was a long table, on which lay a single item—William's magnet, which had been placed into a bag of rope netting. Standing calmly beside the table was Strategist Wang, holding a length of bamboo with a hook at one end. As Lin Mae appeared, he bowed, then used the hook on the end of the bamboo rod to pick up the rope netting bag. He turned towards the cage, in which the Tao Tei was fully awake now, its teeth bared, its tiny eyes wild and rolling, snorts of steam rising from its nostrils as it took long, hard breaths in and out.

As Wang approached the cage, the bamboo rod with its dangling magnet held in front of him, the Tao Tei began to go crazy. It threw itself against the bars of the cage again and again, screaming with fury, its talons raising sparks as it thrashed at the bars and floor.

The four guards blanched and stepped back, the tips of their lances quivering as their hands started to shake. Wang, though, kept calmly walking forward, proffering the magnet as though it was a tasty morsel for the creature to eat.

The creature continued to hurl itself around the cage until the black stone was about eight feet in front of it. Then it stopped. The sudden change from bestial fury to quiescence was astonishing. At first the creature shook its head, confused. Then, as Wang pushed the magnet through the bars of the cage, it sat down. A collective gasp ran around the onlookers as the Tao Tei became utterly motionless, as still as a statue. Wang thrust the bamboo pole into the ground at an angle, pushing it down until it could stand on its own, and then he turned to the crowd with a look of satisfaction.

Lin Mae approached the cage slowly, staring in wonder at the dormant Tao Tei. This creature was her sworn enemy. It was the organizing principle of her entire life, the reason for her existence. She had fought these creatures, of course, but she had never had the opportunity to *study* one before. To stand now, staring into its tiny, dulled eyes, to feel its cold, rank breath drifting over her face, was both eerie and awe-inspiring. There was a part of her that wanted to put her hand through the bars and touch it, feel the roughness of its hide beneath her fingers. She clenched and unclenched her fist, began to slowly raise her arm…

And then the moment was broken as Shen, standing behind her to her right, began to applaud.

"Excellent!" he cried. "We must send it to Bianliang immediately!"

Wang's smile dropped from his face. His brows furrowed. "No! Absolutely not!"

Shen regarded Wang coolly. He moved closer to the Strategist, taking his time, his robes rustling.

"Strategist Wang," he said in the condescending tone of a teacher addressing an errant pupil, "the Emperor must view the Tao Tei immediately if captured alive. It is a standing order of the Imperial Council."

Wang was outraged. "Not now!" he barked. "Don't you see—"

"Does the General agree?" Shen said smoothly, both cutting in on Wang and turning away from him, in order to address Lin Mae.

Lin Mae said nothing. She looked from Wang to Shen, assessing the situation, weighing up her options.

In a pleasant voice, Shen said, "General, I am curious… how will His Majesty react, do you think, when he learns three foreigners have been invited to a military meeting?"

"Didn't you also agree to it?" Wang said acidly.

Shen spread his hands, all innocence. "How dare *I* defy the General's order?"

"Are you threatening the General?" Wang said.

Shen smiled. "I wouldn't dare."

There was a long silence. All eyes turned to Lin Mae. Though her mind was whirring, she stared back at Shen without expression. She was beginning to realize that the position bequeathed to her was not merely a military role but a diplomatic one too. It was a role in which she would not only be forced to make difficult decisions, but also in which, whether she liked it or not, she would be bound to make new enemies.

• • •

The Southern Gate of the fortress was slowly pushed open by a troop of Bear Corps soldiers. It was a job that required some strength. The gate hadn't been opened for some time and drifts of sand had collected against the outside of it.

As soon as the gap was wide enough, a wagon hauled by six horses emerged and began to set off across the desert towards Bianliang. On the wagon bed was a cage covered by a thick canvas tarpaulin. At Lin Mae's insistence a retinue of Deer Corps cavalry escorted the wagon on horseback. At their head, also on horseback, was Imperial Liaison Officer Shen, basking in a smug glow of self-congratulation.

• • •

The huge piles of dirty dishes in the kitchen never seemed to diminish. Peng Yong, at the slop sink, his hands already red and sore from their constant immersion in water, groaned as the door banged open and two Bear Corps warriors entered with a cart laden with yet more dirty dishes.

Peng Yong wondered what his parents would say if they could see him now. His mother had wept with pride when he had left home to become a soldier at the Great Wall, and his father had solemnly shaken his hand.

But he had failed to achieve the standards expected of him. What could he tell them in his next letter home? How could he possibly reveal that instead of protecting Bianliang from the Tao Tei, he had been reduced, because of his cowardice and incompetence, to a menial role more commonly suited to a peasant?

He caught the eye of one of the Bear Corps warriors, who smirked at him. Peng Yong blushed red and lowered his eyes. Oh, the ignominy of his fall was almost too much to bear. He almost wished he had been killed in the first battle with the Tao Tei, torn apart in their huge jaws like so many others.

At least then he would have been looked upon with honor.

At least then his parents, in their hour of grief, would have had a son to be proud of.

• • •

Ribs still aching, William made his way back to the Spartan barracks he shared with Pero. He had been laid up in the infirmary for twenty-four hours, and in all that time had not been visited by his friend. He hoped Pero was all right. Lin Mae had told him the Spaniard was unharmed, but since then he had received no further news. He hoped she hadn't been misinformed, or lying to spare his feelings. Reaching the barracks, he pushed open the door, and was relieved to see Pero slumped on his thin mattress.

"I've been looking for you," William said. Pero did not respond. Indeed, William sensed a chill in the air. Pero was looking at him with resentment, perhaps even hostility. Nevertheless he ploughed on.

"I wanted to say... look, I know you know this, but... *gracias. Gracias, amigo.*"

He held out his hand, hoping Pero would rise from his bed and shake it. Pero, though, simply stared at William's hand darkly for a moment, and then glanced up into his face.

"So sweet," he grunted. "You feel good, huh? A full heart for you." This time he *did* rise from his bed, but he was scowling, confrontational. "Maybe you sing a little song, eh? I'll join you. We'll sing together about how you saved the grateful *Chinos.*"

William was taken aback by Pero's hostility. "You saw what happened out there—and yet this is what you say?"

"I see black powder," Pero muttered. "I see a man forget his friends."

William's ire was rising now. He snapped, "The black powder's not going anywhere."

Pero grinned, but it was a nasty grin; there was no

warmth in it. Jabbing a finger into William's chest, he said, "What's going nowhere, my friend, is you." The grin became a sneer. "You'll never get what you want from this. You think they see you as some kind of hero? A man of virtue? Maybe you can fool them, but I know what you are. *You* know what you are. A thief. A liar. And a killer. And you can never undo the things you have done. And you will never be anything—"

Despite his sore ribs, William moved with lightning speed. Fuelled by rage he smashed a forearm into Pero's throat and slammed him into the wall. Even as Pero was reaching for the knife at his belt, William's other hand was already there, whipping the knife from its sheath, tossing it behind him. As it clinked and clattered across the stone floor, William leaned forward, increasing the pressure on Pero's windpipe. Leaning in close as Pero gasped for breath, he hissed, "Don't ever forget what I'm capable of."

With a final shove he released Pero and stepped back. Pero slumped against the stone wall, his legs sliding from under him. He rubbed his throat ruefully, trying to massage some life back into it. Then he looked up at William and grinned again, and this time the grin was genuine.

"Good to see you again, *amigo*," he croaked.

William glared at him. Though Pero had meant it as a compliment, he didn't appreciate his implication that the *real* William, the ruthless warrior, the beast, was lurking just beneath the surface. No, he was a better man than that. He *would* be a better man than that. Here among the Nameless Order he was discovering there were greater motivations in life than selfishness and greed. There was courage and friendship and loyalty. There was *Xin ren*.

Leaving Pero rubbing his throat, he turned and walked away.

• • •

General Shao's open casket lay in the center of the command tower. The General was laid out in full armour, his hands crossed over his stomach with his sword resting beneath them. The flag of the Nameless Order had been draped over his body, though folded back at the waist. Lin Mae knelt beside the casket, head bowed, her lips moving silently as she paid her last respects.

At last she rose and looked down at the General's peaceful face for a moment. Then she reached out and gently pulled the flag all the way up his body, eventually concealing his features from view. Stepping back, she closed the casket and walked slowly to the edge of the command tower. Below her, lined up on the Wall in their various corps, thousands of soldiers were standing in perfect formation, wearing white mourning headbands and holding long lances, at the ends of which small white pennants fluttered in the night breeze.

• • •

William stood transfixed in the dark doorway of one of the exit towers, watching the ceremony. As ever, he was overawed by the majesty and dignity of the spectacle before him. He saw Lin Mae, having closed the General's casket, descend the stairs of the tower and emerge from it to stand beside Wang. In front of Wang was a platform of some kind, on which were arranged rows and rows of what from William's vantage point appeared to be large white gourds. He looked on curiously as Wang approached the gourds and bent over them. What was he doing?

Then he gasped as the first of the "gourds", lit from within by a soft golden glow, rose into the air. The soldiers nearest the platform began to file forward, and within seconds more of the "gourds" began to rise, one after another, taking to the air and floating out over the Wall and across the desert. As the night sky became illuminated with floating balls of light, William suddenly realized his mistake. These were not gourds at all, but paper lanterns. Looking closer, he saw that beneath each lantern was suspended a small metal dish of black powder, which each soldier was taking his or her turn to ignite.

"As if by magic, eh?" murmured a voice beside him. William turned to see Ballard standing there. The man was smiling wolfishly, his thin hands clasped together.

"The heat from the fire changes the air and makes the lanterns rise. As the fire dies and the air cools, they descend." His voice became a purr of enticement. "Black powder magic!"

William turned back to look at the lanterns. Dozens, perhaps hundreds of them, had taken to the air now, and were sailing away through the night, like the ascending spirits of the dead. It was one of the most beautiful sights he had ever seen.

Black powder magic. Yes, this *was* magic. This whole place was a land of enchantment, complete with its fairy princess, its wizard and its ogres.

As if to consolidate the fantasy in his head, a row of eight Bear Corps soldiers began to beat their drums in a slow, almost soporific rhythm. After a few moments one of the soldiers began to chant words that William didn't understand, but which nevertheless struck him as ancient and soothing—a song of peace and beauty, perhaps a touching lament for the dead.

The soldier's voice was deep and husky, and soon it was joined by other voices, as more and more soldiers took up the song, a rising chorus that spread and echoed all along the Great Wall. William felt a tingle run through his body as he listened to the song of the warriors – a song of love and sorrow and longing – drift out across the vast black desert and into the endless heavens above.

16

The drums were pounding, not slow and steady this time, but hard and fast, calling every soldier along the Wall to their battle stations.

Flanked by Xiao Yu and Li Qing, and escorted by a retinue of Deer Corps cavalry, Lin Mae rode hard and fast along the top of the Wall, leaning forward over her snow-white horse, which was lathered with sweat, its hooves pounding the stony ground.

She was General of the Nameless Order, which meant she was responsible not only for the safety of the million people who lived in Bianliang, but also of the many millions of people who lived in the cities and countries beyond it.

She was ultimately responsible for maintaining the integrity of the Wall, their barrier against the Tao Tei.

But if what she was hearing was true, she had already failed in her duty...

• • •

Soldiers from every corps were rushing to their posts, lining up along the Wall, their shields and long lances gleaming in the firelight.

In a corridor in the fortress, Ballard slunk back into a shadowy alcove as a squadron of Bear Corps warriors rushed past, their boots clattering on the stone floor.

Only when the echoes of their footsteps had faded did he cautiously emerge—to see a dark figure approaching from another walkway that bisected the corridor. Instead of hiding from this figure, he hurried forward to greet him, shrugging to alter the position of the heavy sack whose strap was cutting into his shoulder.

"Nothing?" Ballard asked.

Pero shook his head irritably.

Ballard pulled a sour face. "Do we still need his bow?"

Pero was still walking, and Ballard scuttled to keep up with him. "We wait no longer."

"But how do we know he won't betray us?" Ballard asked.

"We don't."

"He must know that they'll kill him. Now that he's seen the black powder, they'll kill him no matter what."

Pero flashed Ballard a dark look. "The time they

spend killing him is time they're not chasing us," he said grimly.

They hurried on.

• • •

Illuminated by thousands of torches, the Imperial Palace at Bianliang was breathtaking in its beauty and opulence. Greatest wonder of the Ancient World, seat of power for the Middle Kingdom, it was the crown jewel in the heart of the city, its every wall and turret, its every pillar, gate and fountain burnished with gold and carved with intricately elaborate designs.

As Shen led the covered wagon and his escort of purple-clad Deer Corps warriors through the crowded, torch-lit streets of the city, he felt like a homecoming hero. The citizens of Bianliang gaped at him, many bowing, as he rode past. Shen, for his part, primped and preened, offering a haughty nod here, a dismissive waft of the hand there.

The caravan wound through the streets until eventually it came to a wide walkway leading up to the massive golden gates of the Imperial Palace. As they approached the gates they swung wide, a squadron of Imperial Guards in magnificent red and gold armour filing out to flank the caravan on both sides and usher it through to the palace courtyard.

Waiting in the courtyard were what Shen recognized

as the dozen or so men that constituted the Emperor's Council. He had once looked up to these men, had aspired to be one of them, but now he regarded them with lofty disdain. They were lackeys and sycophants, interested only in gaining favor with the Emperor. But they had lived cossetted lives, achieving nothing, whereas *he* had been to the Wall, and returned to Bianliang with a captured Tao Tei. As the Council members jockeyed for position, he smirked, thinking of what the Emperor would say when he saw his prize, of how he, Shen, would be rewarded.

From now on he would be regarded with awe and respect. He would become known in the city as the man who could tame monsters.

• • •

William hurried towards his barracks. He had come to a decision. Hearing footsteps in the corridor ahead, he ducked behind a pillar. A few seconds later there was a flash of red in the gloom of the corridor and a squad of Eagle Corps warriors sprinted past, heading in the direction of the pounding drums. As soon as they had rounded the corridor and disappeared from view, William emerged from his hiding place and hurried on.

• • •

Pero held a torch as Ballard removed the loose stone from the foot of the wall beside his bed. On his knees he stuck his hand into the hole, then leaned forward to push it deeper. He had a look of distracted concentration on his face as he probed about in the gap beyond the wall, and then his eyes widened in triumph. He pulled out one leather bag about the size of his hand, then another, and another. By the time he had finished he had eight leather bags stacked up on the floor, covered with cobwebs and dust.

As he brushed dust from his arm, Pero eagerly lowered the torch to examine the bags more closely.

With a grunt of disdain, Ballard shoved his hand away, causing the torch flame to flap and sending shadows cavorting crazily up the walls.

"Careful with that," he hissed, and nodded at the bags. "They're full of powder."

• • •

William rushed into the room he shared with Pero, but saw he was already too late.

Not only was Pero not here, but all his weapons and his few belongings had gone too.

• • •

A Bear Corps warrior and a Tiger Corps warrior descended a flight of stairs and began to move quickly along the corridor ahead of them. At the sound of approaching footsteps they scuttled into a nearby alcove and crouched down among the shadows.

Moments later a squadron of Tiger Corps warriors ran past, looking neither left not right. The soldiers hurried up the stairs with a deafening thunder of boots, whereupon the carved black bear's head atop the concealed Bear Corps warrior's helmet, its features frozen in a permanent snarl, emerged from the shadows, the face beneath it peering out cautiously.

The face belonged to Ballard. His companion in the yellow Tiger Corps armour was Pero. Both men were carrying heavy sacks, and knew that their disguise would not fool anyone for long. But if the armour deflected attention from them even for a moment, or gave them a few seconds' grace should anyone question them, then the deception would be worth it. Any advantage was better than nothing, and at least the armour would give their bodies extra protection should they be attacked or fired upon.

They hurried on, Ballard leading them along a maze of corridors and down several more staircases. Eventually, ahead of them, they saw a large dark opening on their left, from beyond which came clattering and splashing sounds.

Ballard raised a hand and turned his head to whisper to Pero that this was the kitchen and that they should move past the entrance swiftly, keeping their faces concealed. Pero nodded and the two men marched boldly forward. As they passed the kitchen entrance, Pero glimpsed a forlorn-looking figure in Bear Corps armour washing dishes in a vast sink, dozens of dirty plates and bowls stacked up on his left. As the figure turned to grab another pile of bowls, oblivious to their presence, Pero glimpsed his face and wondered why he looked familiar. The question nagged at him until, a couple of minutes later, he suddenly remembered where he had seen the boy before. He had been the young Bear Corps warrior who had misplaced the keys to the stockade the day he and William had been taken prisoner.

How the mighty have fallen, he thought with a smile.

• • •

Shen stood beside the covered cage in the Main Hall of the Imperial Palace. Ahead of him a flight of marble steps led up to a magnificent golden throne entwined with carved dragons. The Emperor sat on the throne in his golden robes and crown, a boy of fourteen with dark, intelligent eyes but a bored, imperious expression on his face.

Surrounding Shen and the cage was a squadron of Imperial Guards, lances poised, faces tense and alert. Flanking the throne and kneeling on the steps, were the members of the Imperial Council and a collection of eunuchs and courtiers, the ladies in their deathly-white make up fanning themselves furiously, as if pre-empting the swoon that might result from the unveiling of the cage.

Shen looked up at the Emperor, awaiting his response. After perhaps a minute in which no one said anything, the Emperor rose from his seat and began to slowly descend the marble steps. His every movement seemed to send a ripple of excitement through his entourage. His courtiers dropped to their knees as he passed by, each of them bowing so low that their foreheads touched the floor. The boy Emperor ignored them, instead running his eyes over the covered cage, before finally turning his attention to Shen.

Despite his impassive expression, Shen saw excitement dancing in the Emperor's eyes.

• • •

Huge spheres of resin, covered in thick oil and set alight, were lowered on ropes from the Western Tower. They bumped against the Wall a couple of times as they descended, sending sparks flying into the night. Eventually they reached their destination, coming to rest on the sand, a circle of fiercely burning fireballs.

Next, a dozen large metal hooks were latched on to the lip of the parapet, attached to ropes, which were flung down to the ground below. Once all the hooks were in position, Lin Mae clambered up on to the parapet, coiled one of the ropes around her leg and flung herself over the side. With practiced ease she dived headfirst towards the ground, aiming for the center of the burning circle. Within seconds eleven other Crane Corps warriors, their blue armour flashing in the firelight, were diving after her.

• • •

As the canvas tarpaulin was pulled from the Tao Tei cage, the courtiers and eunuchs gathered on the steps and around the Emperor's throne shrank back, uttering high-pitched squeals of terror.

The Emperor, however, not only stood his ground, but moved closer for a better look.

The Tao Tei, the magnet hanging around its neck like a bizarre necklace, was squatting on its haunches, completely dormant. Its great jaws were closed, its eyes were glazed and its breathing was slow and steady, as if it was asleep.

The Emperor walked all the way round the cage, viewing the creature from every angle. His councilors shuffled behind him in a human chain, trilling with excitement. When the Emperor had done a complete circuit he halted and turned to Shen, who was standing there like a proud father.

"How did you capture it?" the Emperor asked.

Shen was about to offer a somewhat creative version of the truth when one of the councilors, a thin, stooped old man with a wispy grey beard, stepped forward.

"The magnet, your Excellency, keeps the beast in check," he said, snagging the Emperor's attention. "This is an incredible discovery and will require our extensive study."

As he prattled on, Shen glared at him, feeling like

a child whose candy had been snatched by a bigger boy. But he didn't dare say anything. The Emperor was listening intently to the old man now, and it wouldn't do to interrupt. All Shen could hope for was that his time would come again. He glanced at the Tao Tei, which squatted placidly in its cage, completely oblivious to its surroundings.

· · ·

Strategist Wang and a squadron of nervous Tiger Corps soldiers holding burning lanterns stood in a close-knit group in the center of the flaming circle as Lin Mae and her Crane Corps warriors alighted, graceful as birds, upon the ground around them. As soon as the Crane Corps warriors had uncoiled the ropes from around their legs, Wang led them across to the rock formation at the base of the Wall. Motioning to the Tiger Corps warriors to illuminate the area, he showed Lin Mae what had been discovered earlier that evening—a huge arched tunnel, which burrowed through the rock at the base of the Wall. A Tiger Corps warrior stepped forward, torch held above his head, firelight lapping the tunnel's ceiling and rocky walls. After several feet, however, the orange glow faded, beyond which could be seen nothing but impenetrable blackness.

Lin Mae looked at Wang, and Wang looked back at her.

"How far does it go?" she asked.

He shook his head. "No one knows."

"Could they have burrowed right under the Wall? Through solid rock? Is that possible?"

His face was grim. "No one knows that either."

• • •

The fortress was almost empty, most of the soldiers now at battle stations. William ran through the maze of corridors, heading downwards, looking for Pero. Sprinting past a large opening on his left, he glimpsed movement, but he was several paces past the door before he registered it.

Wondering whether it was his friend, he doubled back, peeking around the edge of the opening. He was surprised to see the young Bear Corps warrior who had dropped the metal bowl staring at him in surprise. Over his armour the young warrior was wearing a wet apron covered with food stains. He was clutching a pile of dirty plates to his chest, which he had presumably been just about to drop into the huge sink of steaming water beside him.

Hoping the young man wouldn't raise the alarm, William gave him a smile and a wave. "You're much braver than they think," he said.

Turning and hurrying away he heard a crash behind him as the young man dropped the plates.

• • •

Helmeted heads covered tightly by the hoods of their capes, Pero and Ballard crept into the Hall of Knowledge. Ballard had warned Pero that they might have one or two of Wang's assistants to deal with, but all was silent, dark and deserted. Nevertheless they slunk past the display tables of mechanical devices like ghosts, the breeze from their passing bodies causing a dozen or so silk scrolls that were hanging from the ceiling to shift gently as though stirred from sleep.

Scurrying across to the far wall, Ballard moved aside a black silk hanging on which had been painted a depiction of the constellations in the night sky. Beneath it was a hidden door, made of thick wood and inset with a huge iron lock. Pero tried the door, but it was immovable, set so tightly into its frame it didn't even rattle. He looked at Ballard, intending to ask him if he had the key, but Ballard was grinning at him knowingly, and suddenly Pero understood.

He nodded and stepped back, watching as Ballard swung the sack he'd been carrying over his shoulder on to the floor. From it he produced a small copper tube and one of the bags of black powder. Deftly he filled the tube with powder, stoppered it at one end and slid it neatly into the lock. Then he produced a strip of waxed paper from his sack, which he twisted into a fuse and fed into the exposed, open end of the copper tube. Finally he produced a flint and a wad of dirty cotton from his sack, and carefully returned the small leather bag of black powder to it. Although his hands were rock steady, his face was sweating inside his heavy armour.

"Get back and take cover," he said, gesturing towards a nearby workbench.

Pero hurried across to the workbench and crouched behind it. "What now?" he asked.

"Pray," said Ballard. He struck the flint above the wad of dirty cotton once, then again. On the second occasion it ignited. He held the wad of dirty cotton to the fuse, which lit immediately. Grinning, he scooped up his sack and scurried, like a rat chased by a cat, across to where Pero was crouching. Both men lowered their heads and covered their ears as the burning fuse began to hiss.

• • •

Lin Mae stood at the mouth of the tunnel, staring into its depths. On her left were her Crane Corps warriors, and on her right the squadron of Tiger Corps warriors, still brandishing their torches. No one said anything, but as pinpoints of light suddenly appeared in the darkness of the tunnel ahead a few members of the group began to murmur in consternation.

Gradually the pinpoints of light became flickers, which grew brighter, until eventually the dapper figure of Wang appeared, holding aloft a pine oil torch, a squadron of Lin Mae's Crane Corps warriors, armed with long lances, behind him.

Panting for breath, his face haggard with shock, Wang said, "It goes all the way through… They… they've breached the Wall."

It was the worst news possible. There were gasps and moans. One of the Crane Corps warriors who had stayed with Lin Mae slapped a hand to her mouth to stifle a sob.

Her shock turning to fury, Lin Mae barked, "Summon my commanders immediately!"

Li Qing, trying hard to retain her composure, nodded. "Yes, General."

17

Still crouched behind the workbench, fingers in their ears, Pero and Ballard waited.

And waited.

Eventually Pero lifted his head slowly and peered over the top of the bench. Seeing nothing he nudged Ballard, who glanced irritably at him. When Pero raised his eyebrows and pulled a '*What's happening?*' face, Ballard said laconically, "Why not take a look? See if it's gone out?"

"Is it safe?" asked Pero.

"Of course it's safe. Just—"

His words were interrupted by a massive explosion, which buffeted the bench and threw both men backwards. Pero felt as if his skull had been smashed between two sledgehammers. His brain was shaking like a dice in a cup and his ears felt simultaneously to be stuffed with soil and leaking blood. The air was full of smoke and dust and debris; when he breathed in, the air was hot and seemed full of splinters. He clawed at the bench in an attempt to pull himself up on to his knees and peer over the top, but he couldn't see a thing. His eyes were blurred and smarting.

• • •

In the kitchen the floor shook and the pots and pans hanging on hooks from the ceiling began to sway, clanging against one another. Peng Yong gripped the side of the sink to steady himself as a heap of metal bowls slid to the floor with a clash of metal on rock.

When the tremor had passed he looked up. Where had the explosion come from? Though muffled it seemed too close to have echoed down from the top of the Wall. Could it have come from the courtyard then? Somewhere closer? And who could have caused it?

Then he remembered seeing the foreign soldier…

• • •

The air was still full of dust and debris, but it was slowly settling now. Coughing, eyes still stinging, Pero clambered to his feet. He felt bruised and battered, but a little pain was nothing new to him; he was used to carrying injuries.

He was not used to being deaf, though. Not used to

feeling as if his head had been squeezed in a vise. He opened his mouth, rotated his jaw from side to side, and was pleased to find that the pressure in his ears eased a little.

Ballard had already scuttled out from behind the bench and was now crouching beside the door. He was a dark, blurred shape behind a curtain of floating grime. The explosion had blown many of the torches out, transforming the room into a realm of shadows. Flapping at the dust, Pero realized that where the stout wooden door had been was now a charred hole, around which lay pieces of blackened wood, some of which were still burning.

Ballard's head snapped round. His thin face was a soot-smeared mask of savage triumph.

"Shake it off, soldier!" he barked. "To work!"

• • •

William was going round in circles. Somehow, after passing the kitchen, he'd lost his way, got turned around, and was now standing outside Ballard's suite. He banged on the door, then opened it and looked inside. Empty, as he'd suspected. So where—

The *BOOM!* of an explosion, not too far away, caused the flames of the lanterns in the corridor to flap momentarily and the floor to shudder beneath his feet. William didn't exactly stagger, but he put out his arms to steady himself, like a tightrope walker, and turned his head in the direction the explosion had come from.

After a few seconds a waft of warm air barreled down the corridor and rolled over him, causing the lantern flames to shiver again. He caught a faint odor of charred wood. He felt dread seeping through him, curdling his insides.

Oh no, he thought, and began to sprint back the way he had come, homing in on the sound of the explosion and the still lingering smell of burning. He had an awful suspicion, though, that no matter *how* fast he ran, he was going to be too late.

• • •

Peng Yong was frozen to the spot, his mind churning. Should he investigate the explosion, confront the foreigner—if that was who had caused it? But what if the foreigner was armed? In fact, there was every likelihood that the foreigner *would* be armed. He was a soldier, after all, and a good one at that. He would doubtless think twice about cutting Peng Yong's throat if his plans were compromised.

But what *were* his plans? What could he be blowing up inside the fortress? Surely he couldn't secretly be working to undermine the Nameless Order? The Tao Tei were a threat not only to Bianliang and the rest of China, but to the entire world. No matter how ruthless the foreigners were, Peng Yong couldn't believe they would be so foolhardy as to aid the Tao Tei, not even for their own gain. Then again foreigners were inscrutable, unpredictable. Who knew what dark and twisted thoughts went through their minds?

If it was unwise then to confront the foreigner directly, Peng Yong must inform the Order what was happening. But would they listen to him after his previous misdemeanors? He scrunched the bottom of his wet, filthy apron in his hand. He would *make* them listen. And who knew, if he acted quickly enough and thus helped prevent the foreigners from committing whatever heinous activities they were currently engaged upon, he might even be reinstated as a Bear Corps soldier. He might even be honored with—

The foreigner ran past the doorway again—and in the same direction he had been heading last time. Which meant, as far as Peng Yong could tell, that he was heading *towards* the explosion, not away from it. Which further meant that he couldn't have caused it—unless, of course, he had used a very long fuse.

But where had the foreigner been since Peng Yong had last seen him? Had he been running in circles? For what purpose?

Curiosity getting the better of him, he hurried across the kitchen floor and found himself turning not right, towards the route that would lead him up through the fortress, but left, after the foreigner. If he was careful, and kept out of sight, he might be able to ascertain the foreigner's plans. It would be better to give General Lin Mae as much information as he could when the time came.

• • •

"What is this?" Pero asked, peering over Ballard's shoulder at what lay behind the door. He'd hoped it would be an escape route out of the fortress, perhaps a secret passage to the stables, but in fact it appeared to be nothing more than a huge cupboard containing many shelves, each of which were packed with a cornucopia of objects: weaponry, scrolls, tablets, notebooks, various instruments whose use Pero couldn't even begin to guess at...

Granted, there were jars of black powder here too, but surely it would not be too difficult to work out the correct proportions of each ingredient from the powder they already had in their possession, and therefore to make more?

"It's a treasure trove," Ballard said. "Contained here are the fruits of Strategist Wang's studies. It's an invaluable resource. And all for the taking."

Pero shrugged. He wasn't much of a one for learning—though he couldn't deny that some of the weapons Wang had collected over the years looked interesting, and would no doubt prove useful. At Ballard's bidding, he opened the sack he'd been carrying and withdrew the folded-up saddlebags he'd crushed into it. As Ballard began to ransack the shelves, taking what he needed, Pero held the saddlebags open so that Ballard could fill them. Moving between the cupboard and the opened saddlebags, Ballard outlined his plan to Pero. One saddlebag was full and the second beginning to bulge when Pero heard the scuff of a footstep on the gritty dust behind him. He spun round—then smiled.

"*Compadre.*"

His greeting caused Ballard to turn too.

William was standing there, his body, mostly in silhouette, wreathed in dust. He stared at Pero, saying nothing.

Impatiently Ballard said, "So you've come to your senses at last, eh?"

When William still failed to reply, Ballard flapped a hand in irritation. "Well, good God, man, come on, make haste! Grab a bag!"

But William ignored him. He kept his eyes locked on Pero.

Smiling, Pero said, "Ballard has explained it all. He's planned well. The horses are strong. Getting out will be easy. There's a gate twenty miles west. We take that and we can dodge the hill tribes. We can make it, amigo."

Still William said nothing.

Glancing at him, Ballard said, "Where's your bow?" Then to Pero, "Where's his bow?"

But Pero didn't reply, didn't even look Ballard's way. Instead his welcoming smile was fading, becoming a frown. Almost wistfully he said, "Last chance, amigo."

William spoke for the first time. His voice was blunt. "They need us here."

Pero threw back his head and laughed. It was not a pleasant sound. "Oh, they need more than us. These people are doomed."

Still crouched in the doorway of Wang's secret cupboard, Ballard backed up Pero's words. "Don't be a fool, man!"

For the first time, William registered Ballard's presence. He swung round on the little man in his stolen Bear Corps armour, his eyes blazing.

"I've *been* a fool!" he thundered, causing Ballard to recoil. "And I'm *done with it!*"

Pero raised his hands. "Brother, please…"

"Bouchard called it," William snapped. "We've been fighting for nothing. Fighting for greed and gods, and all for shit! This is the first war I've ever seen that was worth it."

"Nothing?" sneered Pero. "Nothing is what we leave behind when we die." He took a breath, made one last appeal. "Come on, let's take our prize and whore away the days we have left. Together."

William shook his head. "I can't do that now."

Pero looked at him a moment, as if trying to find

the man he had once known. Spreading his hands expansively, he cried, "William! My filthy bastard friend! Think of it! What wall, what city, what land could we not take with black powder in our saddlebags? Who would dare to stop us?" He had tears in his eyes now. For him, this was the culmination of a long, hard journey, the fulfillment of his wildest dreams. "We win, *amigo*. After all the pain and cold and blood and shit, *we win!*"

He looked at William hopefully. Had he persuaded him? Had he managed to bring him to his senses? William looked as though he was pondering Pero's words. But so intent on each other were the two men that neither of them noticed Ballard slip into Wang's cupboard and grab a knife from the shelf. Neither of them noticed him creep across to a rope that was stretched taut, holding upright a huge bookcase that was standing directly behind William. Pero only noticed him, as a flash of movement in his peripheral vision, when Ballard suddenly slashed down with the knife.

But by then it was too late. Too late to find out what William's decision might have been. Too late to attempt to persuade him further should he still say no.

Because the bookcase was falling, scrolls and bronze instruments already sliding out of it, raining down on William as he half-turned. Pero saw William's eyes widen, saw him half-raise a hand…

…then the bookcase crashed down, smashing

William down with it, pinning him to the floor.

Once again, dust rose in a great cloud, the crash reverberating through the length and breadth of the high-ceilinged room. Shielding his mouth and nose with his raised arm, Pero moved forward. He felt regret, but also relief that the problem had been taken out of his hands. He saw blood on William's forehead, his closed eyes.

"Is he dead?" asked Ballard.

Pero didn't know, but he bluffed, "It'll take a lot more than that to kill him."

He looked at Ballard, whose eyes were glinting, and who was still holding the knife in his hand. He knew what the skinny man was thinking, and although Pero was disappointed that his friend had proven himself a weak and lovesick fool, even now he couldn't bear the thought of William being finished off in his sleep by this cowardly weasel of a man.

Dismissively he said, "Leave him. Let *them* kill him."

Ballard gave him a long, hard stare. Then he nodded and threw away the knife.

18

As the dawn sun smeared its light across the top of the distant hills, Lin Mae once again stood at the mouth of the vast tunnel that the Tao Tei had bored through the base of the Wall, staring broodingly into its depths. She hadn't slept, but she didn't feel tired. There was so much at stake, so much anger and fear coursing through her system that rest was the last thing on her mind.

To her right stood Wang, who had changed out of the grime-smeared clothes he had been wearing during his exploration of the tunnel the previous evening, and who now looked as dapper and composed as ever, despite the desperate situation. To her left were Commanders Deng and Wu, their capes flapping in the wind. Deng looked shell-shocked, as if he could barely process the horrifying magnitude of the situation, whereas Wu wore a deep scowl, as though incensed at the sheer insolence of their enemy.

Wang was speaking, his voice clipped, with an almost admonishing tone to it. "As I have been trying to tell you, the Tao Tei change constantly. They evolve. All of the attacks up to now have been a diversion while they created this tunnel."

He glanced at Lin Mae and her commanders, but they had nothing to say. They simply continued to stare into the tunnel's black depths, as if unable to believe what they were seeing. He knew what they were thinking, though, because it was what he was thinking too. It was what *everyone* who knew about the tunnel was thinking. He sighed and decided to vocalize it, if only to bring it into the open.

"If the Tao Tei reach Bianliang, they will have unlimited food. There will be no containing them then."

Wu scowled at him, as if he had unveiled a dirty secret —or raised a problem to which there was no solution.

"It will take our army two days to reach Bianliang, even if we sprint all the way," Deng said miserably. "The Tao Tei run twice our speed. If that's where they're heading, we'll never catch them."

Lin Mae looked half-way between frustration and despair. Wang felt sorry for her. This was not the best way to start her tenure as General—not that this situation was her fault. Thoughtfully he eyed the way the capes of the General and her two commanders were curling and snapping at their backs.

"The wind is strong," he said.

All three soldiers turned to look at him. Lin Mae's eyes widened. She knew what he was thinking.

"It blows south, and it will continue to do so all day tomorrow." He shrugged, as though apologizing. "We have to use the balloons. It is our only hope."

There was a tense, heavy silence. Then Lin Mae sighed. "If it worked, how long would it take to reach Bianliang?"

She was looking at Wang, so she didn't see the incredulous looks that flashed in her direction from her two commanders. They couldn't believe she was humoring him, and he didn't blame them. He'd have felt the same in their shoes. On the other hand, he didn't blame Lin Mae for clutching at straws either. After all, as he had already pointed out, what other plan did they have?

"With a wind like this?" he said, raising a finger to test it. "Six hours?"

Commander Wu could contain himself no longer. "Yes!" he snapped. "For those who manage to stay alive." Turning to Lin Mae, he said, "Commander... they have never been tested."

Lin Mae looked at him for a long time. Her gaze was steady and her voice like steel when she spoke. "Then we will test them when we use them. Make it so!"

• • •

When William woke up, his first thought was to wonder whether he was still asleep and dreaming. The last thing he remembered was speaking to Pero in the Hall of Knowledge, before hearing an almighty crash and everything going black.

Now, though, he appeared to be in the Great Hall, chained to a bench, his body aching and the taste of blood in his mouth. Moreover the room seemed to be a hive of activity, though what the Tiger Corps soldiers on the other side of the vast space were doing he had no idea. As far as he could tell, they *appeared* to be stitching together giant masses of pig or sheep skin. Feeling something trickling into his eyes—blood or sweat; it stung at any rate—William closed them, hoping that when he opened them again he'd be able to shake himself free of the odd dreams he was having and remember what had happened. But when he next came round it was to the *clank* of something heavy dropping or stamping down next to him. He opened his bleary eyes, squinted against the light, and through the haze saw something both strange and ominous. Beside his prone body was what appeared to be a guillotine, but one whose blade was in the shape of a snarling, elaborately molded tiger's head with jagged teeth.

Was it real? Or was *this* part of his dream too? He reached out to touch it, wondering whether he'd feel cold, solid metal or whether his hand would pass straight through.

But neither of these things occurred. Because he had barely moved his arm when he felt a sharp tugging at his wrist, and heard the tinkling of metal. He turned his head, and saw that either the dream he'd had earlier was still ongoing, or it hadn't been a dream, after all. There were manacles attached to chains around both his wrists.

As he shook his head, trying to order his thoughts, he heard the pounding of a drum, fast and frenzied, and the next moment his vision became a whirling mass of color as soldiers streamed into the Great Hall, hundreds of them, forming into well-drilled platoons.

William looked at them, wondering why they were here. Was it because of him? Had he done something wrong?

How he wished he could wake up.

• • •

Three horses raced across the desert, moving as fast as the sand and the hot sun would allow.

On the first horse sat Pero, face grim, bent down low over the neck of his steed.

On the second, smaller horse was Ballard, clinging on for dear life, his backside bouncing up and down in the saddle.

On the third horse, which was the biggest and

strongest of the lot, sat no one, yet it was this horse that was carrying the heaviest weight. Attached via a long line to Pero's saddle, the riderless horse's sweat-lathered body was laden down with a dozen bulging saddlebags.

• • •

William looked up dazedly as someone entered the room—and all at once, as if her very presence had kick-started his system, he felt his senses returning to him.

Hands still chained, he shuffled upright into a sitting position, as Lin Mae first spotted him, and then stalked across the room towards him. She looked furious. She looked like an approaching storm. The clamor of activity from a few moments before suddenly ceased as everyone stood, motionless and silent, watching her stride across the room towards him.

She halted about six feet away, as though she had hit an invisible wall. Her face was thunderous with rage and betrayal. Such a rage that she seemed unable to find the words to express it.

The memories were coming back to William now. The Hall of Knowledge. His conversation with Pero. Ballard slashing the rope to bring the bookcase crashing down on him.

"I tried to stop them," he croaked.

Lin Mae's eyes widened. "*You dare speak to me?*"

William looked around. On every face that was

staring at him he saw disapproval, hatred, disgust.

"It's true," he said, pleading with them to believe him. "I went there to try and stop them."

"Yes," said Lin Mae, her voice raw and cold, "and you came here to trade. And you knew nothing of black powder. And you fought for *honor*. What a fool you must think I am."

Her words were like a knife to his heart. He shook his head desperately. "No. I didn't do this. If I was with them, why would I be here? *I tried to stop them.*"

"*Liar!*" she screamed at him, lunging forward. Then she seemed to remember her position, and that all eyes were on her, and with a supreme effort she brought herself under control.

Turning to Wu, who was standing behind her right shoulder, she gave a sharp nod. He marched forward, grabbed William by the left arm and yanked him to his feet.

William glanced at the guillotine to his left. Now that he had recovered his senses, he could see that it was indeed real—very much so. Was this to be his fate then? Was his life to be ended so ignominiously in front of all these people he had tried to help, these people who he admired and respected as he had never admired or respected anyone before? His blood boiled to think he was to be punished for the vile and cowardly actions of a man he had mistakenly regarded as a friend and his snake of an accomplice. It was so unjust.

But life often *was* unjust. He had learned that the hard way.

Lin Mae began speaking again, the full extent of her bitterness clearly not yet expelled from her system.

"I need only think of you from now on to know how ugly the world can be," she said. "You will die as you have lived. For nothing."

Her words again struck home. William felt a dull, heavy sickness in his heart, his soul. He was not afraid to die, but he couldn't bear the thought that Lin Mae would live out the rest of her life harboring these thoughts of him.

Looking her in the eyes, willing her to believe, he said, "Some part of you must *know* that's not true."

But she was unmoved and seemingly immovable. Contemptuously she said, "If I were not the General, I would kill you myself."

William bowed his head, all hope, all energy, draining out of him. That was it then. The sum total of his life. The first time he had tried to do something good, the first time he had found a cause worth fighting for, and it had all blown up in his face.

Maybe Pero had been right all along. Maybe he shouldn't have become involved.

But he didn't regret it. Not for one moment.

"So be it," he murmured. "If you're going to do it, make it quick."

• • •

Lin Mae was trying her hardest to hold it together. She was the General now, and she had to set an example, had to project an air of strength and authority. The breach of the Wall by the Tao Tei was the very worst thing that could have happened. Not only could it signal the end of everything she believed in and held dear, but far more seriously, it could ultimately lead to the end of everything that ever was, or would be.

In relative terms, therefore, William's betrayal on top of this far greater crisis was a minor concern, something that General Shao would have dealt with quickly and efficiently. But she was not General Shao. She had grown to trust the foreign soldier, even to like him. She had begun to believe he possessed integrity, honor.

General Shao had told her she was ready to lead the Nameless Order, but what sort of leader would make such an error of judgment? Clearly she was not fit to lead. She had been betrayed, played for a fool, and as a result she had let down all those who relied on her. Trying not to show weakness in front of all those who fought in her name, she nodded curtly to a pair of Bear Corps warriors, who moved either side of William to hold him while Wu removed his shackles. She watched, face set, as they dragged him towards the guillotine, forced him to his knees…

Suddenly a cry rang out, sharp and shrill in the high-ceilinged room: "He tried to stop them!"

Everyone in the room first froze, and then turned, Lin Mae included. At first she saw nothing. Then she noticed movement over by the door, saw a Bear Corps warrior moving forward, pushing through the ranks.

She felt a flash of anger. Who was this? How dare he—

And then she recognized the young man's face. This was Peng Yong, who had been disgraced and assigned to kitchen duties.

Before anyone could respond, Peng Yong piped up again. "He did. I saw it with my own eyes!"

Lin Mae glanced at William, who, although he didn't speak Mandarin, had raised his head and was looking at Peng Yong with interest. She knew General Shao would not have tolerated such insolence as that shown by this already disgraced young man—but, as she had already established within her own mind, she was *not* General Shao. To the evident disapproval of some of her commanders, she snapped, "Come forward! Speak up!"

Peng Yong scurried nervously past the ordered and motionless ranks of soldiers until he was standing before her. Bowing he said, "The prisoner speaks the truth. I was there when it happened. I saw him try to stop them."

Lin Mae regarded him for a moment. Then she glanced again at William.

"And you did nothing?" she asked.

Peng Yong brought a trembling hand to his forehead. He looked on the verge of tears. "I was afraid… and I am shamed. But I... I cannot let a man be killed for this."

"Are you sure he tried to stop them?" Lin Mae asked.

Commander Wu, who was one of those who had shot her a disapproving look when she had given Peng Yong leave to speak, strode forward and grabbed the young man by the collar of his overalls.

"If you're lying I'll have *your* head first!" he snarled.

Peng Yong looked terrified, but he said, "I swear on the blood of the Nameless Order that I speak the truth."

The room was silent. William was now looking around, baffled but with something like hope on his face. Lin Mae stared at Peng Yong for a long moment, her thoughts churning. Then she again turned her attention to William. What should she do? What was the *strong* thing to do? What was the *right* thing to do?

At last she barked, "Lock him up! Send the cavalry after the two that got away!"

Wu narrowed his eyes, then turned and relayed an order to the two Bear Corps warriors, who hauled William back to his feet.

Aware that all eyes were still on her, Lin Mae shouted, "Back to work!" Then she turned and marched out of the room.

• • •

Despite everything that's happened, William thought, *I find myself back here.*

Last time, of course, he and Pero had not actually entered the stockade, because the young man who had just apparently saved his life had misplaced or forgotten the key. On this occasion, however, there was no such oversight. One of the two huge and silent Bear Corps warriors who had been assigned to escort him produced a key from a loop on his belt, unlocked the door and shoved it open.

It was not an easy task. He had to put his shoulder to the wood and push as hard as he could before the door started to grate inwards over a floor strewn with rubble. Evidently the cells had not been used for a long time. As William was shoved inside, he found himself choking in a cloud of upraised dust, which reminded him of how the air had been in the Hall of Knowledge after the explosion. He was still coughing when the door was slammed shut and locked behind him.

Once his lungs had settled and his eyes had stopped smarting he looked around. The walls and floor were made of rough stone, a slit of a window gave access to a narrow column of sunlight, and on the floor was a thin, rat-chewed mattress leaking filthy straw.

A real home from home, he thought ruefully. Still, he had slept in worse places. And being here was infinitely better than having his head separated from his body. He thought again of the young man, and what he must have said to persuade Lin Mae to stay his execution.

William knew the young man had seen him the first time he had passed the kitchen entrance. He could only suppose, then, that he had seen him the second time too, and had been curious enough about William's presence or the explosion, or both, to follow him. He must have hidden in the shadows and observed William's encounter with Pero and Ballard in the Hall of Knowledge. He wouldn't have understood what was being said, of course, but he must have seen enough to realize that William had not been part of Pero and Ballard's plot.

William wondered where Pero and Ballard were now, whether Lin Mae would send men to pursue them and bring them back. If they had black powder with them it was possible. She had already made it clear how terrible she thought it would be if the secret of black powder were ever to reach the wider world.

How would he feel if Pero *were* captured? William didn't know. He and his friend had been through a lot together, and he certainly wouldn't rejoice in his inevitable execution.

• • •

Pero wondered how much longer it would be before he ended up cutting Ballard's throat and taking the black powder for himself. He wasn't normally so ruthless—in fact, loyalty was his greatest strength (and also, perhaps, his biggest weakness)—but the man was starting to drive him crazy. He had lived a cossetted life among the Nameless Order for so long that he was no longer suited to hardship—if, that is, he ever had been. Almost from the outset he had started complaining—about the heat, the dust, the discomfort of being perched atop a horse, and every other little thing he could think of.

Now, several hours after fleeing the Wall, and with the sun high in the sky, Ballard was falling further and further behind. Eyes rolling and his breath wheezing in his chest, he was slumped over his horse like a man who had had no sustenance for days, his bag-of-bones body sliding about in the saddle as though under constant threat of being dislodged.

They were ascending the side of a canyon in the Painted Mountains, Pero leading the riderless horse laden down with their saddlebags. It was hard going, there was no doubt about that. The horses were panting, their bodies lathered with foamy sweat, and Pero himself had aching shoulders and a throbbing back.

But pain was a given, and something to be endured. You didn't give in to it, especially not out here. In such a hostile environment it was imperative to stay alert and in control. This was bandit country, added to which they weren't yet far enough away from the Wall for Pero to feel safe. Under normal circumstances he would have ridden for at least another three or four hours before stopping for a rest and a sip of water. Ballard, though, was simply not up to the task. Already his horse, some way behind, was starting to wander off to one side.

"*Vamanos!*" Pero called angrily.

Ballard looked up, whining something about his sore ass.

"It will be more than your ass that hurts if we don't move," Pero replied, wishing he had William with him; wishing it was the two of them riding across the desert with the black powder, whooping and laughing as they went.

He felt bad about William. He wasn't sure what he would have done if he had been unable to persuade his friend to join them, but even so he felt bad about leaving him injured and unconscious to face the consequences of his and Ballard's actions. He hoped the Nameless Order would go easy on his friend, but it was odd to think he might never know, might never see or hear from William again. They had been through a lot together, had saved one another's lives more than once.

He glanced back again at Ballard, and his mood darkened. He couldn't imagine Ballard ever saving his life. As far as he was concerned, the sooner the two of them went their separate ways the better.

It took a few more choice insults from Pero before Ballard was shamed into sitting up straighter in his saddle, and getting his horse to at least trot in the right direction. Pero waited impatiently for the older man to catch him up, and then the two of them went on, side by side, in a simmering silence.

After ten minutes, however, Ballard started to fall behind again. If he hadn't claimed to know the quickest and safest route through the Painted Mountains, Pero might have simply gone on and left him to it. Coming to a fork in the canyon trail, he turned back.

"Which way?" he shouted.

Ballard meandered up to him, his eyes narrowing as he tried to focus. With trembling hands he reached into his saddlebag for his canteen.

Pero jabbed at the choice of routes ahead. "Left or right?"

Ballard fumbled the top off his canteen and took a long, desperate pull of water. From the way it sloshed when he lowered it from his mouth, Pero could tell there wasn't much left, that he had drunk far more than he should have done by this stage of their journey.

"Which way?" Pero asked again.

Ballard peered at him, as if he didn't understand the question, then he muttered, "What do *you* think?"

Pero rolled his eyes and spat on the ground in disgust. "What *I* think is that you should save your water." Suddenly, losing his patience, he shouted, "*Izquierda!*" and slapped Ballard's horse hard on the rump.

With a whinny of pain and surprise, it leaped

forward, almost dislodging its rider, and began to gallop up the left hand path. Pero watched it go, then gave a satisfied nod.

"The left," he muttered.

19

It was a massive operation, and incredibly risky. At five staging areas along the Wall, Strategist Wang's desperate plan was coming to fruition.

Lin Mae stood with Wang at the main staging area, watching as a brazier was set above an airbox with a plunger on the side. As the brazier was ignited, the plunger was slowly pulled out, causing a measured amount of black powder to be blown up into the brazier. This in turn caused flames to surge up from the brazier, generating a large quantity of shimmering hot air.

Taking care not to burn themselves, a number of Tiger Corps soldiers, communicating in sharp, staccato phrases, manipulated a huge bag of stitched-together silk and canvas and sheep skin. Lin Mae knew that if they had had more time and more materials the bags would have been more meticulously crafted, the materials more carefully selected, and tests would have been carried out on the resulting constructions. But time had been very much of the essence, and so they had had to utilize what knowledge and materials they could. All she hoped was that the materials used would be good enough to do the job required of them, and that Wang's theories would work in practice.

As the huge bag began to fill with hot air, so it began to bulge and rise, and to tug on the shroud ropes connecting it to the woven basket gondola below. The gondola contained four soldiers, and was equipped with weapons from the black powder armory, which were lashed to the sides.

When the bag was fat enough and round enough with hot air, it launched itself from the Wall and became airborne, tugging the gondola with its human cargo behind it. Just as the gondola began to lift itself from the ground, more Tiger Corps soldiers rushed forward, clipping nets containing yet more weapons to the base of the rising basket. The gondola, Wang had explained to Lin Mae, was equipped with a simple propulsion motor, which acted as a crude tiller. This, he said, would enable the occupants of the craft to steer it in the direction they wanted to go.

Lin Mae watched the first of Wang's hot air balloons lift sedately into the sky, and then looked up and down the line, where more and more balloons were inflating, rising, launching themselves into the air. Propelled by fire and black powder and wind, her army was sailing forth. It was like watching the paper lanterns that had been launched to commemorate General Shao's life, albeit on a massive scale.

She only hoped that the balloons, like the lanterns, would not burn out and die before they reached their destination.

• • •

Taking the left-hand fork may not have been the correct decision, after all. Pero and Ballard had followed the trail for a while, but it hadn't seemed to lead to anywhere in particular, except deeper into the mountains.

Now the sun was going down, and the air was getting cooler, and they needed somewhere to camp for the night. With Ballard all but falling asleep on his horse, Pero had called a reluctant halt to their day's progress, and had told Ballard that if he remained below and looked after the horses, he would trudge up the steep ridge on their right and try to work out where they were. Ballard had agreed with a tired waft of his hand and Pero had set off. Now he was nearing the crest of the ridge and his thighs were aching with exertion. Close to the top he paused and looked back.

Ballard and the horses were nothing but a group

of dark smudges far below. From here the Painted Mountains looked spectacular, striped in vibrant colors. Pero took a swig from his canteen and saw Ballard's stick-like figure doing the same at the foot of the valley. He felt a flash of irritation. Why did the idiot need yet *more* water when he was only sitting there, not doing anything? He'd regret it tomorrow when his canteen ran dry and there was no more water to be had. Putting his own canteen away, Pero ascended the last steep stretch of slope. When he got to the top he sighed.

The view, though spectacular, was not exactly encouraging. To the north were more mountains, marching away into the distance. To their south, beyond the great desert plain glowing gold and red in the light of the setting sun, was the seemingly never-ending black thread of the Great Wall, miles behind them now, but still not far enough away for Pero to feel entirely safe.

Squinting, he saw dozens of black dots in the sky above the Wall. What the hell were they? He couldn't quite make them out. He shrugged. Ah well, they weren't his concern. As long as they didn't interfere with his business, he didn't—

A sound from below cut in on his thoughts. He wasn't sure what it was—movement of some kind—but it set alarm bells ringing in his head all the same. He spun quickly, looking down, half-expecting to see bandits converging on Ballard and the horses. But what he *did* see was even worse—and utterly unbelievable.

Ballard and the horses were riding away. Riding away fast. A great cloud of dust kicking up into the air behind them as they disappeared into the canyon.

"No!" Pero yelled, and started to scramble down the steep slope of the ridge, knowing it was already hopeless. Had Ballard played him along all this time? Pretended to be exhausted when in fact…

"No!" he shouted again as Ballard, the horses and the precious black powder disappeared from view. He raised his head to the sky and howled into the approaching night.

"*Noooo!*"

. . .

William, dozing, was woken by the sound of cheers rising from the top of the Wall. The stockade was located in one of the high towers of the fortress, which meant that the cheering was coming from somewhere below him.

Curious, he scrambled to his feet and crossed to the slit of a window, which overlooked the Wall, hoping to see what was going on. Had the Nameless Order achieved a major victory of some kind? But if the Tao Tei had launched another attack, surely he would have heard it?

His cell was darker than it had been when he'd entered it earlier, the thin beam of light now a deep reddish amber, which meant that the sun was going down. Soon he'd have nothing but the vague flicker of torchlight from outside to puncture the darkness. To all intents and purposes, it would be like being sealed inside a tomb.

For now, though, there was enough illumination to see by, though the window was so narrow, and set at such an angle, that he couldn't see very much. He strained forward, pushing his head into the gap, hoping that it wouldn't get stuck.

And then he lurched backward, scraping his ear and cheek on the rock. A giant had just thrust its face against his window blocking out the light!

That was his first thought. When he looked again, the billowing, rounded head was swinging by. All at once he realized it was made of stitched-together pieces of silk and canvas. And suddenly it occurred to him what it really was. A balloon! An impossibly vast balloon! And below it, rising now, was what appeared to be a basket in the shape of a small boat, containing people.

William laughed. The thing was crazy! Impossible! And yet here it was.

Then there was an enormous *BOOOM!* and the balloon became a huge ball of flame. As William threw himself backward, the heat of the explosion washing across his face, he heard awful screams that instantly faded, became distant, and he imagined the boat-shaped basket with its human cargo plummeting to the earth at the base of the Wall, far, far below.

He stumbled and fell, rolling onto his back. There was

another gigantic explosion, more screams and once again burning white flame, hotter and brighter than the sun, rushed in through his slit of a window, blinding him.

What was happening out there? How could triumph turn so quickly to tragedy? Were the Nameless Order under attack?

He wanted to batter down the door and rush out. He wanted to help in any way he could.

But all he could do was sit on the rocky floor of his cell and listen to the explosions and the screams.

• • •

Perched in her own gondola with Xiao Yu and Li Qing, waiting for their balloon to fill so they could take off, Lin Mae watched with horror as a burning Eagle Corps soldier fell from the sky. He twisted and writhed as he plummeted downwards, burning bolts and arrows and bits of charred gondola falling around him. She tensed as he smashed into the ground, sparks flying into the air. And he wasn't, by any means, the only casualty. In front of them other soldiers and gondolas were falling too, other balloons erupting into vast fireballs.

Yet for every balloon that didn't make it, there were at least three or four that did. The ground might be peppered with the burning dead and chunks of blazing debris, but the sky was filled with the majestic sight of dozens upon dozens of balloons heading like airborne sailing boats towards Bianliang.

Not all of them would get there, of course. In fact, it was questionable whether any of them would. There was a long way to go and the black powder was highly volatile. Even those balloons that survived the initial launch were still at risk of disaster with every second that passed.

But the possibility of a sudden and horrible death didn't deter the warriors of the Nameless Order. Even now they were still filing calmly forward, still filling the gondolas, their faces set and determined, their sense of purpose undimmed. They had been born to fight the Tao Tei, and if this was the only way of fulfilling their mission, then so be it.

The wind was picking up, blowing harder than ever now. Lin Mae looked up at the vast balloon above their gondola, which was billowing and flapping as it filled. Bear Corps soldiers and Tiger Corps soldiers clung on to guy ropes, struggling to contain it, as the wind tried to pluck it, only half-deflated, over the Wall.

If that happened, of course, it would mean certain death for Lin Mae and her crew. The material of the balloon would droop into the brazier and ignite, which would then in turn react with the black powder and cause an explosion.

Yet still the wind tried to drag the balloon from the Wall, and still soldiers clung on desperately to guy lines in an attempt to stop that from happening. And as the balloon rose, became fatter, so the gondola beneath it began to sway and shift, causing its occupants to stagger and stumble about. Lin Mae and Xiao Yu grabbed and held on to the ropes which secured the gondola to the balloon, both to try and regain their footing and also prevent the ropes from tangling. Li Qing, meanwhile, operated the plunger, attempting to manage the surging flames erupting from the brazier.

Slowly but surely, with everyone working together, the balloon fully inflated, becoming round and taut. As it did so it strained towards the sky, dragging the gondola behind it. The soldiers on the Wall held on to the guy ropes for as long as they possibly could, and then, at an order from their commander, they all let go at once.

Propelled by the wind, the balloon threw itself eagerly from the parapet, like a bird launching into the endless sky. Lin Mae felt herself hurtling forward as the gondola swayed and rocked. For one awful moment she thought it would tip over, causing them to fall out and plunge to the ground far below. She saw a rope in front of her and grabbed it, holding on for all she was worth. She was vaguely aware of Xiao Yu stumbling over from the other side of the gondola, slamming into her and ricocheting off, before she too managed to grab hold of a rope and steady herself. Then Lin Mae noticed that the brazier was unmanned, Li Qing having been hurled away from it as the balloon had lurched. Her eyes widened in horror as she saw that the black powder nozzle was open. If the gondola tipped the other way and too much black powder poured out of the nozzle and into the brazier…

"Watch the powder!" she screamed.

Li Qing pushed herself up on to her knees and, as the gondola steadied, launched herself forward. She threw herself against the black powder nozzle and held on, shielding it with her body. The gondola gave another couple of sickening lurches and then began to steady. The wind was still strong, but the balloon was properly airborne now, riding the currents.

Heart thumping wildly, Lin Mae regained her feet and looked around. The sky was filled with balloons that were rising, moving forward, their crews bustling about, manning the braziers and pulling on ropes. Some of them, shockingly, were still blowing up, erupting instantly into flames as the black powder ignited. Many, though, were leveling out, picking up speed, ploughing forward. It was terrifying, but also exhilarating.

She looked behind her. The Wall was getting further and further away. She could still see balloons inflating, launching themselves from the battlements. She glanced at Xiao Yu and Li Qing, who looked back at her, and she grinned. Xiao Yu grinned too, though she had tears in her eyes.

On the horizon the sun looked like a spreading pool of blood.

20

Ballard cackled as he rode through the canyon. He'd shown that idiot who was boss! All the time Pero had thought he was top dog in their partnership, whereas in truth Ballard had manipulated him every step of the way. No doubt the Spanish simpleton had planned to dispatch him at some stage of the process and take the spoils for himself, but if he thought such a possibility wouldn't have crossed Ballard's mind, he was even stupider than he looked. Well, how did he like it now, out in the middle of the desert with no food, no water and no horse? Ballard's only regret about running out on Pero was that he hadn't been there to see the look on his face when he realized he'd been hoodwinked!

He moved quickly along the valley floor, the reins of both Pero's horse and the packhorse attached to the pommel of his saddle. Eventually he came to a ridge and paused to scan the surrounding landscape, raising his hand to shield his eyes from the setting sun.

Suddenly his horse shied, almost throwing him off. He gripped the reins tight, lowering his hand and looking down to see what had startled it.

Trudging up the ridge towards him, converging on him from three directions, were a trio of rangy horses with unsmiling, black-clad men on their backs. The men's hands were not on their reins, however. Instead each of them had their bows drawn and pointed his way. At the sight of the metal arrowheads trained on him, Ballard felt his bowels contract, his balls shrivel into his belly. But he forced himself to clench his teeth in a grin and raise a hand, as if he was greeting old friends.

"What fortuitous timing, gentlemen!" he cried. "I've been wandering all day looking for new partners!"

He kept his smile fixed to his face as the brigands closed in.

• • •

It had gone on for a long time—the explosions, the fierce, brief flashes of flame—but now it seemed to be coming to an end. William still heard the occasional shattering boom, some of which seemed quite close, some much further away, and saw white flashes burst like lightning bolts into his cell, but they were more spaced out now, the periods of darkness between one explosion and the next more protracted.

He still couldn't work out what had been happening, why the Nameless Order had taken to the sky in vast balloons. Had they decided to attack the Jade Mountain from above, to drop black powder into its craters and tunnels, to split it apart? But if so, why? Why take the fight to the Tao Tei? The Wall was a powerful war machine, and a fearsome defence mechanism, and according to Wang, all they had to do was hold out for a few more days and the threat would be over for another sixty years.

Something must have happened, he decided. Something drastic that had necessitated a change of tactics. But what? Was it something to do with Pero and Ballard? Had they used the black powder to... to breach the Wall in some way, perhaps as a distraction to allow them to escape? But that didn't make sense either. That still didn't account for the balloons.

William was still trying to work it out when the key grated in the lock of his cell and the door was shoved grittily open.

He wafted dust away from his face and squinted against the light. It wasn't particularly bright light, merely the pine oil lanterns burning in the corridor, but after being shut up in the dark for several hours, it was like staring into the sun.

As far as he could make out, there were three soldiers

standing in the doorway. Shielding his eyes he saw they were Bear Corps warriors—all big men and all staring at him without expression.

Why were they here? Was his presence required? Were they bringing food? Or had Lin Mae decided to execute him, after all? One of them stepped into his cell and beckoned him with a crooked figure and a guttural phase that he didn't understand. Still blinking, he stepped into the corridor, the Bear Corps soldiers moving back to give him room. He expected to be grabbed, perhaps even chained, but to his surprise one of the soldiers waved a hand at him as if he was a stray dog they were trying to shoo away.

"I can go?" he said. "Go where?"

One of the soldiers barked something at him in Mandarin.

"Where's Lin Mae?" he asked. "Lin Mae? Wang?"

The soldiers conferred among themselves, then one of them jabbed a finger downwards, as though pointing vaguely at the floor.

William knew what the man meant. Lin Mae, or Wang, or maybe both, were out on the Wall. He began to jog in that direction, his mind whirling. To be freed from his cell and apparently given the run of the fortress—essentially to be granted a free pardon. What was going on?

When he stepped out of the tower exit on to the top of the Wall, he was shocked by the scene of devastation before him. He stood for a moment, trying to take it in. The desert beyond the Wall was strewn with wreckage. There were burning balloons, like vast, crumpled animal skins, there were smashed gondolas, and there were twisted, blackened bodies. Not only that, but some of the balloons had clearly lost control as soon as they had lifted off, and had either blown back against the towers or exploded directly overhead. A huge, burning balloon skin was draped over the parapet less than thirty feet away, a cloud of black, stinking smoke rising from it and curling into the night. Drooping from the top of the Northern Tower, from which he had just emerged, was a smashed and smoldering gondola, a body, which had been twisted in its severed ropes, dangling beneath it like a charred puppet.

There were other bodies, or parts of bodies, lying around on the plaza area directly in front of him too, as well as a great many unidentifiable bits of twisted, burning debris. He looked to his right, but with the smoke and the darkness it was hard to see if anyone was still alive out here. And then, through a greasy pall of smoke, he saw someone moving, and he started heading in their direction, picking his way through the grisly obstacle course that lay between them. The smoke cleared for a moment, and he saw the figure was not a soldier but a small man in dark, simple robes and a brimless hat.

"Hey!" he shouted. "Wang! What happened? Wait!"

But if Wang heard him, he chose not to acknowledge him.

William coughed to shift a tickle of smoke in his throat and shouted again, louder this time.

And this time Wang *did* stop and turn. His face was white and drawn. He looked both haunted and impatient.

As if unsurprised to see William there, he said, "We have failed. The Tao Tei are in the city."

William looked at him, stunned. "What? How?"

But Wang ignored his question. Like the Bear Corps warrior a few minutes earlier, he wafted a dismissive hand, as though shooing away a troublesome animal. "You are free. Free to leave. Take what you wish and go. This was the General's final order." As though as an afterthought, he gave a short bow. "Good luck to you."

William stared at him, wide-eyed. *Final* order? What did Wang mean? Once again he took in the carnage around them: the bodies, the burning debris, both here and strewn across the desert. In the night sky, far away, in the direction of Bianliang, he saw winking flames. More balloons? Those that *hadn't* crashed and burned? That were still heading towards the city?

When he turned back, Wang was walking away. William saw that further along the Wall, in a space that had been cleared of debris, a final balloon was being inflated.

"Where is she?" he called.

Wang kept walking.

"Hey!" William broke into a run, going after him. He thought of reaching out, grabbing Wang's shoulder, but he didn't. Instead he said, "Lin Mae? Where is she?"

Wang stopped and sighed. He turned to face William again. Gesturing at the sky he said wearily, "Out there somewhere. Who knows?"

"Has she gone to fight? Is there still a fight to be had?"

Wang shrugged and turned away again, his face exhausted, defeated.

William ran past him, around him, halted directly in front of him and actually *did* put out a hand to stop him this time. Before Wang could react he said, "Tell me—is there a chance?"

"To win? You mean, do I have a plan?"

William nodded.

"We must kill the Queen. Kill the Queen or die together." The little man shrugged, grimaced, as though to convey how utterly hopeless the situation was. "So if I were you, I would make haste and be gone. Tell the world what you have seen. Tell them what is coming."

William heard footsteps behind him, felt hands grabbing his arms, pulling him away from Wang. They weren't overly rough with him, but they weren't gentle either. Wang gave him a sympathetic look, then hurried towards the balloon. It was three-quarters inflated now.

There was just time for him to climb aboard before it drifted away.

"I'll need my bow," William shouted at Wang's retreating figure.

Wang's shoulders twitched briefly—he had clearly heard—but he kept walking.

William raised his voice. "If I'm to join you, I'll need my bow!"

Wang stopped, turned. There was a look of astonishment on his face.

"What?" he said quietly, nodding at William's captors to release him.

William walked forward. He smiled. "Be honest," he said softly. "Have you a better soldier than me?"

• • •

At least he was still alive, which had to be a good sign. If they'd simply wanted to rob him, they'd have killed him there and then, and left his body in the sand for the vultures and wolves to eat. But the fact they'd bound him and brought him along for the ride meant... what? That they wanted to take him somewhere? Question him?

Torture him?

No, no, he wouldn't countenance that. He'd win their trust somehow; make them understand how invaluable he'd be as an ally, how much they could help each other.

Lying on his side on the sand, Ballard squirmed, trying to get comfortable. His feet had been tied together, his hands bound tightly behind him, and a thick wad of brightly-colored but filthy material had been crammed into his mouth, then secured with a strip of brown cloth that stank of sweat and worse. He tensed as a scorpion scuttled towards him from behind a nearby rock, seemed to regard him for a moment, its pincers poised and its sting raised like a question mark above its head, and then, when he twitched, darted away.

Fifteen feet in front of Ballard, just close enough that the warmth of it took the edge off the cold night air, was a freshly built camp fire. Two of the three brigands who had captured him were now sitting around it, warming themselves and roasting lumps of meat on metal skewers. The third brigand was some distance away, tethering the six horses tightly together. He was the youngest of the trio, with a full set of teeth and only a straggle of facial hair.

Ballard had come to think of this man as Brigand 3; he was very much the junior member of the group and performed most of the menial tasks. Brigand 1, who was now biting into the fatty meat on the end of his skewer, making slobbering noises as he chewed, was plump and sweaty with a growling voice. Brigand 2, sitting beside him, was older, skinny and almost toothless. He had a full beard and a jagged red scar down the left side of his face. All three men stank of unwashed flesh and were dressed in dark robes over layers of rags. Ballard had seen them laugh, but only at his discomfort. Most of the time they conversed in guttural, staccato phrases that he didn't understand.

He was hoping that once they removed his gag so that he could eat—which they surely must at some point— he could talk to them, draw them into his confidence. They were unintelligent, uneducated men. Like Pero, they would be malleable, easy to manipulate. All he had to do was bide his time…

His eyes widened in concern as Brigand 3 trudged back over to the camp fire carrying a couple of Ballard's saddlebags, which he had removed from the pack horse. Ballard knew that the saddlebags contained Wang's copious notes about black powder, as well as various black powder based weapons and, of course, large quantities of the stuff itself.

He was worried enough about the notes—he'd need them if he was going to make a long-term profit from his windfall—but what made him far more anxious was the prospect of large quantities of black powder so close to the fire. If it wasn't handled with care they could all be blown to Kingdom Come. But how could he communicate such information to these primitive savages in his current state? He wriggled like a worm on the ground, making frantic sounds in the back of his throat to draw their attention. Brigand 3, firelight playing across his face and across the leather saddlebags he was carrying, glanced his way briefly, but then turned his head dismissively away and sat down next to his companions.

Ballard watched in horror as Brigand 3 opened the first of the saddlebags and began to scrabble at the contents. He pulled out Wang's notes with abandon, tearing the delicate parchment, glanced at them a moment, and then—clearly unable to read or understand them—tossed them away. Some of the rolls of parchment landed on the sand nearby, some were picked up and blown into the surrounding darkness by the wind, and some drifted into the camp fire, where they shriveled and were quickly consumed.

Ballard glared at the man, as if hoping the sheer force of his fury could stop his hand. He wanted to rage at him and his companions, ridicule them for their ignorance, punish them for their presumption, their effrontery, their willful destruction of his precious property. But he was helpless to do anything. All he could do was watch as Wang's black powder formulas, his painstaking research notes, his diagrams of potential weapons, were scattered to the wind, or burned, or crumpled. He felt like weeping in frustration. There was even a part of him that wished Pero would magically appear and dispatch these three filthy primitives, lopping their heads off where they sat.

When Brigand 3 tossed the first saddlebag aside with a snort of disgust and opened the second, Ballard really began to sweat. He saw the man delve inside and rummage about. Then he saw his hand emerge clutching one of Wang's black powder grenades.

In many ways, Ballard knew the worst thing he could do was react, but he couldn't help it. He managed to remain silent as Brigand 3 examined the grenade with a puzzled expression, but when he casually tossed the grenade to Brigand 2, and when Brigand 2 fumbled it, causing it to drop in the sand close to the fire, Ballard screamed. Or at least, he made a shrill, panicked sound behind his gag, which drew his captors' attention. They looked at him at first curiously, and then with amusement, as he attempted to squirm back from the fire, his eyes bulging. They said something to one another, and burst into uproarious laughter. Even when Ballard shook his head frantically from side to side, trying to communicate to them the terrible danger they were in, they only laughed and mocked him.

Brigand 2 picked up the grenade, looked at it, then handed it to Brigand 1, who was grasping for it with greasy fingers. Brigand 1 sniffed the grenade, as if hoping it was something to eat, and then leaned forward with a groan, holding it close to the fire for a better look.

In his mind, as he frantically wriggled backwards until he was squashed up against a sheltering outcrop of rock and could wriggle no further, Ballard was screaming at them. In truth, though, he could only make shrill and muffled noises beneath his gag—noises which they either ignored or laughed at.

When Brigand 3 pulled one of the small leather bags of black powder out of the saddlebag, opened it and tipped a quantity of the powder into his cupped hand, Ballard felt as if the panic trapped inside him would make his heart explode. Then Brigand 1 barked something at Brigand 3, causing Brigand 3 to swing round so quickly that some of the black powder blew out of his hand and drifted towards the fire.

Next instant there was a sound like the world splitting apart and a burst of blinding light. Ballard experienced a brief, agonizing blast of pain and heat, and then he felt no more.

• • •

Pero was marching in the moonlight, following the direction Ballard had taken. The scowl and dead-eyed stare on his face had been in place for the past eight hours. He marched steadily and with great determination, energized by a survival instinct that was second to none and a seething desire for revenge. Horses or no horses, he would track Ballard down. And when he did he would take the black powder from him—but not before he had ripped the man's head off with his bare hands.

Aside from the soft chirruping of desert insects and the occasional faraway howl of a wolf, the night was silent. Suddenly, though, the peace was shattered by a muffled explosion that echoed flatly from the mountains and seemed to cause the very air to ripple.

Immediately Pero's head snapped up. His lips curved in a scimitar-like grin. And then, feeling very like a desert wolf himself—one with the smell of his prey's blood in his nostrils—he broke into a smooth and tireless run.

• • •

William and Wang stood side by side, watching as the final balloon was inflated. In a few moments it would be time to climb aboard, and then there would be no turning back.

William knew, of course, that what this also meant was that in a few minutes he could be dead, his burning body hurtling towards the earth. He tried not to look at the charred corpses and still smoldering debris littering the top of the Wall and the desert plain beyond, tried to blot out his memories from earlier that day of the explosions and the screams he had heard from his cell, the flashes of light that had sizzled like rods of fire through the slit of his window.

At least if he died, it would be while pursuing a noble cause. Which was infinitely better than dying pointlessly for a crime he had not committed. He wondered where

Lin Mae was now. Was she somewhere out there, still drifting towards Bianliang? He wondered where Pero was too, and how he and Ballard were shaping up as partners. He wondered which of them would kill the other first, and whether either of them would end up profiting from their misdemeanors.

Once, such questions would have invigorated him. Now, pursuing such an existence seemed pointless, devoid of both honor and worth.

Behind him, someone spoke his name, or something like it. He turned, as did Wang, to see Commander Wu standing there, resplendent in his shimmering yellow armour and flowing cape. In his arms he was carrying a full set of red Eagle Corps armour, a brace of red-feathered arrows in an Eagle Corps quiver clutched in his right hand. Almost shyly he offered them to William.

William was taken aback. "For me?"

Behind him the black powder was being pumped into the brazier, the flames roaring as the hot air rising from them filled the balloon. Wu gave a single decisive nod and Wang echoed the motion. A little overcome, William stepped forward and took the armour from Wu. Wu clasped his hands together in the traditional gesture of comradeship and respect.

"*Xie*, *xie*," said William, trying to get the pronunciation right.

Wu smiled and nodded, and then at the sound of

raised voices all three men turned towards the Northern Tower. Through the haze of smoke they saw two men standing there, apparently engaged in an argument. Both wore the black armour of a Bear Corps soldier. The smaller and younger of the two, William recognized as the kitchen orderly, who, by speaking up, had apparently saved his life. The smaller man had something in his hand, which the Bear Corps warrior was trying to take from him. William couldn't see what it was at first, and then the smoke cleared a little and suddenly he recognized it.

It was his bow.

"What's that man's name?" William asked, pointing at the kitchen orderly.

Wang all but rolled his eyes. "That is Peng Yong."

"He's got my bow," William said. "What's going on?"

As if Peng Yong had heard, he shouted something across to the three men.

Wang said, "He says that if you wish to thank him, you must tell us to let him join us."

Peng Yong was still shouting. Wang winced, but added, "He is begging you. He says that you owe him this honor."

William looked at Peng Yong, who was still tussling fiercely with the Bear Corps warrior. He felt a sudden wave of almost brotherly affection towards him. Shrugging, he said, "Well, if he wants to come... why not?"

"Look at him," replied Wang, as if that explained everything.

"The less to carry," William said persuasively.

Wang almost smiled.

• • •

Although it was warm close to the brazier, it soon became cold when you moved away from it. They had been travelling now for several hours, and so far things were going well. They had got into a rhythm, Lin Mae and Xiao Yu taking turns to manipulate the ropes and keep them on course, Li Qing working the brazier. Although it was Li Qing who was closest to the source of heat, however, it was she, ironically, who was sitting with a blanket draped across her shoulders. This was because hers was a mainly sedentary role, whereas working the ropes took effort and strength. Having just completed her latest stint, Lin Mae was now taking a break, and hoping that the aches in her arms and back would have lessened by the time her turn came around again.

She stood at the prow of the gondola, looking out across the sky. In the darkness she had done her best to count the balloons spread out around them, and therefore knew that seventy-five (or thereabouts) of her fleet were still airborne. The balloons furthest away were visible only by the constant glow, and occasional flare, of their braziers. Indeed, the occasional hushed roar of the braziers was all she could hear this high above the ground.

If it hadn't been such a risky way to travel, and if there hadn't been such urgency to reach Bianliang before the Tao Tei laid waste to the city, the journey would have been almost enjoyable. Certainly the passing view was one that prompted a feeling of serenity, despite the fact that the balloons were travelling deceptively quickly— more quickly than a horse could gallop, for instance, or, most importantly, a Tao Tei could run.

All at once a flash of light from behind them lit up the sky, which was followed a split-second later by a distant boom. Lin Mae turned to see another balloon become a plummeting fireball, and felt yet another wrench in her stomach at the knowledge that more lives had been lost, that even now friends and colleagues, perhaps people she had known all her life, were hurtling in pain and terror towards the earth.

Then she felt an extra jolt as she remembered that Wang had been planning to oversee the entire launch, before boarding the very last balloon to lift off from the Wall. Had that *been* the last balloon she had just seen suffer a fiery demise? She scanned the horizon behind her. If not the *very* last, it had certainly been one of them.

• • •

The balloon that had gone down had been close enough to the one occupied by William, Wang and Peng Yong for the hot, buffeting wind of the explosion to rock their gondola. With William working the brazier (under instructions from Wang), and Wang himself at the ropes, they had managed to keep the craft on an even keel. Now, as they pulled smoothly away, William and Peng Yong silently watched the stricken balloon flailing towards the earth in flames. It was too dark to see what had become of the crew, but William knew there was no way they could have survived.

Glancing at Peng Yong, he saw that the boy was pale and very scared. William reached across and patted him reassuringly on the shoulder. Peng Yong looked startled for a moment. Then he smiled.

• • •

The ceiling of the Main Hall in the Imperial Palace was composed of panels of rare glass, which made it the perfect laboratory. Dominating the center of the opulently appointed room was the huge iron cage containing the captured Tao Tei. Despite the presence of dozens of scribes and assistants who were making notes, Imperial Councilors, courtiers and various other onlookers, all of whom were surrounding the cage in a wide circle, chattering or simply gawping, the Tao Tei was sitting placidly, its head down, its eyes glazed, its huge taloned paws resting between its knees.

The creature remained inert as Shen edged towards

the cage holding a lacquered pole with a hook on the end. He was clearly nervous, but trying to fight it. This was his moment, after all. His moment to prove his worth, to make an impression on the Emperor's court, and to be subsequently elevated into a position of influence and importance.

When, having walked up to the cage, he realized that the Tao Tei was still not paying him—or anything else—the slightest attention, his confidence grew a little. He drew himself up, standing straighter and squaring his shoulders. Extending the pole slowly through the bars of the cage, he tried to keep his hands steady as he hooked the noose around the creature's neck, to which the magnet was attached, and started to lift it slowly and carefully up and over the creature's head. He sucked in a sharp breath as the dangling black stone bumped against the Tao Tei's snout, but it didn't react.

Stepping backwards, pulling the magnet away from the Tao Tei, he looked around at his audience and indicated the white, carefully measured lines beneath his feet.

"The markings on the floor," he said importantly, "will measure the distance from the beast at which it begins to demonstr—"

He was still looking at his audience when the Tao Tei's eyes blazed, its head snapped up and it launched itself with a bellowing roar at Shen. It slammed into the bars of the cage with such force that the entire construction toppled over. Shen turned in utter terror and let loose a shrill scream—and then the heavy cage smashed down on top of him! The pole with its attached magnet flew out of his hand and went slithering away across the polished floor, out of reach.

Although the Tao Tei had not actually broken out of its cage, people began to scream, to panic, to run in all directions. Inside the cage the Tao Tei opened its vast mouth and expelled shriek after bellowing shriek. Shen, on his back, the lower half of his body crushed, found himself looking up at the glass ceiling. But he was already so delirious with pain that when the ceiling began to shatter, when the glass began to rain down in glittering shards, he wondered if it was real.

· · ·

Through the valleys, across the desert plains, up and down the peaks and troughs of the mountain ranges, came the Tao Tei horde. There were thousands of them, massed together, moving as one. They formed a seething green ocean of teeth and talons, which flowed ever forward at incredible speed, flooding the land, stopping for nothing. Anything that got in their way—any animal, any roaming tribes, any bands of brigands or groups of merchants—were instantly overwhelmed and devoured. Nothing was left.

At the center of this raging sea, this teeming crush of Tao Tei soldiers, was the Queen, surrounded and protected by her Paladins. Her skin rippled with the thousands of eggs she carried. Yet her young didn't slow her down. If anything, they made her more frantic to feed, to procreate, to flood the world with more of her kind.

Suddenly, however, she stopped. And as she did so, as though at an unspoken command, so did the green wave of creatures. She raised her vast head, opened her mouth wide and from it extended a surprisingly fragile and flexible receptor. She could hear something, taste something. It was one of her own. And it was calling to her. Informing her of the feeding ground it had discovered, inviting her to the feast. She felt excitement flooding her, felt her salivary juices flowing in anticipation. A scream erupted from her, high-pitched, ululating, causing fat veins to pulse and bulge all over her bloated body.

Then—a moment of silence as the horde took on new information.

They turned, as one, and began to flow in a new direction.

Towards Bianliang. Towards the feast.

21

The rain of glass had stopped falling. Some of it had landed on Shen—a shard of it had sliced through his cheek—but he barely noticed. He barely noticed the screaming, running crowd either, the crush of people at the door of the Main Hall, trying to get out. All he was really aware of was the overwhelming agony coursing in waves through his body, and the Tao Tei above him, in its toppled cage, still shrieking and hurling itself again and again at the bars.

The bars were buckling now, bending. Soon the creature would be free. Soon the wild beast he had foolishly brought here would break out and rampage through the Imperial Palace, and then the city, ripping people apart with its hooked black talons, crunching them in its vast jaws. It might even kill and eat the

Emperor. Shen might become known not as the man who had tamed the Tao Tei, but as one who had brought a scourge of death and destruction to the Kingdom. He would be dishonored, reviled. Before he died, therefore—for he *would* die, he knew that, and very soon—he must do all he could to redeem himself.

Ignoring the black talons of the creature, which were slashing through the bars of the cage, inches above his body, in an attempt to rip him apart, he craned his neck, trying to look around and above him. The movement sent jagged bolts of new agony through his shattered legs, but he ignored them, blinking away the fug of unconsciousness that threatened to overwhelm him.

There on the floor, just above his right shoulder, he saw the base of the lacquered pole. He stretched his hand up towards it, screaming at the pain it caused him in his stomach and pelvis—so much pain that for a second he thought the black talons of the Tao Tei had reached him and torn him open. He kept screaming as his rapidly numbing fingers gripped the base of the pole and began to drag it, inch by inch, towards him.

Vaguely he was aware of a wrenching sound, and then a heavy metallic clatter. He knew instinctively what it was: one of the bars of the cage had given away—the Tao Tei was breaking loose! But there was nothing he could do except keep on with what he *was* doing. His fingers continued to climb the pole, dragging it down, bit by bit. With pain coursing through him, and the fingers of his hand moving sluggishly, like the legs of a dying spider, the task seemed impossible, insurmountable. He felt darkness closing in on him now, seeping from all sides. But he kept on. Inch by inch. Bit by bit.

And finally, impossibly, his fingers were clutching the top of the pole, finding the hook, the thread of the noose to which the magnet was attached. And here *was* the magnet! He could feel its cold, hard surface, even though the feeling was going from his hands. He gripped it, dragged it down towards the cage...

And the Tao Tei fell silent. Its eyes glazed, it stopped throwing itself about the mangled cage, it slumped as though drugged against the bars. It became utterly docile once more.

And Shen, feeling exonerated, smiled.

He closed his eyes and allowed the blackness to flood in and take him.

• • •

There were maybe only fifty balloons now left in the flotilla. But the survivors, spread out over several miles, powered on, a stiff wind pushing them quickly south.

There had been great excitement an hour ago, just as a pale pink dawn began to break on the horizon, when the green wave of Tao Tei, barreling towards Bianliang, was spotted in the distance. Slowly but surely the flotilla had been gaining on the creatures ever since, and were now almost directly above them.

More alarming, though, was the fact that as the dawn sun rose, awakening the land, it had also begun to glint on the glittering spires of Bianliang. It now seemed to be a race to see who could reach the city first—the Nameless Order or the Tao Tei. With a favorable wind the Nameless Order—or those that were left, at any rate—might just do it. But it was going to be close.

On the other hand, it might not even come to that, because one thing which had encouraged Wang, and which he had pointed out to William and Peng Yong, was that the Tao Tei appeared to be veering slightly off course. Unless they corrected themselves there was a chance they might bypass the city altogether. If that happened, and the creatures ended up in the open plains, it might then be a case of bombarding them from the air with black powder weapons. The Nameless Order had lost so many balloons, and might yet lose more, that Wang didn't know whether they would have anywhere near enough firepower to wipe the Tao Tei out completely. But they might severely weaken them. And if they *could* score a direct hit on the Queen…

His musings were broken by Peng Yong, who was working the ropes. "They're turning! Look!"

Wang, who had been resting, leaped to his feet. He looked over the side of the gondola, and saw that what

Peng Yong had said was true. The Tao Tei were indeed turning—and were now once more heading directly towards Bianliang. It had perhaps been too much to hope that they would miss the city entirely, but even so, he couldn't help feeling disappointed.

• • •

The Reception Hall of the Imperial Palace was a place of beauty and serenity. It was a huge, empty space, shuttered and silent, draped in peaceful, pale grey shadows.

The ornate double doors at the far end of the room were sturdy, bolted from the inside. Anyone in the Reception Hall at that moment might have looked up at the suggestion of an approaching rumble from somewhere beyond those doors; might have wondered whether a storm was brewing on a distant horizon.

But the approaching rumble was no storm. And as it got closer to the doors, it began to break down into individual sounds: screams, pleas for help and mercy, panicked running footsteps.

Then there was a crash, which quickly became a clamor of shouts and banging fists, as something huge and weighty hit the double doors from the other side. The doors held at first—but then, as the pressure and the panic on the other side increased, they began to shake and bend inwards, the gap between them widening. Under immense strain, the bolts that secured them together first started to bend, and then to tear themselves from the wood. And then suddenly they flew off, and went clinking and clattering across the polished floor.

The doors crashed inwards, one of them with such force that it was almost ripped from its hinges. And a flood of people surged through, like a single, flowing entity made up of many parts. The people were screaming, running, falling then scrambling upright again, their faces stricken, their eyes wide. They raced through the Reception Hall as though they had demons at their back.

Which, to all intents and purposes, they did.

• • •

Lin Mae could barely believe it. The Tao Tei had won the race!

They were in the city now, spreading havoc, while she and what remained of her warriors were still drifting above it. What was most demoralizing was that, aside from the many casualties the Nameless Order had suffered en route, it had actually seemed for a short while as if the tide might be about to turn their way. Not only had the flotilla caught up to the wave of Tao Tei, but it had looked as though they might overhaul them, reach the city first. If they had they could have organized Bianliang's defenses, battened down the hatches as much as possible, and hit the Tao Tei from behind the city walls with the full force of their black powder weapons. It still might not have been enough to stem the tide, but at least they would have been in with a chance.

The Imperial Guard, though… they had never had to deal with a threat of this magnitude, and as such they had been ill-equipped, ill-prepared and subsequently overwhelmed. Now all the Nameless Order could do was track the marauding Tao Tei through the city and try to minimize the damage they had caused. But they would have to do it with a severely depleted force. As far as Lin Mae could tell, there were only twenty-five balloons now left out of the entire flotilla. Which meant they had less than a hundred troops to fight thousands of Tao Tei.

It was a hopeless task, but one which she would not give up on; one which she would pursue to the end. She tried not to dwell on the many problems that had beset them on the final stage of their journey, but it was hard not to feel that the gods were against them.

First, the wind had dropped, causing many of the balloons to drift aimlessly, some of them going way off course. Of those that *had* been able to maintain their course, a large number had then started to run out of fuel, and had crashed one by one to the ground. Now those that were left were drifting in over the city, but losing altitude fast, Lin Mae's among them. With Xiao

Yu at the ropes, and Lin Mae and Li Qing guiding her as best they could, they were currently both tracking the Tao Tei and looking for somewhere to land.

Directly in front of them was the magnificent Imperial Palace complex, its glazed roof tiles, shimmering in the sun, stretching nearly a mile into the distance. Several of the flotilla were drifting over this now, the thoughts of their crews no doubt echoing her own: *Can we land here? Do we dare?*

In truth, though, they needed to get to the rear of the Imperial Palace if they could, because interestingly, and perhaps ominously, the Tao Tei had veered around the outskirts of the city to enter Bianliang via the North Gate, which just happened to be the one closest to the Palace itself. Could this be because they knew the Imperial Palace was the Emperor's residence, and that to attack here first would be to strike at the very heart of the Kingdom?

Despite the fact that Wang had said the creatures were evolving, she couldn't believe they were imbued with such intelligence. So what, then, had possessed them to enter the city here? Instinct? Or had it been a random choice?

Then she remembered the way the Tao Tei had all suddenly changed course, as though responding to a signal. And she recalled too the lone Tao Tei, placated by William's magnet, that had been brought to Bianliang by Shen. Could it be that the placated Tao Tei had somehow summoned the others here from the Imperial Palace? If so, then Shen might have delayed the terrible fate awaiting the people who lived in Bianliang's streets, but he had put the Emperor in deadly danger!

Their balloon was sinking rapidly now. In one of the balloons ahead of them, also sinking, she glimpsed Commander Chen. Leaning forward, she yelled, "To the rear! Steer to the rear of the Palace if you can! Stay together!"

She was aware, even as she gave her orders, that her words would probably be in vain. As they lost altitude the balloons would doubtless prove ever more difficult, if not impossible, to steer. She supposed that the best most of her crews could hope for was to reach solid ground—wherever that may be—in one piece. And even if they did manage to stay together and get to the rear of the Palace, what could they hope to achieve? Her plan, such as it was, was the same as Wang's—any chance they got they should bombard the Queen with everything at their disposal. It sounded simple, but Lin Mae didn't think for a moment that it would be. The Queen would no doubt be highly protected. Unless her Paladins could somehow be disabled, they would deflect anything the Nameless Order threw at her.

The balloon at the head of the flotilla drifting over the Imperial Palace was also the one that was sinking most rapidly out of the sky. It was barely managing to crest the tiled rooftop beneath it, though Lin Mae could see three Eagle Corps soldiers struggling tirelessly within the gondola to keep it airborne. She clenched her teeth, hoping they wouldn't be reckless with the black powder—and then just when it seemed they might make it over the roof, after all, the tiles beneath them erupted outwards with a splintering crash, and a Tao Tei burst through, its jaws opening wide.

It leaped into the air like a breaching whale and grabbed the gondola in its teeth. The gondola tipped, all three of its occupants falling out. One fell straight through the hole the Tao Tei had burst from and the other two hit the roof. One of the men landed, bounced and then slithered right off the edge of the roof, disappearing from view. The other rolled over, then manage to scramble up onto his hands and knees.

As the Tao Tei dropped back into the hole from which it had emerged, still hanging on to the gondola, the balloon, yanked downwards, first tore and half-deflated, then erupted into flame. The fireball shot up and sideways, engulfing the surviving Eagle Corps soldier and scorching the roof.

By now Lin Mae was already diving for the ropes and yelling at Xiao Yu and Li Qeng to take evasive action. They steered around the already dwindling conflagration, clearing the edge of the tiled roof with inches to spare—but now they were descending far too quickly towards another rooftop, the one over the North Gate.

Xiao Yu tugged frantically on the ropes as the roof rushed up towards them, while Lin Mae grabbed a couple of long lances attached to the inside wall of the gondola and yanked them free. As Li Qing slashed at some of the ropes secured to counter weights on the outside of the gondola in the hope of reducing the speed of their descent, Lin Mae extended the lances over the side with the intention of using them to slow their fall or perhaps even push them higher.

Thanks to their combined efforts, they managed to slow and steady the balloon, at least a little. As it passed over the roof, however, so close that the black powder weapons that were dangling below the craft scraped and bumped over the roof's surface, a Tao Tei, having scaled the wall to the edge of the roof, suddenly appeared in front of them and leaped.

Caught off guard, Xiao Yu recoiled, letting go of the ropes that controlled the steering mechanism, and the gondola dipped to the side. As it did so, Lin Mae, struggling desperately to retain her balance, thrust one of her lances forward in an attempt to deflect the leaping Tao Tei.

She managed it, the lance piercing the side of the creature's head, and causing it to flip and writhe in the air. It missed the tipping gondola by inches, hit the edge of the roof, then flipped over and plummeted to the ground below.

The danger was not over yet, though. Not only was the gondola still tipping, causing all three of its occupants to lose their footing as they scrabbled frantically for the dangling ropes that would steady them, but now more Tao Tei, alerted to the presence of the sinking balloons, were swarming up the walls and scrambling on to the variously leveled roofs of the Palace.

Fighting to hold on and to get back to her feet, Lin Mae glimpsed two of the creatures loping along the edge of a roof above them. Before she could draw breath to shout a warning, the creatures leaped, talons extended, like cats attempting to pluck a bird from the air.

Shoving herself upright in the tipping gondola through sheer force of will as Xiao Yu tumbled past her, Lin Mae again raised one of her lances and rammed it forward. More by luck than judgment it struck one of the leaping Tao Tei squarely in the chest and deflected it past the gondola, its teeth still gnashing and its claws flailing at the air. The second Tao Tei also missed the gondola, but became briefly entangled in the ropes beneath it, causing the craft to veer even more wildly out of control. The Tao Tei squirmed violently, causing the gondola to rock from side to side, and then, still squirming, it clawed its way free of the ropes, only to plummet past the edge of the roof and down to the ground below.

The balloon, though, was failing badly now, starting to deflate. Glancing up from the rocking gondola, Lin Mae saw that not only was the heat in the unattended brazier now dwindling, which meant there was not enough hot air to keep it afloat, but at some point in the past few minutes the balloon itself must have got caught on a passing spire, or perhaps even been slashed by a Tao Tei's talon, and had sprung a leak.

For now the gondola was still directly above the roof of the Northern Gate—a drop of ten or twelve feet—but as the balloon slumped, its weight and the pull of the wind dragging at it, it would likely be plucked sideways, whereupon it would either ignite or crash down to the ground below, which was teeming with Tao Tei.

Their only choice, therefore, was to jump from the gondola on to the roof and hope for the best. Already she could see more Tao Tei rapidly scaling the walls towards them, but it was still the more favorable of two very bad options.

"Grab whatever weapons you can, and jump!" she screamed, then led by example, launching herself from the gondola, one of her two long lances still clutched in her hand. She saw the roof rushing at her, hit it and rolled, distributing her weight and dispelling her momentum. She looked up just in time to see Xiao Yu falling towards the roof. Her lieutenant, though, looked as if she had not so much jumped from the gondola as tumbled out of it. She hit the roof hard, a flailing mass of arms and legs, the jolt sending her own lance flying out of her hand. As Xiao Yu turned painfully on to her front and pushed herself up on her hands and knees, groggily looking around for her weapon, a Tao Tei dragged itself up over the edge of the rooftop behind her. Before Lin Mae had time to scream a warning, the creature lunged forward, jaws open and swallowed Xiao Yu whole!

Lin Mae froze in horror, but she had no time to mourn. She heard Li Qing's frantic warning, "Behind you!" and the next moment she was wheeling round, instinctively swinging the blunt end of her lance into the gaping maw of a Tao Tei that was rushing up behind her. The creature tumbled away, knocked off balance, but sprang instantly back to its feet. Sensing movement on her other side, Lin Mae turned to see Li Qing using her lance as a vault, jamming it into the crevice between two tiles, then rising in a graceful arc up and over Lin Mae's head. As the Tao Tei leaped forward to attack again, Li Qing hurled the spear she was holding in her free hand with all her might. The spear went straight through the creature's eye and into its brain.

Letting go of the lance, Li Qing completed her arc, which took her over the now-collapsing body of the Tao Tei. She rolled and jumped to her feet, but before Lin

Mae had time to thank her for saving her life, two more Tao Tei loomed up over the edge of the roof, one of them snatching Li Qing with its black talons and stuffing her into its mouth.

Of her three-strong crew that had risked so much to get here, Lin Mae was now the only one left. She had known and trained with Xiao Yu and Li Qing for almost all her life; she had regarded them as friends. But now, within a matter of seconds, they were both gone.

The two Tai Tei to her right, one of them with Li Qing's blood still dripping from its jaws, moved towards her. To her left a third Tao Tei scrambled up on to the other side of the roof. Adopting a fighting stance, lance held out before her, Lin Mae backed up to give herself room to maneuver. As the three Tao Tei closed in, she readied herself for her final battle.

22

"L in Mae! Above you!"

William saw her whirl round, then look up, her eyes widening in surprise as the gondola rushed towards her. The three Tao Tei, who had now been joined by a fourth and a fifth, were closing in on her, blood and drool trickling from their jaws, their small eyes glinting.

Knowing he had only a few seconds, he leaned as far as he could out of the gondola, his arm stretching out.

"Hand!" he yelled, but even as he gave the instruction he knew the gondola was still too high, a good six or eight feet above her, and she would never make it.

She was sprinting towards him now, though, the five Tao Tei springing forward, close on her heels. He saw her jam her lance into a divot between two of the tiles that covered the roof and launch herself toward the gondola.

She kicked her legs, as though pedaling the air, to gain as much height as possible. At the same time she stretched upwards, gritting her teeth in her attempt to make her arm, her hand, her fingers as long as she could.

William concentrated on that slender hand. Right at that moment it was, for him, the only thing that existed in the world. He stretched out his own arm and hand just that little bit further. The slim white hand came within reach…

He lunged and grabbed it! Grabbed it and held on tightly. As he yanked backwards, pulling Lin Mae up towards him, she brought up her legs and tucked her knees into her chest, the jaws of a leaping Tao Tei snapping shut on empty air just a couple of inches below her.

"Hold fast!" he shouted as she dangled below him, like a hunk of meat above a pool of hungry piranhas. Then he heard a cry of dismay from Wang and turned his head to see that the balloon was heading directly towards another roof, one that was a good twelve or fifteen feet higher than the roof they were currently flying over.

Still hanging out of the gondola, still gripping Lin Mae's hand, he shouted, "Pull it up!"

His words were unnecessary. Peng Yong was already frantically cranking the little fuel they had left, while Wang, showing rare speed and nimbleness, had pulled out his sword and was slashing free unwanted ballast.

As the weights fell and the hot air gave the balloon

extra lift, the gondola rose so quickly that it tipped a little, then righted itself. Fortunately for William and Lin Mae, it tipped up rather than down on the side of the gondola where he was clinging to her. As a result, she was jerked up into the air. Before she could fall again, William reached out and gathered her in, then allowed himself to drop backwards.

They tumbled into the gondola in a tangle of arms and legs, William on the bottom and Lin Mae landing on top of him. For a moment their bodies were pressed together, their faces so close that their noses were almost touching. Breathless and stunned, Lin Mae stared into William's eyes, as though unable to believe he was here in front of her.

"I set you free," she said.

He smiled. "And yet here I am."

"Hold on!" Wang yelled before she could respond. Both their heads jerked up. Lin Mae used her now freed arms to push herself to her feet. The balloon had cleared the higher roof, but now, thirty feet in front of them, was one of a pair of huge pagodas, its tiered roofs shining red and gold. The balloon was still rising, but the pagoda was at least a hundred feet high and dead ahead; there was no way they would clear it.

They were going to crash!

• • •

Commander Chen's balloon had passed by the right hand pagoda, and he and another Eagle Corps soldier were now firing arrows at a line of Tao Tei that were running along the rooftops beside them. Most of their arrows were hitting the target, but for every Tao Tei that tumbled dead from the rooftops another sprang up to take its place.

Seeing movement in his peripheral vision, he glanced behind him, and his eyes widened. In the balloon that was closest to his own he could see General Lin Mae, Strategist Wang and the foreign soldier, William, who was dressed in the armour of an Eagle Corps warrior. Yet although this was surprising enough, what really shocked him was that their balloon was heading straight for the pagoda his own balloon had just passed by. If the General's balloon hit the pagoda, Chen knew they would all surely die.

• • •

The fuel was all but used up, but for now the brazier was roaring and the balloon was still rising. Peng Yong, having fed as much black powder to the brazier as he could without blowing it up, was now hauling desperately on the ropes, helping Wang steer the craft.

"Left! Left!" Wang was yelling. "Up the center! Split the pagodas!"

They both hauled hard to the left and the balloon

responded accordingly, heading towards the gap between the two huge towers.

Behind them, closer to the back of the gondola, William and Lin Mae were now both up on their feet. She was still a little shaky, still recovering from her ordeal. She made no attempt to shrug herself free of William's grip as he held on to her.

All at once Wang let out a cry of shock

"What is it?" William asked.

Wang pointed at the ground below. "See for yourself!"

William and Lin Mae exchanged a glance, then the two of them made their way up to the front of the gondola, where Peng Yong was now successfully steering the craft towards the gap between the two multi-tiered towers, which rose up majestically on either side of them. When they saw what Wang had seen they both gasped.

The two matching pagodas were standing either side of the foot of the broad North Steps, which rose up towards the huge and magnificent Reception Hall. Here, on the wide mezzanine in front of the vast double doors was a seething horde of Tao Tei, surrounding the Paladins, which had massed into a protective circle. It was clear the Tao Tei had fought and feasted. Many of them were smeared and splashed with human blood.

Lin Mae's mouth opened in a silent gasp of horror and wonder.

• • •

Having successfully negotiated their way around the pagodas, and seen the General's balloon change course and sail safely towards the channel between the two towers, Commander Chen's craft had now run into difficulties. Passing to the right of the right-hand pagoda instead of steering the balloon between them had meant having to negotiate a forest of jutting spires on the long building that ran parallel to the North Steps. However some of their ropes between the balloon and the gondola had become caught on, and tangled around, one of the spires, and the balloon, though still airborne and billowing impotently in the wind that wanted to push them onward, was now stationary.

This wouldn't have been a problem if it wasn't for the fact that the Tao Tei were now homing in on them, more and more of the creatures swarming across the nearby rooftops to mass on the roof below. As Chen and another Eagle Corps warrior kept them at bay with arrow after arrow, the third member of their crew clambered up on to the side of the gondola and began trying desperately to free the tangled ropes. He couldn't cut them, because it would mean severing the connection between gondola and balloon, but if he didn't free them quickly then it would be only a matter of time before the massing Tao Tei swarmed up the spire and overwhelmed them through sheer force of numbers.

• • •

Peng Yong was still hauling on the ropes, trying to steer a steady course through the twin pagodas. However, it was not proving easy. A strong, sideswiping wind was blowing them back towards the right-hand pagoda.

Wang was all but jumping up and down in desperation and eagerness. "Left!" he shouted. "Left!"

Peng Yong glared at him, sweat pouring down his face. He snapped something in Mandarin, which William didn't need to understand to know that the young man had retorted he was doing his best. By the time he yelled something else, a warning of some kind, William's attention, along with that of both Wang and Lin Mae, had become fixed on the mezzanine area below and ahead of them. They stared in fascination and revulsion as they caught their clearest and closest glimpse yet of the Tao Tei Queen.

She was sitting within her circle of Paladins and appeared to be feeding. The Paladins had allowed a select number of Tao Tei soldiers to come forward and open their vast jaws. Also open was the Queen's mouth, from which had extended multiple tentacle-like tubes, which had reached down into the throats of the uncharacteristically servile Tao Tei. Now the tentacles linking the Queen to her soldiers were bulging and rippling as she gorged on their already partly digested meal.

William didn't know what was more disgusting—the Queen's eating habits or the fact that the belly of her already bloated form was distended yet further by the many thousands of eggs rippling beneath her almost translucent skin. He glanced at Lin Mae, who put a hand over her mouth to demonstrate how the sight made her feel. He grimaced and nodded.

Peng Yong yelled another warning, and William looked up to see that, despite his efforts to steer them the other way, the strong wind had plucked them yet closer to the right-hand pagoda. It was looming up on their starboard side, coming at them both too fast and too quickly. Instinctively William grabbed something solid and fixed with one hand and, as the balloon suddenly swung up in a wide arc, Lin Mae with the other.

• • •

Chen kept firing arrow after arrow, but he knew it was hopeless. The ropes were still tangled around the chimney, the balloon above them was now slumping and sinking, and the Tao Tei were becoming too numerous to keep at bay.

He fired yet another arrow, as did the soldier beside him, as four Tao Tei leaped in unison from the chimney towards the gondola. Both arrows found their mark, the creatures twisting in mid-air before falling back into the seething horde of teeth and claws below, but the remaining pair of Tao Tei clamped their jaws around the gondola and wrenched it sideways. As Chen fell backwards, the last thing he saw was the glowing brazier tipping over onto the container of black powder they had been feeding it with.

Then everything disappeared in noise and blinding white light.

• • •

The balloon missed the pagoda roof by inches, but the gondola didn't. As the balloon drifted up and past the multi-tiered tower, the stern of the gondola, swinging behind it, clipped a protruding ledge, which both knocked off a chunk of rubble, and made the vessel spin and shudder.

Feeling as though he was inside a giant barrel being rolled down a hill, William clung on to both his handhold and Lin Mae. Dragging Lin Mae down with him, he crouched low to better center himself, tucking in his head, and so was only peripherally aware of something large and dark tumbling past behind him. Belatedly realizing it was Wang, he looked round to see the little man slam against the inside wall of the gondola as it tipped, then roll back to lie spread-eagled on the floor as it settled again. From the shocked expression on Wang's face, it was clear he knew all too well how close he had come to falling overboard. If the gondola had tipped just a few more inches, he would have tumbled up and over the side.

As the gondola, though juddering, started to settle, with Peng Yong still hauling heroically on the ropes, William opened his mouth to speak. But at that moment Chen's balloon, which had been somewhere to their right, on the other side of the pagoda, exploded with a shattering roar.

Once again they threw themselves to the floor as their gondola rocked and spun. A black cloud of smoke and dust and debris rolled over them, making them cough, hampering visibility. That was another balloon gone. Another three soldiers of the Nameless Order who had given their lives to the cause. William wondered how many more of them were left. Wondered whether the future of the entire human race now lay solely in the hands of him and his companions.

• • •

Of the many balloons that had launched from the battlements of the Great Wall, only a handful had reached their destination. Following their General's orders they were landing now in the huge open courtyard to the rear of the Main Hall.

It was a scene of utter chaos. As gondolas careered and scraped across the stone floor, trailing ropes and masses of deflating silk and canvas, hundreds of people, perhaps even as many as a thousand, were pouring out of the Palace like ants from a trampled nest. These were mainly the Palace's staff—servants, cooks, porters, footmen, laundresses. They were all sizes, all ages, all types, and they were fleeing for their lives, every single one of them terrified out of their wits.

They were heading as one towards the South Gates, in the vain hope that they might somehow escape the marauding monsters at their heels. The Tao Tei were not here yet, but they soon would be; they were not far behind. As the people flooded from the Palace they screamed and pushed and shoved. Many of them tripped over the trailing ropes or the deflating billows of silk, and fell and rolled, often injuring themselves, only to then pick themselves up and limp or stagger on regardless.

In the midst of this melee the Imperial Guard, or at least those that were left, were trying in vain to restore order. In truth, though, they had been completely overwhelmed by the disaster that had befallen them, and were just as scared and disorganized as everybody else.

As yet another gondola crashed down in the courtyard, the balloon it was trailing billowing up and over it like a shroud, the Guards ran instinctively towards it, their swords drawn.

• • •

The huge mass of stitched-together silk and canvas and animal skin billowed and furled in the wind. Trapped beneath it, Lin Mae felt as if it was smothering her. For a few seconds she was unable to breathe, overcome with panic.

Then she heard William's voice, muffled but nearby. "Use your blade! Cut your way through!"

She forced herself to become calm, to reach for that still point in the center of her being. When she had found it, she reached with her fingers, ignoring the silk slithering across her face, and plucked her short blade from the sheath that was strapped to her leg. She slashed upwards, cutting through layers of dark material, feeling them fall away, finally seeing light penetrate the gloom. Cutting the hole wide enough, she clambered out, like a butterfly from a cocoon, and immediately became aware of William beside her, taking her arm and helping her out of the shredded wads of fabric.

When she looked up it was to see an Imperial Officer and several panic-stricken soldiers staring at her. The Officer, in his beautiful gold armour with its royal red and blue trimmings, was pointing a sword at her, his shaking hand causing the blade to quiver like a divining rod.

His voice shrill with alarm, he demanded, "What is this? Who are you?"

William scowled at him. "Back away!"

It was clear the Officer didn't understand William's words, but his aggressive manner was easy to interpret. Addressing Lin Mae again, he shouted, "Answer me!"

Lin Mae knew that if the man had had his wits about him, he might have recognized her armour, but he was clearly beyond that. Placing a hand on William's chest as an indication that he should stand down, she stepped forward and reached into the collar of her armour, producing the gold medallion that General Shao had passed on to her. Silently she showed it to the Officer, who gazed at it as if hypnotized.

Finally, in something like awe, he murmured, "The Nameless Order."

Instantly the nerve-wracked soldiers behind him dropped to their knees.

"Forgive me, your Excellency, for having eyes that fail to see," the Officer continued. "I deserve a thousand de—"

"Off your knees, man! We've not time for that! Where is the Emperor?"

The outburst came not from Lin Mae, but from Wang, who was now struggling free of the deflated balloon. Behind him, white-faced and blinking and clearly astonished to find himself still alive, was Peng Yong.

As the Imperial Officer merely gaped at him, his mouth opening and closing like a fish, Wang barked, "We need help. All the help that you can muster." He turned to Peng Yong. "Black powder. We need everything you can salvage in three minutes." Peng Yong nodded and scurried away on his mission.

Turning back to the still gaping soldiers, Wang clapped his hands together, like a hypnotist awakening his victims. "Well, come on! Get to it!"

• • •

Cowering behind his throne, shaking uncontrollably, the Emperor no longer projected the aura of an imperious ruler who held sway over the Seven Kingdoms. Now he had been reduced to what he really was: a small boy in fancy robes who was terrified for his life. As he heard footsteps clacking towards him, he drew himself into an even tighter ball, and when a hesitant voice said, "Your Majesty?" he couldn't help but flinch.

For the sake of his reputation he knew he needed to respond, however, and so, after taking several deep breaths, he rose nervously from behind his throne. The magnificent Main Hall, a place that usually bustled with life, was now stark and almost empty. Aside from his Chief Counselor, who was the man who had spoken, and whose hands were pressed together in obeisance, there now remained just a smattering of his Imperial retinue—counselors, eunuchs, attendants—and a small group of soldiers.

Of the soldiers, who were standing at the foot of the throne steps, half a dozen were dressed in the gold, lavishly designed armour of his Imperial Guard. The rest were dressed in variously colored armour—seven in black, three in red, including one foreigner, and one in blue—and they looked battered, bruised and exhausted, as if they had just fought a long and arduous battle. Accompanying them was a small man in dark robes. He and a nervous-looking black-armored soldier were presiding over a pile of ropes and strange weapons and military paraphernalia, all of which were gathered together on what appeared to be a large, crumpled square of torn white silk.

As soon as he looked upon them, the soldiers and the two other men dropped to their knees and bowed their heads. The woman in the blue armour came forward and gave a small, respectful bow.

"I am General Lin Mae," she said. "Your Majesty's humble servant."

The Emperor, recovering a little of his composure now, came slowly down the steps.

"Servant?" he said curtly. "Of what? How have you served me?" Suddenly his long pent-up fear found an outlet, erupting into fury. "The Wall has given way! My Palace is falling! My Kingdom overrun with beasts! Thousands of soldiers and innocents are dead! *This* is your service?"

Lin Mae lowered her head, as if in shame. "Forgive me, Your Majesty."

The Emperor stared down at her with contempt. "How many men have you brought?"

Lin Mae hesitated, as if afraid to answer.

"Your Majesty," the Chief Counselor interjected, "for the sake of the Kingdom, we must leave quickly."

Finally Lin Mae gave him an answer to his question. Her voice was both apologetic and defiant. "I brought many. But these ten are all that remain."

The Emperor seemed to sag, his arms reaching out for support. His Chief Counselor and two attendants rushed to his side to stop him from falling.

As though he had had enough of etiquette and deference, Wang rose to his feet and stepped forward. "Where is the captured Tao Tei?"

Everyone looked at everyone else. No one answered. Wang cast an accusatory look at the Chief Counselor, then at the Imperial Officer.

"Tell me you still *have* the captured Tao Tei!"

The Officer looked at the Emperor for permission to speak, and received a small nod in response.

"Of course. It's been moved below," he said. "To the dungeon."

"Take us there!" ordered Wang.

• • •

In direct contrast to the opulence above, the Palace dungeons were dark and dank. Water ran down the slimy stone walls and dripped from the ceilings, as William, Wang, Lin Mae, Peng Yong and the rest of the

Nameless Order were led hurriedly down a set of wide, slippery stone steps.

The Imperial Officer, leading the way with a torch held above his head, informed them hurriedly of Shen's death, and of how the Tai Tei had wrecked its cage, necessitating its transferal to one of the cells in the Palace dungeon. He said that now the magnet had been placed back around the creature's neck, it was once more dormant and pliable.

It was clear, as a pair of Imperial Guards unlocked and opened the cell, however, how frightened of it the soldiers here still were. They hung back, their faces taut with apprehension, as Wang, William, Lin Mae and (more reluctantly) the Imperial Officer crowded inside.

Lit by torchlight, the slumped Tao Tei did indeed look a fearsome beast. In the enclosed space, the scent that it exuded was musky, bestial. It breathed noisily, its great chest rising and falling, and even in repose they could all see the muscles clenching and rippling in its tree-like limbs.

Perhaps because he felt he had to make up for the terrible losses the Nameless Order had suffered as a result of his suggestion that they use the untested balloons, Wang seemed hyperactive, full of nervous energy.

Indicating the Tao Tei, he said, "We load it up with black powder weapons. We feed it. We pray it returns to the Queen." As everyone nodded, he added, "We have very little time. With every minute that passes the death toll mounts, and the Tao Tei grow stronger. We must act now! Immediately! And may fortune be with us!"

His words had a galvanizing effect. Immediately Lin Mae started barking orders, which were relayed, via the Imperial Officer, to his own men. Within minutes everyone had an assigned role, and preparations were underway.

A dozen men, a mixture of Imperial soldiers and Nameless Order warriors, carried the Tao Tei up the slippery steps of the dungeon and into the courtyard above, where they loaded it onto an open cart. After heaving and pushing the creature into place, they stepped back, many of them unconsciously wiping their hands on their armour as if they had touched something unclean, expressions of disgust on their sweat-streaked faces.

Meanwhile William, Lin Mae, Wang and one of the Bear Corps warriors fashioned an elaborate harness of chains and leather bindings. As soon as the Tao Tei was in place, they fastened the harness tightly around its neck and arms. On the front of the harness was a pouch, designed to nestle snugly against the creature's chest, made from a piece of canvas torn from one of the felled balloons, into which they carefully placed the magnet. That done, Peng Yong dragged the makeshift silk pouch, containing its arsenal of black powder weapons, up to the cart and quickly unwrapped it. He began to hand the grenades to William one by one, who, together with Wang and Lin

Mae, knotted them tightly to the chains attached to the harness. As they were doing that, two Bear Corps soldiers appeared from an arched entranceway, wheeling forward another cart, this one piled up with meat—whole hogs, sides of beef, stacks of plucked and headless chickens.

Once the bulk of the work was done, the last few minutes were spent in a flurry of final preparations. Soldiers checked their swords and lances; torches were lit; Wang fussily re-checked the harness around the Tao Tei, tightening knots here and there. William strapped an ignition device—one of Wang's inventions—to his arm, while Lin Mae, standing beside him, tightened her ropes and the scabbard containing her sword. All around them was a babble of voices, of steel weapons sliding into sheaths, of ropes creaking. In the midst of it, William looked up, to find that Lin Mae too was raising her head, turning to him. She hesitated a moment, and then said, "I was wrong about you."

William smiled. "No. You knew me right away."

She smiled back at him, but hers was an ironic smile, even a little bitter. "If I had been right, you would not be here."

"I'm not here," he said. When she frowned in puzzlement he explained, "The man who first arrived at the Wall is not here. I'm not him any more. I'm someone else now."

Before she could reply, they were distracted by the

creaking sound of a door opening on the far side of the courtyard. Both of them looked across to see the Imperial Officer pushing his torch forward into a dark entrance, illuminating a slope leading downward. William and Lin Mae watched as Wang and the Imperial Officer conferred for a moment, Wang nodding curtly. As Lin Mae translated what they were saying, explaining to William that beyond the door was a tunnel leading under the Palace complex, Wang marched back to a group of soldiers, who were waiting on the far side of the courtyard, and who had been chosen to stay behind as a last line of defense.

"We need all the time you can buy us," he said.

As one, the small band of soldiers, fronted by two Eagle Corps warriors in filthy, battered armour, bowed in obedience, their faces masks of duty and grim determination.

Wang called together the procession that were undertaking the journey into the tunnel, and seconds later they set off. He and the Imperial Officer led the way, the Officer holding up a torch to light the route ahead. Directly behind them came two Bear Corps warriors, grunting with effort as they pushed the meat cart. Following them were Lin Mae and Peng Yong, both of whom, like the Officer, also brandished torches. Then came the three biggest and burliest warriors that the Nameless Order had at their disposal, all of whom wore black Bear Corps armour, and all of whom panted and strained and sweated as they maneuvered the heavy cart holding the recumbent Tao Tei through the tunnels. And finally, bringing up the rear of the group, came William, their last line of defense.

As the heavy door swung shut behind them, he glanced back, watching the block of daylight between door and frame become narrower until finally it disappeared. Now all they had to combat the darkness were their flickering torches, which threw strange, wavering shadows up and down the walls. Their journey had only just begun, and already the tunnel felt hot and stuffy, the air pungent with the stink of raw meat and the Tao Tei's musky flesh.

William wondered what the next few hours would bring, whether this would be his last day on earth. He was all too aware he could be with Pero now, riding free across the desert plains, his saddlebags stuffed with black powder. But he had no regrets. He knew if he was given his time over again, he would still choose to be here—fighting alongside Lin Mae and the Nameless Order. Fighting for a cause that, for the first and only time in his life, actually *mattered*.

• • •

The door to the now empty Main Hall crashed open and the Tao Tei flooded in, their black talons scoring long grooves across the highly polished wooden floor. They crashed into pillars, knocked over pedestals, smashed vases and priceless statues, and tore down hanging silks with their claws and teeth.

Some of them swarmed up the steps to the Imperial throne, demolishing the delicate, ornamental balustrades at the sides. They sniffed at the throne and then around it, and then at the bottom of the steps. Their tiny eyes glinted; their maws opened, lips curling back from their rows of teeth, and they let loose a series of shrieks.

They had picked up a scent.

• • •

The defensive guard around the courtyard door numbered sixteen soldiers. Thirteen were from what remained of the Imperial Guard, and the other three were from what remained of the Nameless Order. Of the three Nameless Order soldiers, two were Eagle Corps warriors, standing at the front of the group with their bows armed and ready, and the other, standing just behind them with an axe in one hand and a mallet in the other, was from the Bear Corps.

None of the men spoke to one another. None of them shifted from their positions. They stood stoic and resolute, waiting for the enemy.

Waiting to fight and die.

• • •

The tunnel was hot and dark and seemingly endless.

Torches flickered. Muscles strained. Sweat poured. Wheels turned.

Silently, determinedly, they went on.

• • •

The silence in the courtyard was suddenly shattered by a sound that was distant, though no less terrifying for it. It was a shrill and hideous screech. Wordless, and yet full of rage and hate and awful, endless hunger.

The men in the courtyard stirred. The Imperial soldiers clutched the hilts of their swords with trembling hands; the Bear Corps warrior took a firmer grip on his axe and mallet; the Eagle Corps warriors drew back the strings of their bows, their focus absolute, their arms rock steady.

Another cry rent the air, closer this time, and was then quickly followed by another, and another. And now the men in the courtyard heard the thump of myriad feet, like the far-off rumble of approaching thunder.

The enemy were on their way.

• • •

There was light up ahead, Lin Mae was sure of it. It was difficult to tell with the flickering firelight of the Imperial Officer's torch limning the rocky walls, but all the same she was certain she could see the faint glimmer of a different light beyond that—one that was softer, purer, more natural.

Was this new light coming from above? Yes, she was sure it was. She felt a pang of alarm as she wondered what could be causing it. Was it coming from a breach in the ceiling that had been created by the Tao Tei? Could their enemy have become tactically aware enough to anticipate their plan and intercept them?

But no. As they neared the light, she saw it was coming from a row of four open iron grates, like barred windows, set into the low ceiling of the next section of tunnel. The corridor broadened out a little here, and looked more man-made. The Imperial Officer turned and held up a hand, instructing them all to halt. When the wheels of the carts had creaked to a stop, he indicated a longer, darker section of tunnel that lay beyond the grated section directly ahead.

"That's where we're heading for," he said. "Fifty more paces will bring us to the cellar of the East Pagoda."

He turned away, holding up his torch, and again they began to move forward, the wheels of the two carts rumbling back to life. Lin Mae glanced over her shoulder at William, who was helping the now weary Bear Corps warriors push the Tao Tei cart the last fifty paces. She saw him glance up at the first of the grilles set into the ceiling—and then she saw him freeze. She glanced up too, following his gaze. Close to the grilles—no more than a few feet away—she saw movement.

At first the light filtering from above was too bright for her to make out what was causing it. But then her vision adjusted and she drew in a sharp breath. So close she could have reached up and touched it had the grating not been there, she saw a mass of shifting green flesh, interspersed with brief flashes of black taloned claws and glistening white teeth.

The area directly above their heads was teeming with Tao Tei!

Eyes widening, she looked at William. Casting a warning glance at the Imperial Officer at the head of the group with Wang at his side, he leaned forward and whispered, "Eyes forward! Keep moving! Tell them!"

But no sooner were the words out of his mouth than the Imperial Officer glanced up at the grating above his head—and froze in terror. He came to an abrupt halt, causing the rest of the procession to stop again too.

There was snuffling and grunting now from above, a new eagerness and awareness among the Tao Tei. Whether the creatures had seen their flickering torchlight, or heard their rumbling carts, or perhaps simply caught their scent Lin Mae had no idea, but all at once the light from above grew dimmer as the creatures moved across to press eyes and snouts against the grates. Next moment scrabbling talons appeared through the gaps between the bars and drool thick as candle wax began to drip down on them.

Wang gave the Imperial Officer a shove in the back and hissed sharply, "Press on! We're almost there!"

The Imperial Officer looked at him, his face stark with terror, and then, with an effort, managed to recover himself. He gave a sharp nod and lurched forward, his movements jerky and panicked, the torchlight veering this way and that.

As they hurried through the long tunnel as fast as they could, the activity above them grew yet more frenzied. The shafts of daylight leaking in from overhead became fewer, and then were blotted out completely, as the Tao Tei crammed forward, turning the gaps between the bars into a slavering, hissing mass of squirming green flesh. More talons poked through, scrabbling at them, causing them to duck their heads. Lin Mae felt alarm lurch inside her as the grilles began to creak and bend under the intense pressure exerted by the weight of dozens of Tao Tei bodies. She felt an urge to run, but the carts were too heavy to push at anything more than walking pace.

Suddenly, in front of Lin Mae, there was a splintering crack and one of the grilles gave way. Instantly a Tao Tei arm burst through into the tunnel, long talons sinking into the shoulder of one of the Bear Corps warriors pushing the meat cart and plucking him up through the gap in the ceiling as easily as a child might pluck a crab from a rock pool. The soldier gave a short scream of agony and then he was gone, his shield, which was too big to fit through the gap, clattering to the floor, followed almost immediately by a pattering rain of blood.

Before anyone could react, a second grille burst open and a second Tao Tei arm reached in and plucked away another of the Bear Corps warriors. Then, in quick succession, several more massive green arms swiped down and grabbed the remainder of the soldiers, one of them snagging the shoulder of Peng Yong's armour with its pincer-like talons and hauling him upwards.

Peng Yong screamed and struggled, his legs kicking wildly as he was dragged towards the drooling mass of Tao Tei. Lin Mae had been unable to act swiftly enough to prevent the sudden and shocking deaths of the rest of her soldiers, but now she tugged her grappling hook from her waistband and instinctively threw it.

The hook flew straight and true, the chain wrapping around the Tao Tei's wrist like a metal shackle, the four prongs of the hook itself securing themselves around the bent and twisted bars of the damaged grille. This clamped the Tao Tei's arm in place, at least temporarily, and prevented it from dragging Peng Yong up through the rent in the ceiling.

Lin Mae knew it would only be a matter of time, however, before the Tao Tei managed to yank itself free. Behind her she was peripherally aware of William running forward, dipping down. She turned just in time to see him snatch up the blood-spattered shield of one of the dead Bear Corps warriors, turn it sideways and hurl it like a discus.

The shield, spinning like a top, flew with such speed and ferocity, that it severed the Tao Tei's arm cleanly at the wrist. As Peng Yong dropped to the floor, the taloned claw still hooked in the shoulder of his armour, the Tao Tei let out a bellowing scream of agony. With green, foul smelling blood gushing from it and splashing over Peng Yong, the creature's arm retracted through the breach in the ceiling. Lin Mae knew, though, that the Tao Tei's injury would not prevent others of its kind from trying to get at them.

"Stay low!" she shouted as she, William and Wang rushed forward to retrieve her grappling hook and check on Peng Yong.

The three of them crowded round the young Bear Corps warrior, who was slumped against the wall, his face contorted in agony. Carefully William lifted aside the mangled, blood-spattered flaps of armour and cloth at Peng Yong's shoulder and examined the wound beneath.

"You'll have one hell of a scar," he said. "But you'll live."

Quickly Lin Mae translated William's words. Peng Yong nodded weakly, his face ashen.

William could tell that the young man, though not mortally wounded, was in no state to jump to his feet and return to the fray just yet – and they had no time to wait for him to recover.

"We'll come back for him," he said to Lin Mae.

She hesitated a moment, then gave a decisive nod.

It was much harder going now that the rest of the soldiers were dead, but with William, Lin Mae and Wang putting their all into getting the two heavy carts down the tunnel, they creaked and rumbled slowly onward.

• • •

With a thundering clatter of clawed feet and a chorus of enraged, ear-splitting screams, the Tao Tei poured into the courtyard. Instantly the Eagle Corps warriors began to unleash their arrows, their hands a blur of motion as they loaded and fired. The Bear Corps warrior gave a roar of his own and waded fearlessly into the fray, swinging his axe and mallet. Even the Imperial Guards, unused to combat, fought bravely, slashing and hacking with their swords.

In spite of their courage, however, the battle was over in seconds, the soldiers managing to dispatch only a few Tao Tei before they were overwhelmed by sheer force of numbers. There was a brief, mad, dark swirling blur of green flesh and blood and screams, and then the Tao Tei were smashing the heavy wooden door from its hinges and flooding into the tunnel.

• • •

The fifty paces to the pagoda cellar entrance were the longest of William's life. Together with Lin Mae and Wang, he hauled and heaved at the two carts, edging them inch by inch towards their destination.

Eventually they crossed the threshold of the long tunnel into what appeared to be a small junction chamber. Directly ahead of them, on the far side of the chamber, an arched opening framed a set of wide, stone steps leading upwards. To their left, set at an angle, was a wet, dripping, spillway tunnel, the ceiling of which, some distance ahead, was inset with more of the grates through which daylight poured like a line of misty white ghosts. From what William had seen of the layout of the Palace grounds from the air, he suspected that this tunnel stretched towards the North Gate steps.

"Here," Wang gasped, stepping back from the cart. His dark robes were crumpled and smeared with grime, and his face shone with sweat.

He looked exhausted, in need of a rest, but William knew there was no time. He was about to reply when, from back down the tunnel, they heard the triumphant screeching roar of the Tao Tei.

All three of them looked at one another, then swung round. In the far distance, beyond Peng Yong's slumped form, they saw flashes of green, rippling shadows, the suggestion of movement.

"They've broken through!" Lin Mae cried despairingly.

"Do it now," William said to Wang. His words were punctuated by another echoing screech, this one a little closer.

"We need more time," said Wang, his voice desperate.

"Look!" gasped Lin Mae.

William turned to see Peng Yong staggering to his feet. The young man clutched the black powder weapons he had been issued with to his body and touched the fuse of one to the ignition device attached to his wrist. As it fizzed into life, he turned to look back at him, his eyes steady in his waxy, sweating face. He said something in a quiet, calm voice, and although they were too far away to hear his words, the message was clear. Peng Yong was both resigned to his fate and determined to do his duty.

The boy had finally become a man.

23

"Turn away!" William yelled, waving his arms.

Wang and Lin Mae did so just in time. The next second there was a massive explosion, and William was swept off his feet and thrown forward by a buffeting wave of heat.

The tunnel filled with debris and dust. For a minute or more, lying on his belly, he couldn't see anything. He sat up gingerly, coughing and spluttering, waving his hands in front of his face. He brushed at his clothes, which were covered in rubble and fine white powder.

Somewhere close to him, through the haze of dust, he heard Lin Mae and Wang coughing too. The sound was muffled, as though his ears were packed with sand. Still coughing, he clambered to his feet and walked a little way back down the tunnel, towards the site of the explosion. As the dust settled and the air became clearer, he realized that the grated section through which they had passed earlier was now completely blocked by a dark mass of pulverized stone. He listened hard, but though his ears were still throbbing he was pretty sure that the bellowing cries of the Tao Tei had now been silenced. He couldn't even hear scratching or scuffling from the other side of the rockfall.

Peng Yong had done it. By sacrificing himself he had given them the most precious thing of all.

Time.

William staggered past the carts and saw two dark figures standing upright, albeit a little unsteadily, in the murk. As he approached them, they looked blearily up at him, their faces and clothes greyed by stone dust.

"Are you all right?" he asked Lin Mae.

She frowned and pointed at her ears.

He raised his voice. "Can you hear me?"

"Yes, yes," she said, though she still seemed a little off-balance.

Wang coughed and wiped his eyes, then peered back through the settling curtain of dust. "Are they…?"

"They're gone," William said simply.

Wang nodded, though he looked dazed, as though he couldn't quite process what William was telling him.

"What now?" William asked, and then, more sharply, hoping to get Wang to focus, "What now?"

Wang blinked. Equally sharply, he said, "We free the beast. We let it feed."

William nodded and ran across to the meat cart, which he dragged, inch by straining inch, across the floor of the chamber to the foot of the steps on the far side. Glancing up the steps he saw that they culminated in a small stone landing, on the far side of which was a large wooden door.

"Does this open on to the courtyard at the foot of the Palace steps?" he asked.

Wang nodded. "Stand back."

He waved a hand, gesturing that William should stand with Lin Mae behind him. William did so, and noticed another narrow opening that he had not previously seen in the gloom. Glancing through it, he saw a winding wooden staircase, which he realized must lead up to the various levels of the multi-tiered pagoda.

Wang moved across to the cart on which the Tao Tei still slumped, oblivious to everything that had been going on around it.

"Ready?" he asked.

Lin Mae drew her sword and William nocked an arrow into his bow and pulled the string taut, aiming it at the Tao Tei. Both nodded.

Wang gave a small smile and leaned forward, stretching out his hands towards the creature. "Here we go."

Moving slowly and carefully, he lifted the magnet from the pouch attached to the creature's chest, then backed quickly away to stand beside William and Lin Mae. Freed from the magnet's influence, the Tao Tei jerked awake and scrambled upright, its dulled eyes suddenly glinting with malevolent life. William, Lin Mae and Wang all held their breaths as the creature suddenly became aware of the harness attached to its body. If it tore off the harness and its cargo of black powder weapons their plans would be in ruins. But to their relief, after giving its body an experimental shake, the creature seemed to forget about the harness, its attention turned to more immediate concerns: food.

Sniffing the air, the Tao Tei turned its massive head in their direction. Then it leaped down from the cart and start moving towards them. William raised his bow, ready to unleash two swift arrows into the creature's eyes, but Wang, holding up the magnet like an offering, hissed, "Wait! Do not shoot!"

The Tao Tei took a couple of steps closer—then abruptly it stopped. Reaching the periphery of the magnet's influence, it flinched back. It turned away as if it was no longer aware of their presence and began sniffing the air again like a hungry dog. Suddenly its body quivered. Denied fresh, living meat, it had found the next best thing. It bounded across to the meat cart, leaped up on to it and began to devour the huge stack of bloody, dust coated carcasses, gobbling up entire pigs in two bites, swallowing mouthfuls of chickens whole.

William, Wang and Lin Mae watched and listened to the Tao Tei eating its fill, Wang wearing a small grimace of distaste.

"You have no real idea where that beast is going when it's done, do you?" William muttered.

Wang looked affronted. "It will go to the Queen."

"You know this for certain?"

"It will," he declared. Then a note of doubt crept into his voice. "It must."

Once it had devoured every last scrap of meat, and even lapped up the blood from the bottom of the cart with its barbed tongue, the Tao Tei leaped down from the cart. Then, as if responding to some unheard signal, it bounded across the stone floor and up the steps on the far side of the chamber.

All three of them heard a crash from above, and then saw the still-drifting dust in the chamber disturbed by an eddy of air.

"Is it clear?" William asked.

Still brandishing the magnet like a trophy, Wang hurried across the chamber and moved nimbly up the steps, his energy restored now that his plan seemed to be coming to fruition. He halted at the top, then half-turned and gestured for William and Lin Mae to join him.

When they had done so, all three moved to the

now open door into the courtyard. "Careful now… Slowly…" William said, and cautiously pushed the half-shattered wooden door all the way open. Peering out into the courtyard that adjoined the Palace steps, they saw immediately that it was swarming with Tao Tei. It was an eerie feeling to be so close to such a huge number of the creatures, only to be completely ignored. William was all too aware that if the magnet should, for whatever reason, suddenly lose its effect, he and his two companions would be torn to pieces in seconds.

Still treading softly, as if that would make a difference, they edged further out into the courtyard until they could see the steps themselves. They too were a mass of green, but whereas they couldn't see the Queen among the bustling throng of Tao Tei, they did see their 'own' creature, with its harness of deadly weapons, snuffling through the crowd. On the wide mezzanine area at the top of the steps, they could also see a circle of larger Tao Tei with fan-like shields on the sides of their heads that were standing shoulder to shoulder, effectively creating a protective enclosure.

Wang murmured something to Lin Mae, who nodded. William looked at him quizzically.

"The Paladins," Wang said, pointing at the circle of creatures. "The guards that protect the Queen. She'll be there, in the center."

William quickly assessed the distance and angle to

the target. "It's an almost impossible shot. We can't risk it from here. We may have only one chance."

Wang nodded in agreement, then glanced up at the huge structure beside them. "Climb the pagoda. Fire from above. But you must hurry. Go!"

William turned away. Lin Mae asked, "What about you?"

"I'll keep us safe with this," Wang said, holding up the black stone magnet.

• • •

William and Lin Mae raced up the winding wooden staircase inside the pagoda, multi-colored light from its stained glass windows washing over them. At the fifth floor William halted.

"This should be high enough."

They ran out on to the roofed balcony that overlooked the Palace steps, which from their elevated position were little more than a rising mass of squirming green flesh. At the top of the steps the extended fan-like shields of the Paladins formed a kind of plated dome with a dark hole in its center. William and Lin Mae caught glimpses of something shifting, pulsating within the hole. They were heartened to see that the Paladins were allowing selected Tao Tei through the barrier one by one, presumably so they could feed the Queen with their partially digested stomach contents. Wang's plan relied on the fact that 'their' Tao Tei would be one of those given access to the inner sanctum. Certainly it had been a good tactic of Wang's to feed the creature until it was fit to bursting. All they had to do now was hope and wait.

They did so in tense silence, watching the teeming horde below. At last William nocked an arrow onto his bow, the fuse of which passed through the ignition device on his wrist and instantly ignited. "Ready."

Peering at the circle of Paladins and the writhing mass around them, Lin Mae asked, "Can you see it?"

"Yes," William said. "It's with the Queen."

He took aim and fired the arrow.

The flaming arrow sailed through the air, describing a perfect arc over the heads of the massed Tao Tei. Bang on target, it dropped unerringly towards the dark hole at the center of the Tao Tei shield. At the last moment, however, just as William was beginning to grin in triumph, the Paladins, sensing danger, moved into position and opened the fan-like shields around their heads. To his dismay William saw the shields pass across his original target area like clouds across the sun. As a result his burning arrow bounced off the shields and ricocheted away into the mass of Tao Tei, where the flames were quickly stamped out under dozens of trampling feet.

William's face fell and he slumped backward. "No…" he moaned.

Lin Mae was equally distraught. "They blocked it!"

But there was no time to dwell on their disappointment. For all at once the Queen rose up from within the protective circle of her Paladins, as if her massive, palpitating body was about to swell and explode. She swiveled her head, her glittering green eyes searching, probing for her attackers. William shuddered as she looked up, directly at them. Even from here he fancied he could feel the icy coldness of her penetrating stare.

There was a long, silent moment of mutual appraisal— and then the web of flesh stretched between the Queen's horns began to vibrate. The sound the action produced was like an ululating screech of such rage, such *purpose*, that both William and Lin Mae had to momentarily cover their ears. Instantly, like a shoal of fish, the Tao Tei turned as one and began swarming towards the pagoda.

"They see us!" Lin Mae yelled.

William leaned out over the balcony and glanced upwards. "We need to go higher."

"Come! Hurry!"

• • •

Down on the ground, standing in the courtyard doorway that gave access to the pagoda, Wang paled as the milling Tao Tei suddenly turned in unison and rushed towards him. Exactly how strong was the magnet's influence? He was about to find out.

Holding the magnet above his head, he stood resolute as the horde bore down upon him. When they got to within eight or ten feet of him, they veered off to one side or the other, forming a semi-circular no-go area around him.

It was working! He was denying the Tao Tei access to the pagoda! But to his dismay, he quickly realized that the courtyard doorway was not the only way to breach the tower. To the left and right of him the deflected Tao Tei were now starting to climb up the outside of the pagoda. There were so many of them that from a distance they must have resembled a voracious, fast-growing fungus.

So numerous were they, in fact, and so eager to reach and destroy their Queen's attackers, that many of those ascending found they were unable to secure handholds through the melee of their fellow creatures' bodies. These unlucky ones began to fall back, like exceptionally weighty autumn fruit shed from a tree. They crashed down in the courtyard one by one, their vast bodies smashing open on impact with the ground. Protected though he was by the magnet, Wang realized it was only a matter of time before a falling Tao Tei body smashed down on top of him. Added to which, the Nameless Order's only realistic hope of preventing the Tao Tei scourge from spreading and devouring the world rested with William and the General. It was *they* who needed the protection offered by the magnet, not him.

Bracing himself, he stepped out into the courtyard and looked up. "General!" he yelled at the top of his voice. "William!"

A pair of heads, perhaps seven floors up, appeared over the top of a balcony and looked down at him.

There was no time to engage in conversation. Wang simply yelled, "It's up to you now!" and then, gathering all the strength left in his body, he hurled the black stone up towards them.

• • •

William looked down in horror as the magnet left Wang's hand and began hurtling upwards. As soon as its protective influence, which Wang had worn around him like a cloak, was removed, dozens of Tao Tei heads turned in his direction. The little man didn't try to run. He simply stood where he was, composed and dignified as ever, waiting for the inevitable. Before any of the creatures surrounding him could pounce, however, a climbing Tao Tei fell from the tower directly above him. William turned away, not wishing to see the man he had come not only to respect but to consider a friend crushed beneath it.

Leaning so far over the balcony that William instinctively rushed forward to grab her legs, Lin Mae pulled free the long lance that was strapped to her back and lowered its metal blade to meet the ascending magnet. Attracted to the metal, the black stone rushed towards the blade and stuck fast to it. Lin Mae pulled the lance back in and gathered it protectively to her chest as William dragged her back to safety. The two of them glanced at each other, a split-second acknowledgement that in order to both justify and respect Wang's sacrifice they had to act now and mourn later, and then they turned and raced up the stairs to the top of the pagoda.

When they were as high as they could get, William nocked another black powder arrow onto his bowstring and gave Lin Mae a determined nod. As the fuse passed through the ignition device on his wrist and burst into life he let fly. The target was larger and wider from this height, but with incredible speed and dexterity the Queen's bevy of Paladins flowed upwards, clambering atop one another like acrobats, and once again deflected the projectile with their fan-like shields.

"We only have one black powder arrow left," William said bleakly. "Give me the lance."

Lin Mae, though, had unclipped the grappling hook from her belt, and was now quickly unspooling the long coil of rope attached to the hook.

"What are you doing?" William asked.

"I have trained for this my whole life. We will fly," she said.

William looked across at the Queen. It was a fair

distance. He couldn't see how they would reach her. "What? How?"

But she was already spinning the grappling hook on the end of its rope to gain speed and momentum, her eyes fixed on an ornamental corner of the overhanging roof above the balcony, which had been carved into a curl that looped up and then back on itself. Without another word, she let fly.

The hook flew straight and true, the rope wrapping itself around the jutting corner of the roof, before the hook itself, having spun round on the rope several times, clamped tightly on to the structure, its metal prongs digging deep into the wood.

William looked dubiously at the jutting curl of wood to which the hook was attached. It was stout and solid, but would it be strong enough to take their combined weight? Turning back to her, he said doubtfully, "Lin Mae, I—"

"Xin ren," she said fiercely. She held his gaze for a moment, and then he nodded at her.

"I'll give you the shot," he said.

With no further argument, he plucked the magnet from the end of the lance to which it was still attached and tucked it beneath the breastplate of his armour, knowing the magnetism would hold it there until he pulled it free. Lin Mae, meanwhile, quickly secured the line around the both of them, binding them together, then drew her lance, around the top of which she tied pouches of black powder with leather thongs. Lighting the long fuse, which ran up the shaft of the lance, she said, "Ready?"

He nodded. Lin Mae transferred the lance with its sizzling fuse to her left hand, and then, with Tao Tei hurtling up the stairs of the tower towards them, their cries echoing in the confined space, they climbed up on to the top rail of the wooden balcony—and leaped.

As they swung away from the tower, looping towards the ground, the first of the pursuing Tao Tei reached the balcony on which they had been standing seconds before. With no thought for their own safety, the Tao Tei hurled themselves one after another from the balcony, their jaws snapping as, like vast eagles attacking smaller prey, they tried to pluck their enemies from the air. William and Lin Mae, however, were moving too quickly, their bodies describing a graceful arc as they swung out over the courtyard. Lin Mae looked down at the Queen and her Paladins. Then, almost casually, she hefted the lance in her right hand, drew back her arm, and nodded at William, who tugged the magnet out from beneath his breastplate and hurled it towards the center of the protective dome created by the Paladins.

With expert precision, Lin Mae hurled her lance, which followed the arc of the black stone as though the two objects were tied together. The magnet landed first, causing the Paladins, the rigged Tao Tei and the Queen herself to freeze, as though hypnotized. With the Paladins unable to maneuver themselves to create a barrier around their Queen, the lance fell straight and true, right into the gap at the top of the dome. There was a pause, during which time William and Lin Mae continued to swing over the Queen and her entourage, as the fuse on the lance burned down…

…and then there was an earth-shattering explosion, mostly contained within the Paladin's protective barrier, which tore the Tao Tei Queen into a million pieces, gobbets of flesh and gallons of green blood erupting into the air like lava from a volcano.

Swinging in a great loop, low over the Palace grounds to the side of the steps, William and Lin Mae were buffeted by the explosion. It bore them back round and up on their return trajectory more quickly than they would have liked, and they crashed against the sloping pan-tiled roof of the pagoda with enough force to smash the breath from their bodies. Lin Mae, the lighter of the two, recovered swiftly, scrambling up and onto the balcony above her even as the now cracked and unstable tiles began to slither and tumble away beneath her feet. William, however, was not so lucky, nor so nimble. Scrabbling for purchase, he found that the already-damaged tiles were shattering and sliding away beneath him too rapidly for him to gain any forward momentum. As a result he found himself skidding back down towards the edge of the roof, knowing all too well that if he fell he would plunge to his certain death hundreds of feet below.

Then he felt a hand enclose his wrist and grip on tight. He looked up to see Lin Mae, her face contorted with effort, leaning over the balcony. "I've got you," she gasped.

With strength that belied her small frame, she began to haul him towards her. Now that his fall had been arrested, William was able to aid her by gripping with his free hand on to the edges of unbroken and still securely fastened tiles on the roof around him and claw his way upwards. A few seconds later he was up and over the edge of the balcony, the two of them gasping with effort and shaking with reaction. Clambering to his feet, he stood beside her, the two of them looking back at the devastation they had caused.

With the death of their Queen the leaderless Tao Tei that had been swarming up the sides of the pagoda had frozen like statues. And now, as William and Lin Mae watched, the creatures, their life force extinguished, began to fall back, to tumble, one by one, layer by layer, to the ground far, far below.

24

As the sun rose over the Southern Plain, thirteen riders moved quickly and purposefully through the morning mist. The beautiful, exquisitely fashioned armour of twelve of the riders flashed gold in the early light. The thirteenth rider wore a dark, padded jerkin, breeches and boots—simple but well made—and had a bow and a quiver of red-tipped arrows slung across his back.

The horses were fine and strong, and they kicked up a thick cloud of dust in their wake as they galloped across the bare and sandy plain. One of the horsemen carried the Emperor's Standard, which fluttered and flapped in the slipstream.

• • •

Lin Mae strolled along the now empty battlements of the Great Wall, close to its outer edge. Occasionally, as she walked, she stretched out a hand, allowing her fingers to trail across the rough stone.

She had come to say goodbye to the home she had known virtually all her life. It was not an easy task. She had so many memories entwined in this ancient structure. So many ghosts of her past haunted its corridors and walkways. She thought of all those she had loved and lost—her commander and surrogate father General Shao; her friends and lieutenants Xiao Yu and Li Qing; stern-faced but wise and kindly Strategist Wang; even Peng Yong, the frightened boy who had eventually discovered that he possessed great courage, after all.

So many gone, never to return. Alone now, she stopped and looked across the desert, at the rising sun shining on the tip of the Gouwu Mountain in the distance.

"General…"

The voice was diffident. It came from behind her.

She took one last look at the mountain, which appeared peaceful now, its green glimmer like cool, glassy water, and then she turned around.

• • •

The Imperial delegation slowed as it approached the towering fortress on the Bianliang side of the Wall. But when the twelve Imperial infantrymen stopped and dismounted a few hundred yards from the fortress's side gate to stretch their aching limbs and tend to their weary mounts, the thirteenth rider rode on.

Slowing his horse to a walk, William looked up at the fortress's forbidding façade, and then scanned the battlements at the top of the Wall, screwing up his eyes against the brightening sun as he looked first right and then left. He saw no sign of life. The Great Wall, unmanned, appeared eerily desolate. He was just beginning to wonder whether the information he'd been given was incorrect when the fortress's side gate opened and a figure appeared.

It was a Bear Corps warrior, one of only a few who remained here now that the threat from the Tao Tei was over. The Nameless Order, decimated in the final battle, was no more. Soon even the last few survivors who still resided here – those members of the cavalry who had pursued Pero and Ballard into the desert; those warriors whose balloons had drifted off-course and landed miles away from Bianliang – would be issued with orders to join new regiments elsewhere.

The Bear Corps warrior gave a nod of respect and led William along a series of familiar corridors to the stockade – to the very cell, in fact, that he had occupied just before Lin Mae had given orders that he be set free. The door was unlocked and opened, and William entered the dusty cell.

And there, standing against the wall, his head secured within a square wooden pillory etched with Chinese symbols, his upraised hands chained to the wall behind him, was his old friend, Pero Tovar.

Pero glanced at him ruefully, then looked away. William couldn't help grinning.

"So?" he said cheerfully. "How's life without me?"

Pero shot him a dark look. After a moment he mumbled, "A little slow."

Both men regarded one another for a moment, and then, in unison, they started chuckling.

"So you've become a hero, after all," Pero said.

William shrugged, but he wore a smug expression, milking the moment. "Looks that way."

"You seem pleased with yourself. So what are they giving you for all your troubles? A bag of gold? A victory parade along the top of the Wall?"

Airily William said, "All the black powder I can carry. And a cavalry escort to get me home safely."

Pero stared at him, his brows beetling with resentment. "Well, congratulations," he said heavily.

"Thank you."

"So what's all this? Are you here to rub my nose in it?"

William spread his hands. "Would you blame me? The last time I saw you, you left me for dead."

"And the time before that, I saved your life," Pero retorted.

"True," acknowledged William. He stared at Pero for a moment, as if weighing up his options.

Eventually he said, "You know, the Emperor gave me a choice. Either I could take the black powder… or I could take you."

Pero stared back at him impassively. "Please tell me you chose the powder."

William sighed. And then he produced a set of keys and began to unlock the shackles around Pero's wrists.

• • •

"The horses are saddled and waiting. Best we ride before nightfall," said William, leading the way back towards the fortress's side gate.

They rounded a corner at the head of a flight of stone steps leading downwards, Pero rubbing his sore wrists – and there they halted. Lin Mae, resplendent in gleaming gold-plated armour, was ascending slowly towards them.

Pero glanced behind him, saw a door standing half-open.

"I'll wait in here. Don't leave without me," he said.

He ducked through the doorway, pulling the door closed behind him, leaving William alone with Lin Mae.

She reached the top of the steps and the two of them regarded one another for a moment.

"I came to say goodbye," she said finally.

William nodded, momentarily tongue-tied. Then he licked his dry lips and said, "I understand congratulations are in order. General of the North West territory. That's quite an honor."

She smiled and nodded at the closed door behind William. "It seems you've made your choice."

William rolled his eyes. "Oh, him? Believe me, I'm already thinking of trading him back for the powder."

"I heard that," came a muffled voice from behind the door.

To William's ears Lin Mae's laughter was like music.

"Perhaps we're both wrong," she said softly. "Perhaps we're more similar than we thought."

William felt such a swell of pride and emotion in his chest that for a moment he couldn't speak. Then he clasped his hands together – the familiar symbol of respect and togetherness and trust. Of Xin Ren.

"Thank you, General," he said.

• • •

Riding away from the Wall, into the Painted Mountains, William paused a moment, reining in his horse and looking back over his shoulder.

Lin Mae was standing atop the Wall, leaning over

the battlements, her raven hair blowing in the wind, her armour flashing as it reflected the light.

"Are you sure you don't want to go back?" Pero asked softly.

"Of course I do." William grinned wryly. "I just don't trust you to make it out of here alone."

Pero laughed, and the two men spurred their horses into a trot, and then a gallop.

In a cloud of dust, with the magnificent Wall stretching to each extreme of the horizon behind them, they rode away.

ABOUT THE AUTHOR

Mark Morris has written over twenty-five novels, among which are *Toady*, *Stitch*, *The Immaculate*, *The Secret of Anatomy*, *Fiddleback*, *The Deluge* and four books in the popular *Doctor Who* range. He is also the author of two short story collections, *Close to the Bone* and *Long Shadows, Nightmare Light*, and several novellas. His short fiction, articles and reviews have appeared in a wide variety of anthologies and magazines, and he is editor of *Cinema Macabre*, a book of horror movie essays by genre luminaries for which he won the 2007 British Fantasy Award, its follow-up *Cinema Futura*, and two volumes of *The Spectral Book of Horror Stories*. His script work includes audio dramas for Big Finish Productions' *Doctor Who* and *Jago & Litefoot* ranges, and also for Bafflegab's *Hammer Chillers* series, and his recently published work includes an updated novelization of the 1971 Hammer movie *Vampire Circus*, the official movie tie-in novelization of Darren Aronofsky's *Noah*, and the Shirley Jackson Award nominated novella *It Sustains* for Earthling Publications.

FOLLOW HIM ON TWITTER
@MarkMorris10
www.markmorrisfiction.com